Crossing the Black Ice Bridge

Also by Alex Bell

The Polar Bear Explorers' Club
The Forbidden Expedition

The POLAR BEAR

EXPLORERS' CLUB

Book 3

Crossing the Black Ice Bridge

Alex Bell

Illustrated by Tomislav Tomić

Simon & Schuster Books for Young Readers
NEW YORK   LONDON   TORONTO   SYDNEY   NEW DELHI

SIMON & SCHUSTER BOOKS FOR YOUNG READERS
An imprint of Simon & Schuster Children's Publishing Division
1230 Avenue of the Americas, New York, New York 10020
Originally published in Great Britain in 2019 by Faber & Faber Limited
First US Edition 2020
For information about special discounts for bulk purchases,
please contact Simon & Schuster Special Sales at 1-866-506-1949 or
business@simonandschuster.com.
The Simon & Schuster Speakers Bureau can bring authors to your live event.
For more information or to book an event, contact the Simon & Schuster
Speakers Bureau at 1-866-248-3049 or visit our website at
www.simonspeakers.com.
Jacket design by Chloë Foglia and Tom Daly
Interior design by Hilary Zarycky
The text for this book was set in Granjon.
The illustrations for this book were rendered in pen and ink and digitally
Manufactured in the United States of America
1020 FFG
2 4 6 8 10 9 7 5 3 1
CIP data for this book is available from the Library of Congress.
ISBN 978-1-5344-0652-0
ISBN 978-1-5344-0654-4 (eBook)

For my cousin, Chris Willrich

Polar Bear Explorers' Club Rules

ALL Polar Bear explorers will keep their mustaches trimmed, waxed, and well groomed at all times. Any explorer found with a slovenly mustache will be asked to withdraw from the club's public rooms immediately.

EXPLORERS with disorderly mustaches or unkempt beards will also be refused entry to the members-only bar, the private dining room, and the gentlemen's billiards room without exception.

ALL igloos on club property must contain a flask of hot chocolate and an adequate supply of marshmallows at all times.

ONLY polar bear–shaped marshmallows are to be served on club property. Additionally, the following breakfast items will be prepared in polar bear–shape only: pancakes, waffles, crumpets, sticky pastries, fruit jellies, and donuts. Please do not request alternative animal shapes from the kitchen—including penguins, walruses, woolly mammoths, and yetis—as this offends the chef.

MEMBERS are kindly reminded that when the chef is offended, insulted, or peeved, there will be nothing on offer in the dining room whatsoever except for buttered toast. This toast will be bread-shaped.

EXPLORERS must not hunt or harm unicorns under any circumstances.

ALL Polar Bear Explorers' Club sleighs must be properly decorated with seven brass bells and must contain the following items: five fleecy blankets, three hot water bottles in knitted sweaters, two flasks of emergency hot chocolate, and a warmed basket of buttered crumpets (polar bear–shaped).

PLEASE do not take penguins into the club's saltwater baths; they *will* hog the Jacuzzi.

ALL penguins are the property of the club and are not to be removed by explorers. The club reserves the right to search any suspiciously shaped bags. Any bag that moves by itself will automatically be deemed suspicious.

ALL snowmen built on club property must have appropriately groomed mustaches. Please note that a carrot is not a suitable object to use as a mustache. Nor is an eggplant. If in doubt, remember that the club president is always available for consultation regarding snowmen's mustaches.

IT is considered bad form to threaten other club members with icicles, snowballs, or oddly dressed snowmen.

WHISTLING ducks are not permitted on club property. Any member found with a whistling duck in his possession will be asked to leave.

Upon initiation, all Polar Bear explorers shall receive an explorer's bag containing the following items:

- One tin of Captain Filibuster's Expedition-Strength Mustache Wax
- One bottle of Captain Filibuster's Scented Beard Oil
- One folding pocket mustache comb
- One ivory-handled shaving brush, two pairs of grooming scissors, and four individually wrapped cakes of luxurious foaming shaving soap
- Two compact pocket mirrors

Desert Jackal Explorers' Club Rules

MAGICAL flying carpets are to be kept tightly rolled when on club premises. Any damage caused by out-of-control flying carpets will be considered the sole responsibility of the explorer in question.

ENCHANTED genie lamps must stay in their owners' possession at all times.

PLEASE note: Genies are strictly prohibited at the bar and at the bridge tables.

TENTS are for serious expedition use only and are not to be used to host parties, gatherings, chin-wags, or chitchats.

CAMELS must not be permitted—or encouraged—to spit at other club members.

JUMPING cacti are not allowed inside the club unless under exceptional circumstances.

PLEASE do not remove flags, maps, or wallabies from the club.

CLUB members are not permitted to settle disagreements via camel racing between the hours of midnight and sunrise.

THE club kangaroos, coyotes, sand cats, and rattlesnakes are to be respected at all times.

MEMBERS who wish to keep all their fingers are advised not to torment the giant desert hairy scorpions, irritate the bearded vultures, or vex the spotted desert recluse spiders.

EXPLORERS are kindly asked to refrain from washing

their feet in the drinking water tureens at the club's entrance, which are provided strictly for our members' refreshment.

SAND forts may be constructed on club grounds, on condition that explorers empty all sand from their sandals, pockets, bags, binocular cases, and helmets before entering the club.

EXPLORERS are asked not to take camel decoration to extremes. Desert Jackal Explorers' Club camels may wear a maximum of one jeweled necklace, one tasseled headdress and/or bandana, seven plain gold anklets, up to four knee bells, and one floral snout ornament.

Upon initiation, all Desert Jackal explorers shall receive an explorer's bag containing the following items:

- One foldable leather safari hat or one pith helmet
- One canister of tropical-strength giant desert hairy scorpion repellent
- One shovel (please note this object's usefulness in the event of being buried alive in a sandstorm)
- One camel-grooming kit, consisting of organic camel shampoo, camel eyelash curlers, head brush, toenail trimmers, and hoof polishers (kindly provided by the National Camel-Grooming Association)
- Two spare genie lamps and one spare genie bottle

Jungle Cat Explorers' Club Rules

MEMBERS of the Jungle Cat Explorers' Club shall refrain from picnicking in a slovenly manner. All expedition picnics are to be conducted with grace, poise, and elegance.

ALL expedition picnicware must be made from solid silver and kept perfectly polished at all times.

CHAMPAGNE carriers must be constructed from high-grade wicker, premium leather, or teakwood. Please note that champagne carriers considered "tacky" will not be accepted onto the luggage elephant under ANY circumstances.

EXPEDITION picnics will not take place unless there are scones present. Ideally, there should also be magic lanterns, pixie cakes, and an assortment of fairy jellies.

EXOTIC whip snakes, alligator snapping turtles, horned baboon tarantulas, and flying panthers must be kept securely under lock and key while on club premises.

DO NOT torment or tease the jungle fairies. They *will* bite and may also catapult tiny, but extremely potent, stink-berries. Please be warned that stink-berries smell worse than anything you can imagine, including unwashed feet, moldy cheese, elephant poo, and hippopotamus burps.

JUNGLE fairies must be allowed to join expedition picnics if they bring an offering of any of the following: elephant cakes, striped giraffe scones, or fizzy tiger punch from the Forbidden Jungle Tiger Temple.

JUNGLE fairy boats have right of way on the Tikki Zikki River under *all* circumstances, including when there are piranhas present.

SPEARS are to be pointed away from other club members at all times.

WHEN traveling by elephant, explorers are kindly asked to supply their own bananas.

IF and when confronted by an enraged hippopotamus, a Jungle Cat explorer must remain calm and act with haste to avoid any damage befalling the expedition boat (please note that the Jungle Navigation Company expects all boats to be returned to them in pristine condition).

MEMBERS are courteously reminded that owing to the size and smell of the beasts in question, the club's elephant house is not an appropriate venue in which to host soirees, banquets, galas, or shindigs. Carousing of any kind in the elephant house is strictly prohibited.

Upon initiation, all Jungle Cat explorers shall receive an explorer's bag containing the following items:

- An elegant mother-of-pearl knife and fork, inscribed with the explorer's initials
- One silverware polishing kit

- One engraved Jungle Cat Explorers' Club napkin ring and five luxury linen napkins—ironed, starched, and embossed with the club's insignia
- One magic lantern with fire pixie
- One tin of Captain Greystoke's Expedition-Flavor Smoked Caviar
- One corkscrew, two cheese knives, and three wicker grape baskets

Ocean Squid Explorers' Club Rules

SEA monster, kraken, and giant squid trophies are the private property of the club, and cannot be removed to adorn private homes. Explorers will be charged for any decorative tentacles that are found to be missing from their rooms.

EXPLORERS are not to fraternize—or join forces—with pirates or smugglers during the course of any official expedition.

POISONOUS puffer fish, barbed-wire jellyfish, saltwater stingrays, and electric eels are not appropriate fillings for pies or sandwiches. Any such requests sent to the kitchen will be politely rejected.

EXPLORERS are kindly asked to refrain from offering to show the club's chef how to prepare sea snakes, sharks, crustaceans, or deep-sea monsters for human consumption. This includes the creatures listed in the rule immediately above. Please respect the expert knowledge of the chef.

THE Ocean Squid Explorers' Club does not consider the sea cucumber to be a trophy worthy of reward or recognition. This includes the lesser-found biting cucumber, as well as the singing cucumber and the argumentative cucumber.

ANY Ocean Squid explorer who gifts the club with a tentacle from the screeching red devil squid will be rewarded with a year's supply of Captain Ishmael's Premium Dark Rum.

PLEASE do not leave docked submarines in a submerged state; it wreaks havoc with the club's valet service.

EXPLORERS are kindly asked not to leave deceased sea monsters in the hallways or in any of the club's communal rooms. Unattended sea monsters are liable to be removed to the kitchens without notice.

THE South Seas Navigation Company will not accept liability for any damage caused to their submarines. This includes damage caused by giant squid attacks, whale ambushes, and jellyfish plots.

EXPLORERS are not to use the map room to compare the length of squid tentacles or other trophies. Please use the marked areas within the trophy rooms to settle any private wagers or bets.

PLEASE note: Any explorer who threatens another explorer with a harpoon cannon will be suspended from the club immediately.

Upon initiation, all Ocean Squid explorers shall receive an explorer's bag containing the following items:

- One tin of Captain Ishmael's Kraken Bait
- One kraken net
- One engraved hip flask filled with Captain Ishmael's Expedition-Strength Salted Rum
- Two sharpened fishing spears and three bags of hunting barbs
- Five tins of Captain Ishmael's Harpoon Cannon Polish

Crossing the Black Ice Bridge

CHAPTER ONE

S TELLA STARFLAKE PEARL DECIDED she did not like the courthouse in Coldgate one bit.

Not only was it a looming, imposing, ugly building, with high ceilings, paintings of serious-looking, disapproving judges, and stone statues of justice griffins everywhere, but the people who worked there were stiff and serious and seemed to have their collars buttoned up too tight. Perhaps that's why the staff all had that sweating, slightly throttled look—including the panel sitting behind the bench.

The panel consisted of the Polar Bear Explorers' Club's president, Algernon Augustus Fogg, along with three other retired explorers. They were all men, gray-haired, with disapproving expressions that caused their mustaches to bristle from time to time. They all stared down accusingly at Stella's father, Felix, who stood alone before them, dressed in his pale blue explorer's cloak.

The courthouse was normally used for putting criminals on trial, but the members of the Polar Bear Explorers' Club were allowed to use it for occasions like this, when one of their own was under investigation for rule breaking. Felix had, unfortunately, broken quite a few rules recently when he mounted an unauthorized expedition to Witch Mountain. And Stella and her junior explorer friends— Shay, Ethan, and Beanie—had done the same when they followed him in case he needed rescuing.

It was now three weeks since they had returned from their fateful expedition and all the trouble had started. Felix and Stella had both found that their very membership in the club hung in the balance. They had found themselves on trial for rule breaking, and now their very membership in the club hung in the balance. After two visits to the courthouse, last week they had received a telegram informing them this would be the final meeting and that a decision would be reached by the end of the day. Stella saw that everyone had come to see the result, including the president of the Jungle Cat Explorers' Club and his odious son, Gideon Galahad Smythe. Shay, Ethan, and Beanie were there too, along with Beanie's mum, Joss, a slender elf with long blue hair and pointed ears.

Stella was shocked to see her friends. Today was Beanie's birthday, and he had been planning his party for ages. When Stella found out they were due to appear in court, she'd sent a messenger fairy with a note saying she couldn't come. She had assumed the party would go ahead without her, yet here they all were in this horrible place instead.

This was the third time she and Felix had been to the courthouse now, and it seemed to Stella that it had been specially designed to make her feel insignificant and small. The very air—thick with a long history of disagreements and arguments and misery and grievances—made Stella feel all twitchy and itchy inside her clothes. Most of all, she *hated* the fact that they were treating Felix like some kind of criminal. It was so unspeakably unfair. Yes, he may have broken a few rules, and he may have gone to Witch Mountain against the wishes of the Polar Bear Explorers' Club, but it had all been a matter of life and death, and any explorer ought to be able to understand that.

Stella adjusted her position on the chair and tried to persuade Mustafah, Hermina, Humphrey, and Harriet to settle down in her lap. Unbeknown to her, the four jungle fairies she'd met on their last adventure had stowed away in her pockets when they left home, and she was quite concerned they might get into mischief. She'd already caught Hermina with her slingshot out, aiming a stink-berry at one of the brooding stone griffins adorning the walls.

The other people in the courthouse kept throwing disapproving looks at them too—the jungle fairies kind of stood out with their green skin, leaf tunics, and impressive blue spiky hair. And while there wasn't a rule against fairies being inside the courthouse as such, it was certainly the case that the building had a dry, life-sucking air—probably on account of all the lawyers—and that it felt somehow wrong for something as magical and marvelous as a fairy to be there.

Shay, the wolf whisperer, caught Stella's eye and waved at her from across the aisle. It was warm and stuffy inside the courtroom, and yet Shay was still wearing his cloak and seemed to clutch it to him, as if in need of the warmth. Stella raised her hand back, trying not to show her stab of unease at the sight of the white streak in Shay's hair. Had it spread a little more since she'd last seen him, or was it her imagination? Either way, there was no time to lose.

Koa, Shay's shadow wolf, had been bitten by a witch wolf just as they were leaving Witch Mountain, and Shay would almost certainly turn into a witch wolf himself if they didn't do something to help him. But they had tried everything they could, with no success. The only possible chance to save Shay was to travel over the cursed Black Ice Bridge—a forsaken place that no explorer had ever managed to cross. Somewhere on the other side was a mysterious person called the Collector, who had stolen Stella's birth mother's Book of Frost, which contained a spell that might save Shay's life. But it was a formidable task—most said impossible—and they ought to be finishing their preparations for it, not stuck in this stupid courtroom wasting their time. Stella couldn't help gritting her teeth in frustration.

"You knew the club did not want you to go to Witch Mountain," one of the old explorers on the panel was saying to Felix. "And yet you went anyway."

"Is that a question, Nathaniel?" Felix asked mildly.

"This is your final chance to offer some explanation or justification for your behavior," the explorer replied.

"There are some things in this world that are even more important than the Polar Bear Explorers' Club," Felix replied. "As I have already told this court, I went to Witch Mountain because I believed there was a witch there who meant my daughter harm. I feared for her life."

President Fogg's mouth formed a thin, straight line, but he shuffled some papers around on the bench in front of him, peered down at the top sheet, then looked back at Felix and said, "You have taken full responsibility for your adopted daughter—the ice princess known as Stella Starflake Pearl—and you do not deny that she broke into the Polar Bear Explorers' Club and stole a valuable artifact—"

"I deny both those points, sir," Felix interrupted sharply. "As a junior member of the club, Stella should never have been denied access in the first place. Furthermore, the artifact she took was a tiara that belonged to her and was only on loan to the club temporarily. It's not possible to steal your own property—"

"What about my dirigible?" cried a voice from the other side of the courtroom. Stella turned and saw that the speaker was Wendell Winterton Smythe, the president of the Jungle Cat Explorers' Club. "You're not going to argue that belonged to the girl too? And what about my son? He was magically assaulted."

"*I'm* the one who assaulted him!" Stella's friend Ethan Edward Rook rose to his feet, scowling. His black Ocean Squid Explorers' Club cloak gleamed beneath the sickly glow of the courthouse lights. "It wasn't Stella; it was me. And I'd do it again too. In a heartbeat!"

Unfortunately, Gideon Galahad Smythe had been on board the dirigible when the young explorers had used it to flee from the guards at the Polar Bear Explorers' Club. He was a few years older than them, and very handsome, rude, and mean. To their dismay, he had tried to sabotage their rescue attempt by turning the dirigible back around. So Ethan had used his powers as a magician to transform him into a wonky squish-squish frog, and he'd spent most of the expedition stuffed inside someone's pocket.

Stella knew that Ethan had not really acted properly there. He should have turned Gideon back into a boy the moment they arrived at Witch Mountain, but the magician claimed to have forgotten the spell. The others had all known deep down that this wasn't true, but no one had tried very hard to persuade him to turn Gideon back because they had evil witches to worry about, and vampire trolls and ice spiders, and no one particularly wanted to listen to him complaining while they attempted to scale the mountain.

Stella could still see the pure hatred that had blazed in Gideon's eyes as he'd glared up at Ethan from where he lay sprawled on the salted planks of the pier after they got home and he was human once again.

I'll get you back, he'd said. *One day, I swear I'll get you back for what you did to me.*

And now here he was, making life difficult for them. If Gideon hadn't been so furious about the whole thing, perhaps the president of the Jungle Cat Explorers' Club might not have made such noisy complaints and this might all be going very differently now.

Gideon stood up from his chair, completely ignored Ethan, and addressed the judge instead. "The magician had nothing to do with it," he said. "He's just trying to take the blame for the ice princess. No doubt she's bewitched him somehow." He pointed at Stella. "*She's* the one who attacked me."

"I can't turn anyone into a frog!" Stella exclaimed. "I can only use ice magic—"

"Who knows what the girl can and cannot do?" President Smythe said. "We hardly know anything about ice princesses. Except for the fact that they're dangerous."

"Your son is a filthy liar!" Ethan exclaimed.

An annoyed ripple went around the courtroom at that, and Stella saw Beanie's mum pull Ethan back into his seat and urgently whisper something in his ear.

"I tell you, it was her!" Gideon insisted.

Stella didn't know how to make them listen. She'd already been through everything that had happened at earlier meetings. No one seemed to want to hear anything she had to say.

President Fogg picked up his gavel and hammered it down briskly. "Silence!" he cried. "There will be no more of these outbursts, or I will have the room cleared." He turned his gaze on Felix and said, "There can be no excuse for stealing President Smythe's dirigible. None. Not only was it stolen, but it was also lost during the course of the expedition. The craft was hand-carved by Tikki nymphs from the Tikki Zikki River. It was invaluable."

Stella flinched. Upon arriving at Witch Mountain, they had traded the dirigible at Weenus's Trading Post. It had seemed vital at the time to have a camel and a magic fort blanket for the expedition that lay ahead, but now she was starting to think that perhaps they ought to have made more of an effort to bring the dirigible back with them. She had been so focused on rescuing Felix that she'd barely given it a moment's thought.

"I accept that Stella took the dirigible," Felix was saying, "but precedent states that when another explorer's life is at stake, in an emergency situation it is permissible to—"

"Thank you, Pearl, but we do not require a law lecture," President Fogg snapped. "We are here merely to summarize the facts and to give our decision." He set down his gavel and drew himself up a little straighter in his chair. "When I admitted this girl into our club—against my better judgment, I might add—you told me you would take full responsibility for her. She has committed countless infractions and breaches of the rules. Countless. She has led other junior explorers astray." His gaze flickered toward Beanie, Shay, and Ethan, who all got to their feet and started to protest together. President Fogg didn't even pause for breath—he merely raised his voice and steamrolled over their explanations. "As a result, there has been an official complaint from the Jungle Cat Explorers' Club, and you have left me no choice but to take action. Both you and the girl are to be expelled from the Polar Bear Explorers' Club."

The others all stopped talking, and for a moment there was stunned silence. Stella felt like her chest might burst with the unfairness and *wrongness* of it. She remembered Felix's words to her just before her very first expedition:

If anything goes wrong with the expedition as a result, I will certainly lose my membership in the Polar Bear Explorers' Club. . . .

She had promised him that wouldn't happen. She knew

how much the club meant to him—she knew that exploring was Felix's whole life. The other people in the room were exclaiming around her—some in outrage and some in satisfaction.

"Your cloak, sir," President Fogg said in a cold voice. "You have lost the right to wear it. I must also ask that you hand in your explorer's bag and card at the confiscation desk before leaving the courthouse."

Stella saw Felix's fingers shake slightly as he fumbled with the clasp, and before she knew what she was doing she was on her feet, scattering the fairies, who tumbled to the floor in an indignant heap.

"No!" Her voice rang out across the courtroom, and everyone turned to stare at her. "No!" she said again. "This isn't right! *I* was the one who stole the dirigible. *I* was the one who broke into the club. Felix only went to Witch Mountain because of me. It isn't fair to punish him for something *I* did!"

"You do not get to decide what is fair," President Fogg said sternly. "In fact, you have no say in this courtroom at all."

Stella knew it was hopeless to try to make the panel see reason when they were all so clearly determined not to. For a wild moment, her fingers strayed to the charm bracelet at her wrist. When Felix had finally found the witch he had set after, she had turned out to be Stella's old nanny, Jezzybella, and he realized it had all been a big misunderstanding; she had never meant Stella any harm. When they were reunited, Jezzybella had given Stella the charm bracelet. She'd even come home with them and told Stella that each charm on the bracelet created a different spell. Perhaps she could use one now to fight against the panel somehow.

"Stella," Felix said quietly, his voice full of warning.

She looked at him, and he shook his head just slightly before his eyes flicked over to where Shay stood. Stella felt her anger drain away uselessly. She knew what Felix was saying—she had to stay out of trouble because she was the only one who had any hope of saving Shay's life. *If* they managed to cross the Black Ice Bridge and *if* they found the Collector and *if* they managed to steal the Book of Frost, then Stella was the only person who would be able to use the ice-melting spell to counteract the witch wolf's bite.

"I do not regret a single one of my actions, and I will gladly give up my membership if that is the price," Felix said calmly as he carefully folded the cloak and placed it on a nearby table.

"That's so typical of you, Pearl!" one of the retired explorers on the panel said with a sneer. "If you ask me, the Polar Bear Explorers' Club is better off without mavericks like you. You damage the integrity of the club, attack our traditions, and make a mockery of our history."

Stella knew this explorer. His name was Quentin Bodwin Moore, and he was a fairyologist like Felix, only Quentin favored things like pinned fairy displays and killing jars. He'd been furious when Felix had persuaded the Polar Bear Explorers' Club to remove their pinned fairy display and had nursed a vendetta against Felix ever since.

"Let me be quite clear," Felix said. "I have nothing but the utmost respect for the Polar Bear Explorers' Club. For all the exploring clubs, in fact. But sometimes it is surely desirable that we rethink the attitudes of our past and adapt with the times—"

"What nonsense!" Quentin exclaimed. "Perhaps without you putting stupid ideas in people's heads we will be able to bring back the pinned fairy display that stood in our lobby for more than a hundred years!"

"Perhaps you will, Quentin," Felix replied with a sigh, and Stella didn't think she had ever heard him sound quite so sad or so tired.

Before anyone else could say another word, however, Mustafah flew up into the air, slingshot already in hand. Stella saw what he was about to do, but before she could even think about whether she wanted to stop him or not, he drew back the elastic band, took aim, and fired a stink-berry straight at Quentin. Stella supposed the jungle fairy was a little peeved at the suggestion that a pinned fairy display should be reintroduced into the club, and she couldn't really blame him.

Even so, a tiny fairy catapulting a stink-berry at a member of the panel was perhaps not the most helpful thing that could have happened at that moment. The red berry shot straight across the room and hit the explorer on the cheek, where it burst and let loose a vile smell. It's hard to describe a stink-berry stench to someone who has never actually smelled it, but it's a bit like polar bear poo, walrus breath, and camel vomit all rolled into one, with a sprinkling of unwashed feet and cheese that has moldy bits growing on it. It filled the entire courtroom and immediately sent everyone heaving and rising to their feet, tripping over one another as they raced toward the exit.

CHAPTER TWO

AVING LIVED WITH THE jungle fairies since their return from Witch Mountain, Stella and Felix were a little more used to the smell than everyone else, and Felix walked over to Stella, offering her a small half smile.

"Don't look so upset," he said, squeezing her shoulder. "We knew there was every chance this might happen."

"I didn't . . . I just didn't think it actually would," Stella said, hating the fact that her voice shook. "It's so unfair."

"Life is not always fair," Felix agreed. "But you and I have bigger things to worry about right now."

He glanced past her to the corridor, where they could see their friends waiting for them with handkerchiefs pressed over their noses.

"Let's join the others," Felix said.

Stella beckoned the fairies over, and they happily piled

into the front pocket of her dress—an extra-large one her dressmaker had made for just that purpose. They walked out to the corridor, where Beanie's mum gave Felix a quick hug.

"It's an outrage," Joss said quietly. "They've got to see reason and let you back in eventually. They've got to." She smiled over at Stella and gave her arm a squeeze. "You were so brave in there, my dear," she said.

Stella tried to smile back at her, but there was an ache in her throat that she couldn't seem to shift. Still, she was glad in her soul that her friends were there, and she was pleased to see Joss, who was always resolutely cheerful. She noticed that Beanie's mum wore one of her own knit creations today—a woolly sweater so big that it practically swamped her tiny frame. She'd stitched a big, friendly looking yeti on it, with actual fluffy white bits for the fur.

"What's done is done," Felix said. "Let's grab our coats and get out of here. Courthouses make me itchy."

They made their way to the coatroom, where they handed over their tickets and collected their hats and bags.

"Pearl."

They all turned around to see President Fogg standing behind them, his eyes still watering from the pungent reek of the stink-berry. It had even made his mustache wilt a little.

"You've been expelled from the club," he said, dabbing at his eyes with a handkerchief. "I trust you understand what that means? You have lost the right to mount any expeditions into the unknown. Only qualified explorers are permitted that privilege." He glanced toward the front doors, where President Smythe was lingering, looking smug, with his son, Gideon. "And you've made yourself a powerful enemy, Felix," Fogg went on in a quieter voice. Stella thought she saw just a hint of regret in his eyes as they rested on her father. "You know I can't risk jeopardizing our friendly relations with the other clubs—we're on thin enough ice as it is with the Ocean Squid Explorers' Club after that Snow Shark Expedition fiasco." He sighed. "You are a fine explorer and the Polar Bear Explorers' Club was glad to have you, but you've left me no choice in this matter. If I hear that you're planning any kind of expedition, I will have to apply for a warrant for your arrest."

Stella gasped. It was, technically, the law that only explorers were allowed on expeditions, but it wasn't usually a law that was enforced. After all, what harm did it do? If some foolhardy person wanted to buy themselves a raft, tie a flag to it, and go sailing off into the ocean, never to be seen or heard from again, then surely that was their own affair?

"I understand," Felix said in a quiet voice.

"Please don't make me arrest you, Felix," the president went on. "Explorers' prison is not a happy place. You don't want to be locked away with poachers and pirates and bandits and—"

"Indeed not," Felix said, placing his top hat on his head. "Good day, President Fogg."

The others trailed after Felix toward the lobby, all feeling rather crushed and subdued. Stella felt particularly bad for Beanie, because it was a terrible thing to feel crushed and subdued on one's birthday.

"I just have to hand these things in," Felix said, gesturing to his explorer's bag. Somehow, he managed to still make his voice sound cheerful. "And then we'll go."

He went off to the desk on the other side of the room. Unfortunately, President Smythe and his son walked across the lobby at that very moment, buttoning up their cloaks as they headed for the front doors. Stella felt Ethan twitch beside her.

"Don't say anything to them," she warned. "It's not worth it."

Perhaps Ethan would have done as she'd said if Gideon hadn't deliberately barged into him on the way past, muttering an insult under his breath and almost knocking him over. The magician staggered slightly but was quickly righted by Joss. Before anyone could stop him, Ethan spun around on the spot and threw a magic spell at Gideon's back. It hit the older boy square between the shoulders. Stella wasn't quite sure whether the magic made his clothes invisible or caused them to disappear entirely, but either way the effect was that Gideon suddenly appeared to be standing in the middle of the lobby wearing nothing but his underwear—a pair of boxer shorts with elephants and bananas printed all over them.

"Ha!" Ethan cried triumphantly. "I've been practicing that spell for weeks!"

Some of the people in the lobby burst out laughing, while others tutted disapprovingly. Beanie's mum gasped, President Smythe swore, Beanie tugged at his pom-pom hat in agitation, and Gideon's face turned flaming scarlet.

"Ethan!" Joss exclaimed. "Take that spell off at once!"

The magician shrugged, but he clicked his fingers and Gideon suddenly had all his clothes back again.

"I will have you all thrown out of your clubs in disgrace if you carry on like this!" President Smythe said, rounding on them. "You'll never go on another expedition again, any of you! As soon as I am home I will write official letters of complaint to all your—"

Felix suddenly appeared beside them, and Stella could tell he had seen what had happened because he said quietly, "Sir, please let's not continue our quarrel any further. For my part in it, I apologize unreservedly. The children are only young and they will learn. I'm sure we both did things in our youth of which we are not proud. These petty feuds don't do anyone a bit of good, and I am thrown out of the club now at any rate, so might we not let bygones be bygones?"

Felix held out his hand. President Smythe stared at it like it was something dirty and distasteful.

"The plain fact of the matter is, Pearl, that they should never have allowed a man of your sort to be admitted into the club in the first place."

"Ah." Felix slowly lowered his hand. "I see."

Stella gasped, suddenly breathless with outrage.

"You, sir," President Smythe went on, "are no gentleman."

Before Stella could leap to his defense, Joss exclaimed, "How utterly shameful. Felix Evelyn Pearl is one of the best explorers—one of the very best *men*, in fact—that I have ever had the pleasure of knowing! You're . . . you're nothing but a blasted nincompoop!" The tips of her ears had turned scarlet, which Stella knew meant she was furious.

"It is quite all right, Joss," Felix said in a mild voice. "The president is entitled to his opinion."

"Come, Gideon," said President Smythe, fixing Joss with a frosty look before turning and stalking toward the doors.

Stella thought that might finally be the end of the unpleasant encounter, but then Gideon spat on Felix's coat, a long white trail running slowly down the front.

"That's it!" Ethan cried, raising his hand. "I'm going to—"

"You'll do nothing," Felix said calmly, pushing the magician's hand back down again.

Gideon hurried after his father before anyone could hex him, and the next second they had both gone.

Felix took a handkerchief from his pocket and wiped the spit off without a word. Then he glanced at the others and said, "It seems to me that some birthday cake is in order."

"He . . . he *spat* on you!" Ethan exclaimed, outraged, as they made their way toward the door.

"I was sneezed on by a yeti once, you know," Felix said, looking thoughtful as he recalled the incident. "After that, a little bit of spit hardly seems like anything to make a great fuss about."

"I wouldn't have let him get away with it!" Ethan fumed, as they stepped out into the street. "I would have—"

"You would have made everything worse, just like you always do!" Shay burst out. He looked genuinely angry, which wasn't like him. "Hasn't it even occurred to you that if you hadn't turned Gideon into a frog in the first place, then maybe Felix would still be in the club?"

Ethan looked suddenly stricken. "But . . . but I—"

"All right, gather around, everyone," Felix said, drawing them together on the frosty pavement. He bent down slightly to their level, and Stella immediately found herself comforted by the warmth that was always there in his eyes. "Now, listen," Felix said. "Courthouses bring out the worst in people—that's just the way of it for some reason—

but sometimes it's stronger not to show strength, *especially* when facing someone weaker than ourselves." He fixed Ethan with a pointed look, and Stella noticed that the magician couldn't help squirming a little. "If we must humiliate another person in order to make ourselves feel big, then we have become very small and scared indeed. So let's leave all that squabbling behind us." He glanced at Beanie's mum and said, "We have far more important things to discuss right now, and we will need each other—more than ever—for what's to come."

The sun was setting as Felix led the way down Coldgate's cobbled streets. The courthouse was a place for dry lawyers and crusty old judges—people who were fond of rule books and regulations and being safe and secure inside. Explorers, on the other hand, needed to be out in the fresh air, where anything might happen and grand adventures were only ever a footstep away.

They walked to a restaurant near the train station called the Ice Yeti. Stella was pleased to see it had a miniature model of a yeti perched on the roof, complete with shaggy fur and glistening canines, and that it roared and thumped its chest every time someone walked by.

"I don't think we'll be able to get in there, you know," Joss said. "There's a waiting list for tables."

"The owner is a friend of mine," Felix replied.

They went in through the front doors, and a thin man in a red waistcoat immediately came around from behind the front desk to shake Felix's hand.

"Mr. Pearl!" he exclaimed, beaming. "Welcome, sir, welcome! How many in your party today?"

"Thank you, Gil. There's six of us," Felix said.

From Stella's pocket, Mustafah cleared his throat loudly. Felix immediately said, "Sorry, I meant there's ten of us. We're celebrating a birthday."

"How marvelous! Let me show you to your table."

Gil led the way through a blue curtain, and they found themselves in what appeared to be an ice cave. Stella saw that it wasn't real ice, but was actually plaster designed to look like the inside of a snowy Icelands cave. There were even big yeti footprints carved into the floor and a frozen waterfall filled with savage-looking plastic piranha on one wall. Stella loved the place immediately.

They settled themselves down in the booth Gil showed them to, and once they had ordered their food and some breadsticks had arrived, Felix looked at Joss and said, "Well, first things first. What on earth are you all doing here? I thought you were meant to be celebrating Beanie's birthday back home."

"We wanted to come and support you," Beanie said. "Some things are more important than birthday parties."

"But, Beanie," Stella said. "You were so looking forward to it. There were going to be piñatas and paper hats and party whistles. And I thought Cadi and Drusilla were coming too?" Cadi was a witch hunter they'd met on their last adventure, along with Dru, a young witch.

"We sent messages saying the party had been postponed," Joss said.

"But Shay and I said we'd come over anyway, and we all traveled to Coldgate together," Ethan explained. "My father is on an expedition right now, so he won't even notice I'm gone."

"*My* mother only let me leave on the strict understanding I'd be back home tomorrow," Shay said with a sigh. He ran a hand through his dark hair, and Stella found herself startled, once again, by the streak of white in it.

"Where's Koa?" she asked, suddenly thinking it was strange she hadn't seen Shay's shadow wolf.

"Under the table," Shay said.

Stella lifted the tablecloth and saw that Koa was indeed there, tucked beneath Shay's chair with her snout between her feet. No one quite knew for sure why whisperers had shadow animals, but many people believed that they were part of the whisperer's soul given a separate shape. The two shared a unique bond and were even able to communicate with each other inside their heads. Shadow animals had no physical substance and couldn't be touched, but they never strayed far from their human whisperer.

"She hasn't been right since the wolf attack," Shay said. "And my mum thinks . . . Well, the truth is, since the minute I got back she's been treating me like someone who's already dead; fussing and crying and grieving over me." He looked up and said, "I've tried talking to her about the Black Ice Bridge. I've explained that we think there's a book there that might contain a spell that can help me. She just says we can talk about it more once Dad is home, but he's only been away for two months and he's expected to be gone another month at least. He had already left by the time I got back, so he doesn't know about the witch wolf's bite, but I know he would agree with me—I just know it."

There was a brief silence—broken only by the sound of jungle fairies noisily munching on breadsticks.

"Well," Felix finally said. "I can understand your mother might feel that way." He looked right at Shay. "But what do *you* want to do?"

Shay met his gaze. "I want to try," he said firmly. "I want to at least try to get the Book of Frost and find a cure. I definitely don't want to go home and sit around waiting to die. Or turn into a witch wolf."

If an ordinary person was bitten by a witch wolf, they would eventually become one themselves—frozen in wolf shape for eternity, destined to roam the world looking for other souls to devour. But Shay was no ordinary person—he was a wolf whisperer and the witch wolf hadn't bitten him but his shadow wolf. And so none of them knew exactly what was going to happen. They only knew that it wasn't going to be anything good.

"How have you been yourself?" Felix asked in a kind voice.

"I'm cold," Shay replied. "All the time."

Stella recalled how he had still been wearing his cloak in the courtroom.

"And sometimes it's . . . difficult to eat. I just don't feel hungry."

Now that she looked at him more closely, Stella noticed that Shay's normally lean face did look even more angular than usual. She felt a flare of worry deep in the pit of her stomach. She was, after all, partly to blame for what had happened. When the witch wolves had attacked them, Stella had used her ice magic to freeze the pack, but the act of doing so had chilled her heart so she no longer cared about her friends. She had hesitated before stopping the final witch wolf—and that moment of hesitation had been all it took to allow the wolf to bite Koa and put a piece of ice into her heart.

Shay had said he didn't blame Stella for what had happened, but she blamed herself enough for both of them. Her ice princess tiara was a powerful weapon that had come in handy on their expeditions, but Stella hated the way it twisted her soul and turned her into someone she had no wish to be.

"Well, then," Felix said quietly. "What are we to do? You all know what Stella and I learned a week ago. Jezzybella told us there's a spell in the Book of Frost that might undo the witch wolf's bite. So there's a chance there, but it's a slim one. First of all, Jezzybella—bless her heart—is not the most reliable person in the world. Sometimes I think the poor thing's mind is quite addled. But she *was* there when the snow queen's castle was attacked, so perhaps what she says is accurate. If that's the case, though, there's still the fact that no explorer in our history has ever successfully managed to cross the bridge."

They all glanced at Beanie. His explorer father, Adrian Albert Smith, had attempted the journey eight years ago, but his expedition had disappeared partway across the bridge. The rescue party that went after them had found their camp abandoned and frozen in the snow—all their belongings scattered about as if they'd only just left—but there was no sign of the explorers. They had simply . . . gone.

They did find Adrian's travel journal, however. In it he'd recorded a log of the doomed expedition, including the fact that the men said they could sense an evil presence on the bridge, which got stronger and stronger the farther they went. Others said the bridge was cursed and haunted and that strange monsters lived in the water below it. No one had any idea what was on the other side, and most said it was better not to know. Ever since his father's disappearance, Beanie had nurtured the hope that he would one day be the first explorer to cross the bridge, no matter how many people told him it was impossible.

Stella recalled what Shay said his father, Captain Khan Conrad Kipling, had told him once:

There are some lands so forgotten, and forsaken, and forbidden that even explorers shouldn't venture there.

"Mother thinks that nothing good can come of setting foot on the Black Ice Bridge," Shay said. "I tried to tell her about the Book of Frost, but she . . . well, I don't think she believes it even really exists."

"It's a gamble," Felix agreed. "In more ways than one."

"But it's better to gamble than to simply give up," Shay said. "If my dad were here, I know he would understand that, and he'd organize an expedition to the bridge. But he's not, so I've just got to do it on my own." He looked at the others. "I *have* to go on to the bridge, because I'll die if I don't. But it's not fair to ask you all to risk everything for me."

Ethan punched his shoulder. "Don't talk nonsense!" he exclaimed.

Felix's mouth twitched. "Ethan, please don't hit people," he said. "However, I agree with your sentiment." He looked at Shay and said, "Let's not forget that if you hadn't accompanied Stella on her mission to save me, then you would never have been bitten in the first place. We both owe you a great deal, and we will certainly be going on to the bridge in pursuit of the Collector, whether or not anyone else decides to come with us."

Stella gave Felix's arm a squeeze. She didn't think she'd ever loved him more than she did at that moment. The jungle fairies seemed quite taken with the idea too and started emptying the sugar bowl into a napkin, which they then fashioned into a bag by tying it to a drumstick bone they stole from Stella's plate.

A waiter appeared just then to clear the table.

"Someone tells me we're celebrating a birthday here today," he said cheerfully. "Who's the lucky one?"

All four jungle fairies immediately put up their hands, no doubt hoping some kind of dessert-shaped reward might be involved. Stella rolled her eyes at them and said, "It's Beanie over there."

The waiter gave him a smile. "Happy birthday, young sir." Then he produced some paper party hats from his pocket and scattered them over the table.

They were all human-size, and the jungle fairies immediately started to kick up a great fuss, but the waiter said, "Hold your horses."

"I haven't got any horses," Beanie said, looking confused. Some of the odd things people said really didn't make sense when you took them literally, like Beanie tended to.

"He means wait a moment," Stella said.

"Here you go." The waiter reached into his jacket pocket and dropped four fairy-size hats on the table. "I'll be right back with your birthday treat."

Felix immediately picked up one of the hats and set it straight on his head. He loved absolutely anything to do with birthdays, including hats. The others followed suit, and Stella felt glad that Beanie was managing to have a bit of a birthday party, in spite of everything.

"I'm going with you," Beanie said as he straightened his hat. "I said I was going to cross the Black Ice Bridge, even before this happened. And of course we must do everything we can to save Shay."

"Well said." Ethan snapped his fingers and a tiny party hat immediately appeared on Aubrey—the carved narwhal Beanie's father had made for him during his final expedition, which now sat on the table in front of him.

The medic looked delighted and gave Ethan a smile. The jungle fairies had each put on a party hat and were doing their new favorite chant of doom over in the corner of the table while performing backflips and somersaults.

"*Fee*-fi-fo-fo! *Fee*-fi-fo-fo!!"

It was a bit distracting, but everyone did their best to talk over them.

"Well, I've already lost one loved one to that bridge and I don't intend to lose another," Joss said.

Beanie immediately looked crestfallen. "Mum!" he said, sounding shocked. "You wouldn't stop me from going—"

"Of course not, Benjamin," Joss replied, looking quite offended. "I'm coming with you. I know I'm no explorer, but I'm a nurse, after all, so I'm sure I can make myself useful."

Due to their elf heritage, both Joss and Beanie had magic of their own, but it was quite different from Ethan's. As a magician, Ethan could perform a variety of spells—from turning someone into a frog to producing magical arrows in a crisis—whereas Beanie had healing magic and was training to be a medic like his mother. He could patch up cuts and take the pain away from bruises, and as such he was an extremely valuable member of their team.

"So that's decided," Ethan said, looking pleased and grim at the same time. "We're all going on to the bridge."

"I am a little concerned about your mother, however," Felix said, looking at Shay. "If she has said she does not wish you to go—"

"She hasn't *forbidden* me from going," said Shay. "She just wants to wait for my father to come home. She's scared and she doesn't know how to help. But it's not up to her. It's my life, and my shadow wolf. I have every right to try to save them both."

"Yes," Felix replied. "But parents also have the right to decide what's best for their children sometimes." He chewed his lip and said, "And there's also the fact that you're not well, and the Black Ice Bridge will be very dangerous. More dangerous than anything any of us has ever faced. I just wonder whether perhaps you should sit this one out. Go back to your family and wait for us to—"

"Felix!" Stella was shocked. "How can you say that? You've always said you should never ask someone to do something you wouldn't be prepared to do yourself, and *you* wouldn't sit around at home, would you?"

"I don't have parents who'd be worried about me, Stella," Felix pointed out.

"I understand what you're saying," Shay said. "Really I do. But you're thinking about it all wrong. It's not a question of me going with you. I'm going no matter what you say. So you can come with me if you like, but the one place I'm not going is back home." He looked pleadingly at Felix and said, "We can't know for sure how much time I've got left, but I know somehow that it isn't long. I can sense it. If I don't go now, then it'll be too late. I'll send a message back home, of course, telling my mother what I'm doing. But I *am* going. If anyone is not going to go, then really it should be you. President Fogg said he would issue a warrant for your arrest if you went on an expedition."

"Never mind about that," Felix replied. "They can arrest me upon our return, and we'll worry about it then." He drew in a deep breath, then slowly exhaled. "We're cornered by circumstance here, and none of our options is ideal," he said. "But I won't stop you from trying to save your own life. I only hope your mother can understand." He glanced at Ethan and said, "You'd better send word to your father, too."

"When will we leave?" Beanie asked.

"We've got a room booked at the Ice Cave Hotel here in town," Felix said. "I say we organize rooms for you all tonight too and then tomorrow we'll return home to fetch the supplies that Stella and I have already started to gather. There are a few more things we could do with procuring before we set off, though we'll have to be careful how we go about that now that we've been expelled from the club. We might have to complete our shopping elsewhere. And then we'll have to think about how we're going to get to Blackcastle."

Blackcastle was the village on the mainland, farther down the coastline, where the known side of the Black Ice Bridge joined the rest of the world. It was named for the black castle that brooded alone on the cliff top and had once been the home of Queen Portia—a snow queen who'd frozen all the members of her village in a sudden, inexplicable attack more than two hundred years ago. When they discovered what she'd done, an angry mob from the neighboring village had chased her onto the Black Ice Bridge, and she hadn't been seen or heard from since.

Blackcastle had been a forsaken, forgotten place ever since. No one went there anymore, and none of the young explorers relished the idea of visiting it, either. But it was the only way to get to the bridge.

"Can't we leave at once?" Ethan said. "Surely there's no time to lose?"

"This is no normal expedition," Felix said. "We can't go rushing straight on to the Black Ice Bridge like fools. We must do our best to prepare first. I know it's hard, but I really think that we should take another week, maybe two, to gather our supplies, plan our strategy, and have a serious think about how exactly we're going to—"

"Felix Evelyn Pearl!"

They all turned around in their seats to see President Fogg advancing toward them with two police constables in tow. Stella did not like the grim look on his face one bit.

"Good heavens, what is it now, Fogg?" Felix said, a rare note of frustration creeping into his voice as he threw down his napkin. "Can't you see that we're trying to have a birthday party? Don't tell me there's some other rule I've managed to break in the last half hour. It can't be anything to do with mustaches, because I don't even possess one."

President Fogg's own impressive mustache twitched as he looked down at them. "It's not you," he said. "It's the girl."

"Excuse me, sir." A waiter slid past President Fogg and

placed a plate covered with a silver dish onto the table. "For the birthday boy!" he said cheerfully, before whipping off the domed lid.

They all looked down at a little yeti, about five inches tall. It was made entirely from cake and wore a rather fetching red waistcoat with a black bow tie. The restaurant was well known for these magic puddings, and the next moment the yeti waltzed straight off the plate, a lit birthday candle clutched in one shaggy paw, and began to serenade Beanie with an enthusiastic chorus of "Happy Birthday," all while doing an energetic tap dance.

Stella had longed to see one of the restaurant's singing yetis ever since Felix had first told her about them, but her attention was quickly drawn away by President Fogg's next words.

"Stella Starflake Pearl," he said. "I'm afraid I'm going to have to place you under arrest."

CHAPTER THREE

EVERYONE WENT ABSOLUTELY SILENT — ALL except for the yeti cake, which was still happily performing its song and dance routine.

"If that's a joke," Felix said slowly, "then I must say it's in very poor taste."

"It's no joke," President Fogg said in a clipped voice. Stella saw that he was sweating, and he tugged at his collar as if it were too tight. "Look. Could you take off that ridiculous hat? I can't have a serious conversation with you when you're wearing it."

Felix slid the hat off, and Stella did the same. The last thing she wanted was to be arrested while wearing a party hat.

"What are the charges?" Felix asked.

"She's an ice princess," the president said.

"That in itself is not a crime," Felix said through gritted

teeth. "We do not put people on trial simply for being born a certain way."

Stella's eyes went to the police officers, and she couldn't help noticing that one of them had a bear-prod hanging from his hip. These were sometimes used as protection to ward off wild polar bears, but Stella didn't like the way the man's hand twitched toward it as he stared at her. These weapons delivered a shock big enough to take down an eight-hundred-pound bear. Surely he wasn't planning to use it on her?

"She's also been accused of theft," President Fogg went on. "At the celebration dinner upon your return from that joint expedition, there was a dancing penguin named Monty—"

"*I* took Monty from the club," Felix said. "You were going to have him stuffed otherwise. It was me. I take full ownership. You can't have him back, either, by the way. He's nesting in our parlor."

"It doesn't matter," President Fogg said brusquely. "Someone has made an application to the Court of Magical Justice in the Black Spells Forest to have certain . . . restrictions placed on the girl's movements, on account of her being a danger to society."

The others all began to protest, and Stella felt frustrated tears fill her eyes. Her throat ached with the effort of not giving in to them.

"That's a lie!" Beanie cried, blinking rapidly. "It isn't right to tell lies! Stella isn't a danger to society!"

"Well, that is what the Court of Magical Justice will look into—"

"The prejudice and bigotry of Wendell Winterton Smythe, and others like him, is far more of a threat to society than Stella will ever be!" Felix exclaimed.

"That's for the court to decide," President Fogg said. He looked at Felix. "Be reasonable, Pearl," he said in an imploring tone. One finger twirled his mustache in a restless manner. "When you took the girl from the snow, you didn't know what she was—everyone realizes that. But one can't have ice princesses simply running about loose in civilized society—oh, for goodness' sake, could whoever's birthday it is, please blow out that yeti's candle?" he snapped. "The wretched thing won't stop singing and dancing until you do."

"Don't forget to make a wish!" called out a passing waiter cheerfully. He was clearly quite oblivious to the context of the moment, because he deftly popped paper party hats on President Fogg and the two constables as he walked by.

Beanie glanced at Stella before looking back at the dancing yeti. He muttered his wish quietly beneath his breath, but Stella saw his lips moving and understood what he'd said.

"I wish for a diversion."

The moment Beanie blew out the candle, the yeti went silent and still, becoming just an ordinary piece of birthday cake. . . .

But then there was a scuffling sound and one of the constables gave a shocked yelp. Stella thought he was perhaps just impressed with the yeti cake at first, but then she looked at him and saw there was a bug-eyed, web-footed snow goblin determinedly wriggling out from beneath the

paper hat. The constable tore it off, and several more snow goblins tumbled out, clinging to the constable's sleeves and collar. They looked momentarily stunned, blinking in the bright light, before they did what snow goblins do best and sank their teeth into the man's skin. The goblins had needle-sharp teeth, so it was no surprise that the constable let out a howl and lurched back into a nearby table, sending an entire sugar castle crashing to the floor. The goblins tumbled onto the table and immediately snatched up toothpicks, which they brandished like swords. The family who'd been eating there quickly pushed back their chairs with shrieks of alarm.

"Oh, sorry! Sorry!" The waiter hurried about, flapping his hands in agitation. "I didn't realize those were snow-goblin hats."

"Good *gods*, man, why would you have snow-goblin hats to begin with?" the president cried. He tore off his own hat, and a dozen snow goblins fell down the front of his coat with little giggling sounds.

"They're for troll parties!" The waiter groaned. "Their little nips are extremely ticklish to troll children, you see, and—"

"Aarghh!" The second police officer let out a scream as he tore off his own hat to reveal a particularly wild-looking snow goblin biting his head. "Little *nips*? This one's actually biting my head off!"

At the same time, one of the other goblins leapt from the table and started jabbing at ankles with its toothpick. As the waiter flapped around, trying to deal with three panic-stricken men at once, Stella and the others hurriedly got to their feet. Felix threw some money down on the table and then they were slipping away, racing out through the door and into the street. It had gotten dark while they'd been having dinner and snow was falling again, drifting past them in the light from the lampposts. It was ferocious, biting, savage snow—the type that might have goblins in it—and it seemed to have driven most people indoors, for there was hardly a soul around. It muffled all the noise too, and everything seemed still and quiet, as if they had suddenly found themselves trapped inside a snow globe.

"They'll be right behind us," Felix gasped. "We're going to have to leave now. Tonight."

"But how?" Joss said, looking around. "We won't be able to get a train at this time. And we can't outrun them, either."

They heard the sound of raised voices from the restaurant behind them, and Stella knew that President Fogg and the police officers would come bursting out of those doors at any moment. She couldn't go to prison. Not now when she needed to find the Book of Frost to save Shay. Without her, the whole plan fell apart.

She glanced down at the charm bracelet around her

wrist. There were fourteen silver charms on it altogether, all related to some kind of magical spell. Jezzybella couldn't remember what most of them did, and she and Felix thought it was too dangerous for her to try them out. But her old nanny *did* remember a couple of them, and now Stella's attention fixed on one charm in particular.

"I know what to do," she said.

Nestled beside a yeti charm and a fairy charm was a tiny silver carriage. Stella had practiced doing this particular spell in the garden back home with Jezzybella but had never managed to make it work.

"You don't want it enough," the old witch had said. "That's why it ain't working. You've got to want it more than anything else in the world."

At the time, what Stella had wanted most had been to go for a gallop on her unicorn, Magic. Right now, though, she wanted that carriage as much as she wanted to breathe. Her desperation and panic made her heart pound hard inside her chest, and adrenaline surged all the way through her as she placed her bare fingers on the charm, cold as ice to the touch, closed her eyes, and concentrated with everything she had.

There was a soft *pop* right in the pit of Stella's stomach, and then the *swish* of blades on snow. Stella heard the gasps of the others. She opened her eyes to see a massive polar bear standing directly in front of her, tipping back its head and roaring into the night sky, shattering the silence into little broken pieces.

The others all shrank back, but Stella wasn't afraid of the polar bear. In fact, there were two of them, and they were tethered to a magnificent ice sleigh. It shone silver and white in the moonlight, with a great curved frame from which hung deadly looking icicles and an elaborate front engraved with snowflakes and crowns and yetis. A troll carved from ice crouched there, hunkered down against the cold, clinging to the front of the sleigh with one hand and holding out a lantern with the other. Its large, bat-like ears sparkled in the bright white light cast by the lantern. In fact, the entire ice sleigh glittered in the night like diamonds.

The second polar bear pulled her black lips over her gleaming white teeth and snarled into the snow, and Stella realized that these bears were not like Gruff, her beloved pet back home. They hadn't been brought up in captivity, and they had no interest in cuddles and fish biscuits. These were snow queen bears, savage and wild and untamed. Yet Stella felt no fear as she walked toward them. One of her companions—probably Beanie—gave a frightened squeak and the jungle fairies promptly started up their chant of doom, but nobody tried to stop her from approaching them.

Like Gruff, these bears were gigantic, and even standing on all fours they looked Stella straight in the eye. She could hear them both growling slightly, lips pulled back in an uncertain snarl, thin lines of drool stretching between their teeth. Slowly, Stella held out her hands, offering her palms to the bears.

Up close, she could see that there was snow encrusted on their coats, around their paws, and on their backs, as if they'd come straight through a blizzard to get here. She noticed that their huge paws had made bear prints in the snow, their breath smoked in the freezing air, and steam rose from their wet coats. They were real flesh-and-blood creatures—not shadow animals like Koa.

Silver harnesses clinked around their massive shoulders, and both bears continued to growl while sniffing at Stella's skin and peering at her. She thought she should probably be more frightened—after all, either one of these animals could kill her instantly with just a single bat of a great paw—and yet she knew, somehow, that they wouldn't harm her.

After a couple of breathless moments, the quiet, rumbling growls ceased. Stella could still see plenty of dangerous wildness gleaming in their dark brown eyes, but some small shift seemed to take place so they were suddenly calmer and quieter, and she could see wisdom in their gaze now. She knew she'd never be able to cuddle these bears, but she thought they were wonderful even so, and the sight of them snorting their frozen breath in the lamplight filled her with a deep sense of pleasure. Best of all, there was no chilling sensation around her heart, as there had been when she used ice magic. She still felt completely and truly herself, which wasn't something she took for granted anymore.

"Everyone," Stella said, speaking quietly so as not to alarm the bears. "Get onto the sleigh."

There was a moment of hesitation, but then Felix stepped tentatively forward and the others followed him.

"Amazing!" Shay breathed, resting one gloved hand on the edge of the sleigh. He glanced at Stella and gave her a wide grin. "You're amazing, Sparky," he said.

Stella gave him a pleased, slightly embarrassed smile back. It always gave her a small flutter of delight when someone reacted positively to her frost magic, and it was good to hear Shay's old nickname for her again.

But then the door burst open behind them and President Fogg came rushing out, with the two police officers right on his heels. One of them had the bear-prod in his hand, although it dangled loosely from his grip, like he wasn't quite sure what to do with it. The other officer had a furious expression and a toothpick sticking out of his neck—a parting gift from some snow goblin.

"Quick!" Stella gasped, urging everyone to climb into the sleigh.

They tumbled in to land on the silky, soft reindeer skins piled up on the seats. The sleigh was so big there was easily room for all of them.

"Don't just stand there!" President Fogg roared. "They're going to get away! Stop them!"

Standing in the snow by the bears, Stella glanced over her shoulder to see the officer with the bear-prod step forward with a great air of reluctance. She guessed he had never confronted a real live bear before, let alone an ice princess. He had the look of a man whose day was not going at all to plan, and Stella saw that his face and neck were covered in goblin bites. She felt a momentary flash of sympathy for him, but then he brandished the bear-prod at her, and she saw in his eyes that he meant to use it.

CHAPTER FOUR

THE NEAREST POLAR BEAR opened its mouth wide and roared so ferociously at the police officer that bear drool speckled his face.

The bear-prod fell from his fingers, and he leapt back into the other officer. President Fogg jumped as if he'd been shocked and fell backward, landing on his bottom in the snow with a grunt.

"Come on, Stella!" Felix said, reaching down to her. She grabbed hold of him, and he pulled her up. The bears were off the moment her boots left the ground, charging forward as if suddenly released from a spring, their great paws thundering along, making the ground tremble, the blades of the sleigh sliding through the snow.

Stella landed beside the others with a thump, but quickly propped herself up and looked back just in time to see President Fogg and the police officers disappear as they rounded a corner.

Felix snatched up the reins. "Stella, the sleigh," he said. "I think you've got to steer it. They won't respond to me."

"Steer it where?" Stella gasped, as Felix pressed the reins into her hands.

"We just need to get out of Coldgate," Felix said. "Preferably without running anyone over."

The streets were quiet, but they weren't deserted. Fortunately, a snow queen's sleigh led by two polar bears made quite a bit of noise, even over snow, which gave people a fair amount of time to get out of the way.

The problem, though, was that the streets of Coldgate weren't really wide enough to have two massive polar bears stampeding down them. Stella tightened her grip on the reins and did the best she could, but they were going so fast and the air was thick with swirling snow and the yellow glow of the lampposts seemed to flash by with alarming speed.

Despite her efforts, the sleigh knocked against several shop fronts, which unfortunately caused it to rip down awnings and break a few windows. At the end of one street there wasn't room to turn the sleigh to avoid a gentleman on the pavement who hadn't gotten out of the way quickly enough. Stella was forced to swerve away from him and

straight into a fountain, which smashed into pieces beneath the bears' paws and the blades of the sleigh.

Finally, though, they reached the outskirts of the city, and Stella recognized the pier where she and Felix had disembarked from their ship earlier that day. It had been morning then, and the market stalls had been busy and bustling as traders peddled their wares. Now the stalls were all closed up, though some still contained their stock locked within crates. The bears burst straight through one of these, filling the sleigh with piles of rolled-up treasure maps and mermaid flowers.

"Stella, what the heck are you doing?" Ethan cried, plucking petals from his hair. "We're heading straight for the water!"

"I know, but I can't. . . . They won't stop!" Stella cried.

She was yanking on the reins, but the bears weren't listening to her anymore. They seemed absolutely determined to race straight down the pier leading directly to the open, iceberg-filled sea.

"Should we jump . . . ?" Joss asked.

But it was too late for that. The bears had reached the end of the pier. There was a moment of breathless silence as their paws left the boards, and the sleigh followed. For a moment, they hung suspended and sparkling in the moonlight, before landing with a tremendous splash in the sea below, sending freezing, foaming water everywhere. Fortunately, the sides of the sleigh prevented them from getting too wet.

Stella expected the sleigh to sink like a stone, and Ethan obviously did too, because he unhelpfully shouted out, "We're all going to drown!"

"Twenty-four Polar Bear explorers have allegedly drowned in the last two decades," Beanie instantly said. Stella knew that he only recited explorers' deaths as a way of calming himself down, but it wasn't very comforting to anyone else. "Although no one can be certain that figure is accurate," Beanie went on, "because some of them might have been strangled by mermaids, or pulled apart by kraken, or gobbled up by—"

"Look!" Shay cried, pointing over the side. "It's not sinking. It's growing!"

Stella leaned over and saw that he was right. The sleigh bobbed and rocked unsteadily in the water, but underneath it all, there was a crackling sound and she realized that the ice under the sleigh was spreading out, stretching and changing, until the sleigh stood upon its own little iceberg with freezing salt water pouring down its sides. Without even pausing, the two polar bears began swimming steadily forward, tugging the sleigh farther and farther from the pier.

A great laugh burst from Felix, and Stella found she was smiling too. They may have been thrown out of the

Polar Bear Explorers' Club, and they may be on the run, and their entire situation might look pretty bleak, but there was adventure and excitement thrumming through their veins—and in their hearts they were still explorers, and an explorer loved nothing more than an exquisite moment filled with uncertainty and danger.

For the first few minutes, everyone was buzzing with the victory of their escape, but as they got farther out to open sea, the mood became somewhat less exuberant.

"Well," Ethan finally said. "This is a heck of a mess. What are we going to do?"

"We can't risk going home," Felix said, scratching his chin. "They'll send guards there. I'm afraid we've got no choice but to proceed straight to the Black Ice Bridge."

"But we've got nothing!" the magician replied. "No wolves, no tents, no sleds, no provisions, no—"

"There is a long list of things we do not have," Felix agreed. "But how about we start with what we *do* have? Everyone empty their pockets and bags."

Their shared supplies didn't come to an awful lot, but Ethan had brought the magic fort blanket they'd gained on their last expedition, in case they'd been unable to find a place to stay the night in Coldgate, so despite what he'd said a moment before, they *did* have a tent large enough to accommodate everybody, along with Ruprekt the genie who lived in it and magically produced marvelous cooked dinners and packed lunches on demand, as well as hot baths and hot chocolate and—if he was in a really good mood—foot soaks.

"Why, this is fantastic!" Felix exclaimed, staring in delight at the magic fort blanket, which mostly looked like a tatty old rag in its natural state. "This will provide us with all the essentials. Well done for bringing it, my boy."

"It's always wise to be prepared," Ethan said pompously. "Especially since you Polar Bear explorers seem to enjoy sudden emergencies and unexpected disasters."

They all diplomatically ignored the barb and counted up what else they had. Beanie had brought lots of jelly beans, but also had his medic kit. Joss had some bandages and party whistles. Shay had his boomerang, and Stella had her charm bracelet and compass. Shay also had an updated copy of *Captain Filibuster's Guide to Expeditions and Exploration*, and Felix had his usual kit of telescope, magnifying glass, emergency mint cake, matches, and ball of string, which he had transferred into a satchel before handing over his explorer's bag.

"Yes, all in all, this is a much better state of affairs than it might have been," Felix said, sounding pleased.

"We've got a magic fort blanket and some jelly beans," Ethan said in a sarcastic tone. "That'll be a great help when we come across whatever fearsome monster lives on the Black Ice Bridge."

"We don't know for sure that there's a monster on the bridge—" Shay began.

"There's *something* there," Ethan said. "There's got to be some explanation for all the explorers who've gone missing over the years."

"Four hundred and fifty-six," Beanie said quietly. "More explorers have disappeared on the Black Ice Bridge than anywhere else in the known world."

Joss exchanged a look with Beanie. They knew better than most how dangerous the bridge could be.

"Exactly," Ethan said. "So what are we going to do when we come face-to-face with whatever the heck it is? Throw jelly beans at it?"

Beanie frowned. "I don't think that's very likely to work," he said.

"Stella doesn't even have her tiara!" Ethan pointed out.

"No, but I've got this." Stella touched her charm bracelet. "And I'm better doing magic with this because it doesn't chill my heart."

"Yes, but you don't really understand the magic or how it works," Ethan said, looking suddenly serious. "Look, I keep trying to tell you—magic is tricky, and difficult, and it takes a lot of practice to properly master it."

"You should know," Stella said, feeling a bit offended. "You're always creating polar beans by mistake, or conjuring up sea cucumbers instead of spears, or—"

"Indeed," Ethan snapped. His pale face had turned a little pink, meaning he was getting irritated. "I know you lot think I mess up spells because I'm an idiot, but the truth is that none of you has the faintest idea how difficult magic actually is to even touch, let alone control."

"No one thinks you're an idiot," Stella said, trying to be conciliatory.

"I sometimes think you're an idiot when you're mean to other people," Beanie volunteered. "But I don't think you're an idiot for getting spells wrong. Everyone gets things wrong while they're still learning."

"All right, everyone, I think that's enough bickering for now," Felix said. "We can all agree that our situation is not ideal, but we're stuck with it, I'm afraid, so we'd better make the best of things. Now, my suggestion is this: We make our way back toward the mainland and pull up on the coast somewhere. From there we can make our way to the nearest village to gather whatever additional supplies we can find—"

"Large spears," Ethan interrupted. "I think we should definitely have at least one large spear."

"Perhaps, but let's talk about that later," Felix said. "Once we're equipped, we can catch the train to Blackcastle."

Everyone fell quiet, lost in their own thoughts and concerns about what lay ahead. They'd left the lights of

Coldgate far behind them now, and the dark ocean stretched out disconcertingly in every direction as far as the eye could see—which, admittedly, wasn't all that far since it was very dark, with only the lantern at the front of the sleigh to light their way. Now that Stella looked at it more closely, she saw that the lantern dangling from the troll's hand had a single pale candle inside it, which also seemed to be made from ice. An odd white flame flickered from the wick, shedding a sparkly, frosty light dancing over the waves, and when Stella put her hand to the glass side, it was cold to the touch rather than warm.

She kept peering at the ocean, worrying that she had glimpsed the silent, deadly glide of a shark's fin or the splash of a squid's tentacle momentarily breaking the surface. Beanie's thoughts were obviously going the same way because he said:

"Captain Caspar Jasper Caratacus and his team were killed by snow sharks in the Icelands during the ill-fated Snow Shark Expedition. Guess how many shark teeth they found embedded in their ship?"

"Beanie, remember what we talked about the other day?" Joss said. "About how sometimes, in certain situations, this kind of conversation can make people uneasy?"

Beanie paused, then nodded slowly. Stella very much wanted him to change topic, especially since he might go on to mention Ethan's brother, Julian, who'd been killed in the Poison Tentacle Sea by the screeching red devil squid.

"Perhaps you could think those facts inside your head rather than saying them out loud?" she suggested.

Beanie nodded again. "All right. But it was two hundred and four," he said. "Shark teeth, I mean. That's how many they found embedded in the ship."

Ethan turned to Stella and said, "Do you even know where these bears are taking us? They could be swimming straight toward the Land of Pyramids for all we know."

"It turns out there's no such thing," Shay said. "It's been discredited."

"What do you mean?" Felix asked.

"I read about it in one of Father's scientific journals," Shay said. "Captain Filibuster took an expedition to the exact reported coordinates for the Land of Pyramids, but there was nothing there. People are saying that perhaps Lord Horace Hogarton Jennings made the whole discovery up to get accolades and credit. He might even be expelled from the Desert Jackal Explorers' Club."

"But that can't be right," Felix said, frowning. "I've *seen* the Land of Pyramids. From a distance, granted, and many years ago, but I definitely saw it. Besides which, most explorers don't give tuppence for accolades and credit."

Stella knew that Felix didn't care about those things himself, but she wasn't convinced that they weren't terribly important to some of the other explorers.

"Well, the bears aren't taking us to the Land of Pyramids, real or not," she said, squinting down at the compass in her hand. Her eyes seemed to itch with tiredness all of a sudden and her shoulders felt heavy, as if there were a weight resting on them. "I've set this for home," she went on. "I know we're not actually going back there, but we need to aim for the nearest shore down the coast. The bears are going the right way and seem to be listening to me again. We'll be there in no time."

"It'll take all night and most of tomorrow," Ethan replied. "We're still miles and miles away, and these bears are going at about six miles an hour."

He was right. Polar bears were strong swimmers, and Stella knew that they could keep going for days and days. But they weren't exactly the fastest swimmers in the world.

"Well, we'll get there eventually," Stella said, doing her best to sound cheerful at the same time as wondering why on earth she suddenly felt so exhausted. "And that's the most important thing."

The moment she finished speaking, however, something odd started to happen to the sleigh. Stella felt her fingers sinking into the seat like it was made from putty rather than ice. It seemed smaller than it had been a moment ago too. There were cries of dismay from the others as they realized that the sleigh was shrinking around them. The splashing noises made by the polar bears disappeared as the two animals faded away in a twinkling of blue lights, leaving them drifting without direction.

As the sleigh shrank, they were forced to clamber out onto the little iceberg and, moments later, the sleigh had vanished entirely, leaving them with nothing but a floating lump of ice that was barely big enough to contain everybody, and rapidly getting smaller.

CHAPTER FIVE

D O SOMETHING!" ETHAN SAID to Stella. "Get them back!"

"I'm trying!" she gasped. She was clutching the silver charm on her bracelet and concentrating as hard as she could, but it was as if the magic was suddenly slipping through her fingers. Without the carriage's lantern, it seemed very dark out on the ocean, with only the stars shining softly overhead.

Ethan groaned. "I knew this would happen," he said. "I tried to tell you that magic wasn't easy."

"The iceberg is disappearing too," Beanie pointed out.

Stella saw that he was right. The piece of ice beneath them was melting away at an alarming rate. If it carried on like this, they'd all be in the sea within moments. She looked at the icy black waves lapping hungrily against the iceberg and felt a little shudder of dread run through her.

"What are we going to do?" she asked. "We've got no boat, nothing to use as a raft, nothing that will even float!"

"I've been practicing my raft spell," Ethan said. "Allow me."

He drew himself up a little straighter and with a superior, self-satisfied look clicked his fingers. Everyone looked at the water hopefully, praying that a strong, sturdy raft with a nice big sail would materialize, but instead an inflatable hippopotamus appeared—the type children play with in swimming pools, only ten times as big. It had an extremely grumpy-looking face and bobbed awkwardly in the water beside them.

Everyone looked at Ethan.

"Well, it's something, isn't it?" he said defensively.

"Perhaps if you'd spent a little more time practicing your raft spells and a little less time working on humiliation spells for Gideon, we might be in a better position right now," Shay growled.

Ethan scowled. "I've been practicing a shield spell too," he said, a little sulkily. "And I can do it really well."

"It's better than swimming," Felix cut in. "Everyone climb on quick, or else it will float away."

The hippo did look as if it was about to bob off without them, so they all hurriedly climbed onto its back—an extremely awkward procedure, involving a lot of slipping, sliding, and squabbling. Finally, everyone was on—with

Ethan right at the front and Felix and Joss at the back—and only just in time, because moments later the iceberg melted away into nothing.

With all of them on it, the hippo sat a bit lower in the water and their boots only just hovered above the surface of the ocean. Shay sat right behind Stella, and she could feel he was trembling through his cloak. She looked around at him and whispered, "Are you okay?"

"Don't worry about me, Sparky," he replied. He looked paler than before and Stella felt guilt stir in the pit of her stomach again, but he offered her a smile and said, "Just cold, that's all."

It *was* cold out in the middle of the freezing ocean with a salty breeze scraping roughly over their skin. And yet no one else was shivering like Shay.

"Hopefully no sharp shark fins will go by," Beanie remarked. "Because if they do, they'll pop this hippo like a balloon."

There were no handholds for them to grab on to, meaning that everyone had to tighten their grip with their legs and balance precariously where they sat.

"So, what do we do now?" Stella asked. She looked at Ethan and said, "I don't suppose you've got another spell to get this thing to swim forward?"

The magician shook his head, causing the moonlight to glint off his white-blond hair. "I'd probably just make things worse," he said in a morose tone. "As you were so keen to point out, my magic doesn't always go to plan."

"Could we fashion a sail out of a petticoat?" Beanie suggested hopefully.

They considered it for a moment, but Beanie's mum was wearing trousers and although Stella was perfectly prepared to give up her petticoat, it wouldn't be big enough by itself to form a sail.

"A ship is bound to pass us eventually," Felix said. "They'll stop and pick us up."

"What if pirates find us before a respectable ship does?" Beanie said.

"Even if a respectable ship discovers us, they'll probably hand you two straight in to the authorities," Ethan said, glancing over his shoulder at Felix and Stella.

"Perhaps you could use your frost magic to make paddles?" Beanie suggested.

"Frost magic only makes things out of snow," Stella replied. "And snow paddles would disintegrate. Besides, I don't think I'm able to do any more magic right now. It feels like that carriage spell took everything."

"That was pretty big magic," Ethan said with a grunt. "It's no wonder it used up all your reserves."

A miserable silence descended upon the group. Stella didn't think there was anything guaranteed to make you feel small as much as bobbing around helplessly on an inflatable hippo in the middle of a freezing sea.

They were just debating whether the jungle fairies ought to be sent to fetch help and, if so, who exactly they should be sent *to*, when suddenly Joss said sharply, "Did anyone hear that?"

The group fell quiet.

"I don't hear—" Ethan began.

"I do," Beanie said, all the color draining from his face. "It's mermaids."

Elves have better hearing than humans, but after a few moments the others heard it too: an eerie, whispering, lilting song that sent shivers across their skin. Beanie didn't recite any facts this time and Stella was relieved. They all knew how dangerous mermaids could be. They all knew that they would sometimes drag sailors and explorers beneath the waves to drown them for no reason.

"Stay calm," Felix murmured beneath his breath. "And don't jump to conclusions. There are lots of dark rumors about mermaids, but I met a fellow once who said a mermaid had saved his life. They may not all be bad."

The singing got nearer and louder. It was beautiful, but strange too, and Stella couldn't decide whether she liked it or not. It made her feel odd inside her head, like she might float away at any second. She'd seen paintings of mermaids in books and little pictures of them printed on maps, but she'd never seen one in real life before and part of her was thrilled—while the other part was terrified that a hand might suddenly shoot up from beneath the water, wrap around her dangling foot, and drag her straight down into the sea.

"There's one!" Shay cried.

They all followed his pointing finger. Stella thought she saw a flash of something, but it was hard to tell in the darkness.

Then there was a splash and a ripple just behind them, followed by another and another.

Stella looked down and this time clearly caught sight of a mermaid's tail, wet and shining in the starlight, for a brief moment before it disappeared back beneath the surface.

"They're surrounding us," she whispered.

A bigger ripple rocked the inflatable hippo, and they all squeezed it with their legs a little tighter. The next second, a mermaid's head broke the surface of the water.

Her hair was a tangle of green and blue braids, knotted with shells and pieces of coral. She wore a necklace of tiny pearls around her throat and her halter-neck top was woven together from strands of seaweed. Her skin was almost as white as Stella's, and her dark eyes seemed too big for her face somehow. Like their singing, the mermaid was both strange and beautiful.

For a moment, there was a strained silence while they stared at each other.

Then Felix said, "Hello. It's an honor to meet you. My name is Felix Evelyn Pearl. My companions and I are explorers."

Everyone held their breath as the mermaid gazed back at them. Finally, she said, "I've never known explorers to travel on an inflatable hippo before."

Her voice was low and gravelly, like she had sand in her throat.

"Ah," Felix said. "Well, that was somewhat of a mistake. You see we—"

"Can we have our flower back, please?" the mermaid said.

"I beg your pardon?"

"That boy has one of our flowers." She pointed at Ethan.

"I most certainly do not," he protested.

"It's down the back of your cloak," the mermaid said.

Stella leaned forward and, ignoring Ethan's yelp of complaint, thrust her hand down his cloak. Her fingers immediately made contact with something smooth and cool, and she carefully drew out the mermaid flower.

"It must have happened when we crashed through the market," she said.

Mermaid flowers were made from sea glass, and this one had a blue stem with jade petals. Stella thought it was glorious.

"Here you go," she said, holding it out.

The mermaid took it and immediately slid it behind her ear.

"Thanks, I guess," she said. "Although I wish you people wouldn't steal them from us in the first place."

Stella swallowed hard. "I'm sorry," she said.

She noticed that another couple of mermaids had broken the surface just behind the first one. She could only see their outline in the darkness, and it was impossible to tell how many of them there were altogether. They didn't seem as if they were going to attack, but Stella wasn't sure what they wanted, either.

"You shouldn't be out here on that hippo, you know," the mermaid said. "It's not safe."

Had Stella imagined it, or was there just a hint of a threat in those words?

"We're trying to find our way to the Black Ice Bridge," said Felix.

The mermaid gave him a strange look. "On an inflatable hippo?" she said. "It'll take you a very long time. Besides which, only fools go to the Black Ice Bridge. You'll perish, for sure."

"That's our business," Ethan said. "Look, how about a bargain? We need to get to shore somehow. What would it take for you to pull us there?"

There was a little gasp from the mermaids, and the one in front looked horrified. "*Pull* you?" she said. "Like some

common sea cow?" Her eyes went cold. "You talk of bargains, but what's to stop us from simply taking everything you have after we've drowned you?"

Stella gulped.

"I beg your pardon, madam," Felix quickly said. "I assure you there was no offense meant. We have only the utmost respect for merfolk."

"And I really don't want to be drowned by a mermaid on my birthday," Beanie said miserably.

"Birthday?" the mermaid said sharply. She sighed and glanced over her shoulder. "One of them has their birthday today."

There was a soft sigh from the gathered mermaids behind her.

"We cannot drown a person on their birthday," the mermaid said, turning back to them. "It's against mermaid law."

The mermaid swam slowly over and peered up at Beanie with her impossibly large eyes. Now that she was closer, Stella could see that her skin was covered in scars, and a fresh open wound stretched down her right-hand side.

"We have to give you a gift," she said, sounding disgruntled. "It's the law. So name it—what would you have us give you? A ride back to shore, I suppose."

Beanie slowly shook his head. "Thank you," he said.

"But I'd rather not have a gift that someone was forced to give me. We'll find some other way of getting there."

"Beanie!" Ethan hissed.

The medic ignored him and said to the mermaid, "How were you hurt?"

"It's all the ships passing back and forth," the mermaid said. "Sometimes we can't get out of the way in time. Sometimes fishing boats hunt after us deliberately, hoping to catch us as curiosities to sell to the Ocean Squid Explorers' Club."

"I'm sorry," Beanie said, sounding stricken.

The mermaid narrowed her eyes at him suspiciously. "Why?"

"You shouldn't be hunted. Or have your flowers stolen. It's cruel and wrong." He reached out his hand. "Do you mind?"

The mermaid slowly shook her head, and the next second green sparks fizzed from the end of Beanie's fingers as he used his healing magic to knit the mermaid's torn skin back together. Apart from looking a little red, it seemed like she'd never been injured at all, and Stella found herself thinking that Beanie's healing magic must be getting stronger.

The mermaid ran her webbed fingers over her side in surprise, before looking back at Beanie, blinking her large eyes rapidly. "Why would you do that? What do you want in return?"

"You needed help, and I was able to help you," Beanie

said simply. "I don't want anything in return. There's no reason why explorers and mermaids can't be friends."

Some of the other mermaids had come closer to see what was going on. Stella saw that they had gills in their neck and that there was something fishlike and cold about their eyes too.

"There is every reason in the world why we can't be friends," the mermaid said. "Not least of which is the many hundreds of years of bloodshed between us. However, that doesn't apply to you today, little elf, so we would *like* to give you a gift, please."

"Taking us back to shore?" Ethan asked hopefully.

The mermaid ignored him and said, "We will give you the gift of not harming your friends. It's not *their* birthdays, after all." She smiled. "*And* we will take you back to shore."

In a flurry of ripples, the mermaids had attached seaweed ropes around the hippo, and the next moment it jerked forward and they were racing over the surface of the ocean so quickly it felt like the hippo barely skimmed the surface. It seemed, unsurprisingly, that mermaids could swim much faster than polar bears.

"Well done, my boy," Felix said approvingly to Beanie. "A little kindness can go a long way in life, I've found."

Joss leaned forward to briefly touch Beanie's shoulder, looking proud.

They traveled on beneath the stars for much of the

night. Somehow, they managed to doze a little by sitting propped against each other, but it was a precarious business when you were bobbing about on an inflatable hippo that was being towed by mermaids in the middle of the sea. Stella found she couldn't relax enough to sleep even though she still felt extremely tired. Felix had mastered the art of sleeping anywhere, and Stella could hear him snoring softly at the back with the jungle fairies curled up in his pockets, echoing his snores. Beanie had slumped forward over the hippo's head, and she wasn't sure about Shay and Joss.

Ethan was definitely awake, though. He sat directly in front of her and seemed too restless to settle. Eventually, Stella felt obliged to lean forward and ask, "What's wrong? Have you got an itch you can't reach, or something?"

Ethan glanced back at her. "Do you think I'm a bully?" he asked in a low voice.

"Oh." Stella was taken aback by the question. "Well . . ."

"You do," Ethan said with a sigh. "Don't you?"

Stella couldn't help thinking of Gideon, standing in the lobby in his pants, ashamed and humiliated as everyone pointed and laughed at him.

"I don't want to be," Ethan said. "A bully, that is. But I'm afraid it's not something I have any control or choice over. It's just something I *am*."

"I don't think that's true," Stella whispered, thinking of her snow queen heritage.

She'd always wanted to know what had happened to her birth parents, but when they found their abandoned castle during their first expedition, they had discovered that Stella's biological mother and father had been cruel, cold people. And if Stella used her ice magic too much, it would freeze her heart and the same thing might happen to her, too.

"Do you remember when you said that if you'd known about Julian's death, you would have made allowances for me when I was being obnoxious?" Ethan asked. "Well, the truth is that Julian's death didn't make me this way. I was like this before—long before—from the very beginning, I think. There's this big mean streak running right down the middle of me, and sometimes I can't stop it from taking over. And I don't even want to. I'm just as bad as Gideon Galahad Smythe."

Behind Stella, Shay stirred and leaned forward slightly. "The difference is that you think about it later and you're sorry," he said. "You realize you made a mistake. Which means you can resolve to do better next time."

"He's right," Stella said. "We can decide for ourselves that we're not going to be a certain way."

"It's that easy, is it?" Ethan grunted.

"It's that easy," Stella replied. "And it's that hard."

Shay gripped the magician's shoulder. "You're nowhere near as bad as Gideon Galahad Smythe, Prawn."

Ethan flashed him a grateful smile, and they continued on through the night. By the time they reached the shore, the sun was just starting to peek above the horizon, painting the waves gold. Felix leapt off when they got to the beach, his boots splashing into the shallow water as he dragged the hippo up onto the sand. The others scrambled to help him and then turned back to thank the mermaids, but they had already gone, melted away like the morning fog.

"They're going back out to sea. Look," Stella said, pointing at a mermaid's tail that flashed briefly above the waves.

"Do you think they really would have drowned us if it weren't for Beanie?" Shay asked, staring after them.

"Who knows?" Felix said.

He stretched, and Stella heard something pop loudly in his back. They were all feeling the aches and pains of having clung to an inflatable hippo for most of the night. In fact, Stella's legs were like jelly, and from the wobbly look of the others, she thought they probably felt the same. The sun was climbing higher in the sky now, and they all flopped down on the sand to enjoy the warmth for a moment and to catch their breath before getting up and picking their way across the beach to start the next part of their journey.

CHAPTER SIX

THEY SOON DISCOVERED THAT the mermaids had dropped them off on the outskirts of Cragstaff, the neighboring village to Blackcastle. The explorers scrambled up the cliff—which wasn't the easiest climb in the world and not much fun doing on an empty stomach, either. When they reached the top, they could see the small collection of buildings that made up Cragstaff just a short walk away. And in the other direction was the incredible sight of the Black Ice Bridge itself, stretching out across the sea.

It was said to be the largest bridge in the world, and Stella could definitely believe it. It was simply monstrous—like a bridge built for a giant—with great towers that were so tall their tops were lost in the clouds placed along it at regular intervals. Thick cables ran down from these, attached to black marble railings running all the way to the bridge.

Stella had heard stories about the bridge, of course, but it was a very different thing seeing it in real life. Faced with its humongous size, she wondered whether there might actually be giants on the other side of it, after all.

"Felix," she said, looking up at her father. "Have you ever seen a giant?"

He slowly shook his head. "We used to hear stories about giants many years ago," he said. "But no one's seen one for centuries."

"Do you think that's what could be on the other side of the bridge?" Stella asked.

"My dear, I really have no idea."

"It's one of the theories," Beanie said. "Some people believe the Black Ice Bridge leads to one of the Land End Giants."

Although no one could know for certain what shape the

world really was, one of the most popular theories was that it was a flat square, with each of its four corners held up by a tremendous giant.

"Captain Munro of the Desert Jackal Explorers' Club claimed to have seen one of the Land End Giants with his own eyes just a few months ago," Beanie said.

"He also claimed he traveled through the treacherous Tambuctoo Desert with nothing but a compass, a rifle, a blue dress coat, and a wide-brimmed hat." Ethan snorted. "Father says he's a liar who ought to be expelled from the club."

"There did seem to be a convenient lack of evidence," Felix agreed. "You know, there's a new theory I read about in a scientific journal recently. It was penned by the secretary of the Royal Academy of Science, who suggests that the world isn't flat at all, but actually a sphere."

Everyone laughed at the preposterousness of such an idea. Stella was grateful to Felix for sharing the theory just then—seeing the bridge for the first time was extremely frightening, and it was a relief to break the tension for a moment before she turned her attention back to the gigantic structure.

Built from black ice, it gleamed like an oil slick in the sunlight. Everyone knew black ice was particularly treacherous due to the fact that it contained evil magic. The bridge stretched out a long way over the cold sea, before disappearing into the freezing fog on the other side. It had been there for hundreds of years, and suddenly it seemed so strange to Stella that no one knew who had built the bridge, or why, or where it went. But she knew that looking at it now sent a chill racing down her spine and made her hands sweat and her skin crawl. There was just something wrong about it. Something bad. Something unnatural that wordlessly screamed at them to stay away.

Then Stella heard a soft sniffle and looked up to see that Joss was crying. Beanie had noticed it too and moved closer to her.

"Mum," he said quietly. "What can I do to help?"

"Oh, my dear, don't mind me," Joss said, suddenly flustered as she fumbled in her pockets for a handkerchief. "I never thought seeing the bridge would turn me into such a silly . . ."

"Here," Felix said kindly, pressing a clean handkerchief into Joss's hand. "There's nothing silly about it. You lost someone very dear to you."

Joss blew her nose with shaking hands. Stella felt quite dismayed to see her so upset, especially as she was usually so cheerful. She moved closer to wrap her arm around the elf's waist.

"He promised, you see," Joss said softly. "Adrian, I mean. He promised he'd come back to Beanie and me."

Beanie slipped his hand into his mother's and squeezed her fingers.

"I mean, I knew he couldn't really make a promise like

that," Joss went on. "No explorer can." She glanced up at the bridge. "And yet . . . I still . . . I always believed he *would* come back. Sometimes, even now, I expect him to walk through the front door, stamping snow off his boots, grinning that big grin, and saying it was all a mistake."

"He's gone, Mum," Beanie said in a quiet voice. "He's been gone for over eight years. He's never coming back."

"I know, dear," Joss said with a sigh. "I know that really. It's just sometimes I forget to know it." She took a deep breath and handed the handkerchief back to Felix. Then she straightened her shoulders, gave Beanie's hand a squeeze, hugged Stella a little closer, and said, "Right, that's quite enough of that. Adrian would be ever so cross if he could see me making such a fuss. Let's get going."

"Do we . . . do we still think we should do this?" Shay asked, sounding uncertain.

Stella turned toward him. A low whining sound attracted her attention, and she saw that Koa had appeared beside him. She was trembling from head to foot, and frost iced her black fur.

Shay knelt down and spoke to her in a low voice, trying to soothe her, but the wolf was clearly freezing.

"I've never seen her affected by weather before," Ethan said, staring. "Even in the Icelands she never seemed cold."

"It's the witch wolf's bite that's making her cold, like me," Shay replied.

Stella thought back to those fearsome wolves, with their white coats, frozen silver eyes, and snarling rage, and she shivered.

Soul eaters, Cadi had called them. Doomed to roam the wilderness, trapped as wolves forever. They couldn't let that happen to Shay or to Koa.

"Yes," Felix said. "I think we all still want to do this, but if anyone's changed their mind, now is the time to turn back. It may be too late once we step onto the bridge."

No one wanted to turn back, so Felix suggested they go into Cragstaff and pick up whatever last-minute supplies they could get their hands on. Stella was quite comfortable in just her traveling dress, but the others could all do with some extra layers under their cloaks. Everyone thought that weapons and some mode of transportation would be a good idea too.

"I don't suppose we'll be fortunate enough to find a Weenus's Trading Post set up outside the bridge," Felix said as they made the short walk to the village.

Unfortunately, Cragstaff wasn't much of an explorer stronghold, either, and the little shops seemed to have more in the way of knit sweaters and tea cozies than spears and sleds. To make matters worse, the shopkeepers started casting curious looks at Stella, clearly recognizing her as the ice princess who'd been in the papers recently.

"Perhaps some of you should wait outside the village with Stella," Felix said. "It doesn't take all of us to pick up supplies."

Stella was reluctant to go, but she could see Felix was making sense. So, after a brief discussion, it was agreed that Stella, Shay, and the jungle fairies would wait on the road leading to Blackcastle while Felix, Ethan, Beanie, and Joss went to pick up whatever supplies they could.

When they met again about an hour later, the shopping party didn't have all that much to show for their trip except for a few bars of mint cake, some extra sweaters, and a battered-looking sled attached to a piece of rope.

"Not a single weapon to be found anywhere," Ethan said, kicking the sled in disgust.

"But we do have food and shelter thanks to the magic fort blanket," Felix said. "That's the main thing for now."

They continued on their way to Blackcastle, taking the winding path along the cliff top and casting frequent nervous glances at the Black Ice Bridge. As they got closer, they began to pass signs telling them that the village was permanently closed and warning them to turn back. Naturally, they ignored these and continued to trudge through the snow toward their destination. Beanie pulled the sled part of the way, but it was so crumbling and rotten that it fell to bits less than a mile out of Cragstaff.

Ethan picked up a broken plank of wood with a nail sticking through it and sighed. "At least we can use this as a weapon," he said, stuffing the plank into his bag.

No one said much, but Stella found she was chewing her

lip nervously. This was their most dangerous expedition yet, and they were less prepared than they had ever been before. It was not the arrangement any of them had hoped for.

Finally, they rounded a corner and found themselves looking over a crest at the village walls below.

"Oh, look!" Stella cried, pointing. "There's a child."

"That's not a person," Joss said. "Not anymore, anyway."

As they descended, Stella realized Beanie's mum was right. The small figure in the snow had *once* been a woman, but now she was as frozen and lifeless as any doll. She half crouched in the snow, an expression of terror still fixed upon her face as she stared up at some long-gone threat.

Stella knelt in the snow before the woman and peered into her face, hoping for some flicker of life. Her lacy collar and bonnet were items from two centuries ago, and her eyelashes were delicate threads of ice. She seemed so real—almost as if she might blink at any moment.

"Perhaps you could unfreeze her?" Beanie suggested.

"I've got no idea how," Stella replied. "And I don't want to risk making it worse, but . . . I don't think there's anything left to unfreeze. She's made completely of ice now—even her clothes."

She rested her fingertips lightly on the woman's sleeve and could sense, somehow, that it was hopeless.

"I think she's been too cold for too long," Stella said, removing her hand. "There's nothing left to save."

She suddenly had a bad taste in her mouth, which got worse as they made their way through Blackcastle's gates and into the village itself. Everything there was made from the same shiny black rock as the bridge, meaning it had stayed well preserved even though no one had lived there for years.

But the shops and houses stood silent and deserted, and the only sound was the distant roar of the ocean. It was eerily quiet, and as the explorers walked through the streets they found more and more people—frozen just like the woman.

The story was that Queen Portia's attack had been unprovoked and sudden—and here was the proof. These people had clearly just been going about their everyday business. Stella saw women with baskets slung over their arms, dogs frozen midbark, and children caught in a game of hoop-rolling. All had the same horrified expression on their faces, even though whatever they'd been looking at had vanished.

Stella felt a sense of shame prickle over her skin. It was one thing reading about the evil deeds of snow queens in a report, but it was quite another to come face-to-face with the reality. All these people's lives just . . . ended. On a whim.

I will never become this, Stella thought to herself, as hard as she could. *I'll never become a monster.*

They made their way through the village, taking care not to knock into any of the frozen people. They glanced through windows as they went, but anything that might be useful to them had long since gone. Shops had been picked bare and houses cleared out. All that remained were husks—just the shell of the village that had once stood there. Even the carpet of snow was clean and crisp and perfect, and it felt almost wrong to leave their footprints behind. Ice magic had torn through the place, scouring jagged gouges along the walls as it went and leaving behind an ice trail that still glittered.

"It looks like the Black Ice Bridge is through there," Shay said, pointing at a little arch in the walls.

"Good," Ethan said. "Let's get out of this creepy place."

"Surely we're going to look at the castle first?" Felix said, pointing. Everyone looked up at the castle built into the mountainside above, menacing and unfriendly, the windows dark and lifeless. It looked as if the magic had exploded right out of the castle wall, cracking open the bricks on the top floor and coating them in enchanted ice.

"Queen Portia was evil," Stella said. "It seems to me that we should stay well away from her castle."

"We still don't have any weapons or transportation, though," Ethan pointed out. "Perhaps we should take a look."

There was a momentary silence.

Stella couldn't deny that weapons and transportation would be extremely useful on the Black Ice Bridge. Maybe even the difference between life and death. . . .

"All right," she said with a sigh. "I guess we could take a quick look. But everyone just . . . keep your wits about you."

CHAPTER SEVEN

THEY MADE THEIR WAY up the cliff, flashing nervous glances at the castle as they went. The last snow queen's castle they'd visited had been all towers and turrets, spindly and elegant. This one, by comparison, was a squat, square thing, hunched against the side of the cliff.

They reached the front doors and stopped. Snarling gargoyle faces were carved into the black marble surface. Shay reached out to try the door handle, but it didn't budge.

"Locked," he said, glancing at Stella.

She stepped forward and reached out her hand. Before she could even touch the handle, it clicked down and the door swung slowly open into a hall, chilly and dark and deserted. Remembering what had happened the last time they'd entered a snow queen's castle, Stella took a deep breath as she stepped over the threshold. Sure enough, the moment her boot touched the floor, the castle came to life in front of their eyes. Dust vanished from the floor, cobwebs disappeared from the chandelier, and the ice that had formed over the paintings cracked and fell away.

The candles in the chandelier and the wall sconces suddenly lit themselves, casting a flickering glow over the polished black floor, stretching away from them as still and shiny as a lagoon. Dominating everything was a huge portrait of Queen Portia herself. The life-size painting was so vibrant and realistic that Stella jumped, mistaking it for the real thing.

Despite her fear, she was curious about what this other snow queen had looked like and stepped closer to the painting. Like most snow queens, Queen Portia was very beautiful and elegant. She was wearing a purple velvet dress trimmed with white fur. Around her neck hung a splendid golden locket, with a silver dragon curled around it, clutching a single starflake in one clawed foot.

Queen Portia's skin was extremely pale, but unlike Stella, this snow queen's hair was coal-black, pulled back in a complicated arrangement of plaits threaded with purple beads. A white tiara glittered in her hair, and there was a haughty look in her green eyes, which seemed to gaze right out of the canvas at them, as if she could actually see them.

As she stared at the painting, Stella saw that Queen Portia wore a charm bracelet that looked very similar to her own.

The only noticeable difference was that not all of the charms were silver—a single gold heart hung there too. An idea occurred to Stella, and she spun around to face the others.

"Do you think this snow queen had her own Book of

Frost?" she asked. "Jezzybella said that most snow queens have them, didn't she? Just like witches have a Book of Shadows?"

"That's certainly what she implied," Felix agreed.

"Well, if Queen Portia had her own Book of Frost, and it's still here, then perhaps it might contain the spell we need to save Shay! We might not need to cross the Black Ice Bridge at all!"

A small buzz of excitement rippled through them. Perhaps their journey need not be so long and perilous. Perhaps it could end right here in this castle. Stella would still be wanted for arrest, of course, and Felix would still be expelled from the club, but if they cured Shay, then at least that was one less thing to worry about.

"We should conduct a search," Felix said. "Together, I think. It'll take more time, but it's probably best that we don't split up."

They began to explore and quickly found that the castle was just as lavish as the one that had belonged to Stella's birth parents, with countless maps upon the walls and expensive-looking old globes on stands.

"It looks like Queen Portia liked traveling too," Stella said, reaching out to spin one of the globes. "I thought snow queens were supposed to stay in their frozen kingdoms."

She didn't much like the idea of having anything in common with this snow queen, and the thought nagged at her as they made their way upstairs to explore the upper floors. On the third level they quickly found the room with the broken outside wall. It seemed like some kind of magical explosion had taken place there. Enchanted ice spilled out from the center across the floorboards like fingers, spreading toward the wall, which had smashed apart beneath the impact. Icy air whistled in through the gap.

"What's with all the dragon images?" Shay asked, running his hand over a wall tapestry depicting a fearsome-looking white dragon. "I noticed them downstairs, too."

"Perhaps Queen Portia liked them," Stella said.

They went on to explore the rest of the castle, hunting high and low, but there was no sign of a Book of Frost or anything magical at all. Even the queen's bedchamber had been stripped bare, with only an empty jewelry box on display.

"Perhaps she took the book with her when the mob chased her away," Beanie suggested. "It looks like she took her tiara and charms and things."

They made their way back downstairs feeling a bit deflated.

"I feel like there's something else here," Stella said, gazing around. "But I don't know what. . . ."

She led the way back to the library.

"Queen Jessamine's castle had a secret passageway leading out of the castle," Stella said to the others. "You just had to pull the right book out. Maybe this one has something similar?"

They all started to pull books from the shelves at random.

"These books are all terribly old," Beanie said. "We should take some of them with us. They might be useful."

"How much use can a book about goblins be?" Ethan asked, throwing the book on the floor in disgust.

Beanie ignored the remark and stuffed a few books into his bag. They were just starting to think that perhaps there was no secret door after all, when Beanie pulled out a book about dragons—one of the bookcases immediately slid back with a groan to reveal a passageway.

"Well done, Beanie," Stella said, already stepping inside.

There was a stone dragon perched on a shelf just inside the doorway, and the lantern in its hand lit up as soon as Stella appeared.

"It's not a passageway, after all," she said, looking around at the others. "It's a staircase."

It was cut straight into the rock and curved away from them, down into the darkness.

"Does this lead *into* the cliff?" Ethan asked, peering over Stella's shoulder.

"Looks like it," she said. "Let's find out."

Stella knew the staircase could just be another way out of the castle, but there was a chance it could lead to a secret room where the queen's precious Book of Frost was hidden.

They made their way down, with Stella at the front and the jungle fairies bringing up the rear. More dragon lanterns came to life as they went past, casting their flickering light over the shiny stone. The steps were damp with moss, and they had to move carefully so as to avoid slipping. As they went farther, Stella thought she could smell water and hear the soft *drip-drip* of droplets landing on stone.

The staircase seemed to go on and on. They were just beginning to worry that they might never reach the bottom when finally they arrived at an arched doorway. As Stella stepped through, hundreds of candles sprang into life around them.

"It's a grotto!" she exclaimed.

The others followed her, gazing around at the cave hollowed out of the rock. Spindly stalactites stretched down from the ceiling and sharp stalagmites reached up from between the rock pools below. There were shells scattered everywhere, of all different colors—pearl and pink and blue and coral. The air smelled of salt and damp, and they could hear the roar of the ocean coming from not far away.

"And it's a . . . a kind of carriage house too. Look."

Shay pointed, and they saw there were indeed a variety of sleighs and carriages lined up at the far end of the cave. They were beautiful glittering creations made from sea crystal, all of them fit for a queen.

"They must have belonged to Queen Portia," Stella said.

They walked over to examine the vehicles and saw that, along with the more traditional sleighs they were familiar with, some of them were actually shaped like boats, complete with sails that hung limply from the masts. But it looked as if these boats were designed to run over ice rather than water, because they had steel blades attached to the bottom, the same as the sleighs.

"If only we had some expedition wolves, we could use one of these things to travel across the bridge," Ethan said, pointing at the harness attached to the boat's prow.

Stella frowned. "The harness looks too small for wolves. I wonder what type of animal it's for."

She reached out, and the moment her hand touched the reins there was a clanking noise behind them. The explorers turned in time to see a group of gargoyles peeling themselves from the walls, their clawed feet landing on the shell-covered ground with a crunch. They were all slightly different shapes and sizes—strange things, with horns on their heads, large pointed ears, and wings that groaned as they unfurled. There were seven of them, all yawning and stretching, as if they had just woken up.

"Astonishing," Felix said.

At his voice, the gargoyles looked around sharply, and soon they were clambering over the rocks toward the explorers, peering at them with their stone eyes and snuffling at them with their stone snouts.

"They look just the right size for these harnesses," Shay pointed out. "Perhaps Queen Portia had gargoyles rather than wolves."

"Do you think they're friendly?" Beanie asked nervously.

"They seem to recognize Stella," Shay said.

Indeed, the gargoyles were scraping and bowing in front of her.

"Hello," Stella said. "It's nice to—oh!" She broke off in surprise as one of the gargoyles gripped her hand and started tugging her over a stone bridge, the others close behind her. The gargoyle pressed Stella's hand against part of the wall that looked smoother than the rest. Before their eyes, a large chunk of stone slid back, and sunlight poured through the small gap.

"Hang on!" Stella tugged her hand free. "We can't leave just yet. First we have to explore the cave. Perhaps you can help us. You see, we're looking for a special book that—"

She broke off because, shaking its head, the gargoyle pointed at Stella and said something. The words came out all gravelly and clanky, like rocks knocking together.

"Oh dear, I'm afraid I can't understand you," Stella said.

The gargoyle pointed at her again and repeated whatever it had just said. When it realized she still couldn't understand, the creature shook its head again. Then it suddenly grabbed Stella's wrist and jabbed a stone finger at her charm bracelet.

"That . . . that's my bracelet," Stella said. The gargoyle seemed to be getting quite agitated, so she added, "It's all right; it can't hurt you."

"It's pointing at a particular charm, I think," Shay said.

He was right. The gargoyle was tapping its stone fingernail urgently against the silver dragon charm and then pointing back down into the cave. Stella recalled all the dragon motifs back in Queen Portia's castle and then she looked at the rocks the gargoyle was jabbing at. A dreadful thought occurred to her.

"You don't suppose—" she began.

But then Felix said sharply, "What was that noise?"

Everyone fell silent, including the gargoyles. Above the distant roar of the ocean and the *drip-drip* of the damp walls was a new sound: a groaning rumble that made the ground tremble beneath their feet and tiny stones and pieces of shell shower down on them from the ceiling.

And then a huge white dragon's head appeared from over the top of a pile of rocks, trails of steam drifting from its nostrils as it poked its snout into the air. It blew out a great blast of glittering icy breath that snapped off stalactites as if they were made of sugar, covered all the shells in a layer of frost, and chilled the air throughout the entire cave.

CHAPTER EIGHT

T HEY ALL STARED AS the dragon slowly stood up and unfurled its wings. It was massive—over a hundred feet long from snout to tail, with sharp spines along its back, hundreds of teeth, and a dangerous spiked tail. It seemed to be made entirely of ice—all except for its eyes, which were a cloudy, milky blue. It had been buried beneath a layer of shells, and now it shook itself free, staggering slightly as the shells cascaded from it like water. Its tail whacked against the wall of the cave so hard that it cut a gouge right out of the rock, exposing a shining layer of sea crystal hidden beneath.

Finally understanding what the gargoyles had been try-ing to warn them about, the explorers fled toward the exit.

But it was too late. The dragon had realized they were there and let out a great bellow of anger. Its monstrous head whipped around, and it blew a freezing ice cloud at them, which quickly formed into a thick wall of dangerously glittering ice. It didn't hit anyone, but Stella saw a stalactite snap off from the ceiling and go plummeting, like a blade, straight toward Joss.

Stella cried out a warning. Felix spun around, and seeing what was about to happen, dived toward Joss, knocking her out of the stalactite's path just in time. They toppled off the edge of the little bridge, landing upon a slab of rock beneath. Before they could even stand up, the dragon blew ice at them again, and this time it solidified all the way from the top of the bridge right down to the rocky slab, effectively creating a wall that sealed Felix and Joss behind it.

"No!" Beanie screamed.

His shout drew the dragon's attention, and it raised its huge head, turning to face them. Its pale blue eyes wandered straight over them blindly, and there was a grayish tinge to the ice around its muzzle. Stella realized the dragon was old, and she wondered whether it could even see them.

Ethan raised his hand and threw some magic arrows at it. They had fiery tips, and the dragon bellowed as they landed on its back. Its breath came in rapid gasps, and Stella suddenly saw that the dragon was afraid.

"Stop!" she cried.

She ran to the edge of the bridge and raised both her hands. She couldn't do any ice magic without her tiara, but she knew she had to do *something* to show the dragon that she was an ice princess and that she wasn't a threat.

"It's okay!" she cried. "We're not going to hurt you!"

Perhaps the dragon was deaf as well—or else it simply didn't understand or believe her—because it roared out another blast of ice, passing so close to Stella that she had to duck in order to avoid being struck down by it.

Before the dragon could lash out again, Stella straightened back up, raised her arms, and concentrated as hard as she could. The air crackled around her hands and, magically, a butterfly appeared in the air before her. It was as large as an eagle, its wings formed of sparkling strands of pale blue frost, delicate and beautiful as spun fairy silk.

The butterfly immediately fluttered toward the dragon, landing on the very tip of its snout, where it beat its wings gently. The dragon went still, and everybody held their breath. Something about the motion seemed to calm it, and after a moment the dragon slowly lowered its head to rest it upon the stone bridge, snorting out icy air in agitated puffs.

Aware of the others watching from a distance, Stella walked over to the dragon.

"It's okay," she said, gently laying her hand on the creature's snout. The ice was freezing to her touch, but it didn't burn or blister her skin as she stroked up and down with her fingers. "We're sorry for disturbing you," she said. "You're safe. You can go back to sleep now."

The dragon started to make little rumbling sounds of

contentment, and a few minutes later it had fallen asleep, drooling slightly. The delicate frost butterfly seemed to melt away into the air.

Stella stood up carefully and slowly, without waking the dragon, and the next second the young explorers hurried down to the wall of ice below, slipping and sliding over the shifting carpet of frost-covered shells.

Beanie reached the ice wall first and hammered on it with his fist. "Mum!" he yelled, forgetting to be quiet. "Felix! Are you okay?"

Fortunately, the sleeping dragon didn't move a muscle. The others reached the wall in time to hear Joss call back, though her voice could only be heard faintly through the thick wall of ice.

"We're all right, Benjamin."

"How do we get them out?" Shay asked, looking at the others.

"If only there had been some weapons in the castle," Ethan said. "An axe on the wall, or something."

"This ice is too thick," Felix called back. "You wouldn't be able to break through it, even if you had an axe."

He let out a muttered curse, and Stella could hear anger in his voice, which wasn't like Felix.

"Can you do anything?" Beanie asked, looking at Stella.

She shook her head. "I don't know the ice-melting spell, remember? I can't do it without the Book of Frost."

They all stared at the wall in dismay. It seemed that the same spell they needed to save Shay was the one they now needed to free Felix and Joss from their ice prison.

"Well, I've got to at least try," Stella said. "I mean, I didn't know how to cast a spell to create a frost butterfly, but it just sort of happened on its own. Perhaps I need to think about it really hard."

She hoped no one would bring up what had happened when she'd tried this with Koa's witch wolf's bite. Koa had started howling almost as soon as the spell began and Shay had begged her to stop. But the desire to at least try to do something was overwhelming.

"I don't think you should," Ethan said at once. "Remember what happened when—"

Stella rounded on him with more bitterness than she'd meant to. "Well, what do *you* think I should do?" she demanded. "You're always telling us what shouldn't be done, but I never hear you suggesting anything that might actually be useful! It's like Shay said—all you ever do is make things worse!"

Ethan looked taken aback. "I'm sorry," he said. "I don't know what to suggest. I only know that magic can be dangerous—"

"Being sealed up inside an ice cave isn't the safest thing, either," Stella said. "And it's not one of *your* parents trapped in there. So be quiet and let me do this!"

Ethan shrugged but said nothing. Stella felt a small flutter of regret at the way she'd spoken to her friend—she wasn't really angry with him, but at the situation. They should never have come to the snow queen's castle. She shouldn't have let herself be talked into it.

"You'd best step back just in case," Stella said, glancing at the others.

They did as she said. Stella noticed that Koa had appeared at Shay's side, and this time she was sure that the white streak in her dark fur had gotten bigger. The wolf was panting, which Stella didn't remember ever seeing her do before.

She tried to push all her guilt and worry out of her mind as she turned back to the ice wall in front of her. They may not have discovered the Book of Frost in Queen Portia's castle, but perhaps the ice dragon had provided her with the opportunity to discover the magic spell all on her own.

"Felix, Joss, you'd better stand back," she yelled. "I'm going to try to get you out."

She raised her hands and concentrated, as hard as she could, on melting the ice in front of her. She wanted so badly to be able to fix all of this right here and now—to magically make it better for everyone.

She could feel the magic fizzing in her fingertips and her hands were growing warm, but nothing seemed to be happening at first, until Felix called out in an alarmed voice,

"Stella, whatever you're doing, I think you'd better stop! It's getting very warm in here."

"But that must mean it's working!" Stella said. The thought of success gave her an extra burst of determination as she threw all her strength into the magic.

But then there was a sudden shriek from behind the wall, and Felix shouted, "Stella, for goodness' sake, stop!"

Both her hands dropped to her sides as her heart seemed to plummet into her shoes. "What's wrong?" she called, suddenly terribly afraid of what the answer might be.

"Joss's hair was on fire!" Felix called back.

"*What?*" Stella gasped.

Beanie groaned and rushed forward toward the wall. "Mum, are you okay?"

"It's all right," his mum called back. "I'm fine. Felix put the fire out. But, Stella, dear, I don't think you can get through here with magic."

"All right, I won't try again." Stella bunched her hands up into fists. "Are you sure you're okay?"

"Perfectly fine," Joss replied.

"What do we do now?" Stella said hopelessly.

There was a brief pause.

Then Joss called, "You'll have to go without us."

"But we can't!" Beanie cried. "We can't leave you in there, Mum!"

"He's right," Shay said. "The journey across the bridge

and back will take weeks—if we even manage it at all. They'd both starve."

One of the jungle fairies tugged on Stella's sleeve. She looked down and saw it was Hermina holding up a plate of piranha cupcakes. The fairies seemed to be able to produce these whenever they liked, as if by magic. Hermina pointed to herself and then up at the gap in the wall, which, Stella saw, was large enough to admit a jungle fairy. As she watched, the other three disappeared through the gap, all carrying their own plate of piranha cupcakes.

"The fairies are going to stay behind with us," Joss called.

"But . . . but you can't just live off piranha cupcakes!" Stella called back. "Felix?"

"I've lived off worse in my time," Felix replied. His voice sounded strained as he swore again. Stella didn't think she'd ever heard him do that before. "Gods, Stella, I'm so sorry, but I don't think there's anything we can do. You'll have to go by yourselves."

"But what about water?" Stella called.

"The cave stretches back quite a bit," Joss replied. "One of the rock pools has got spring water in it."

The young explorers looked at one another.

"I don't see another way," Shay said.

Stella looked back at the wall. This couldn't be happening. It had been bad enough thinking they would have to cross the Black Ice Bridge when they were all together, let alone with the adults stuck here in Queen Portia's castle. She childishly felt there had to be *something* Felix could do to fix this. She needed him beside her for this adventure.

"Felix, you have to come," she said, even though she was very aware of how useless those words were.

"My darling, I wish that I could," Felix said. "But it isn't possible. Once you get the book and cure Shay, you'll just have to come back here and set us free."

"But what if we don't get the book?" Stella asked. "What if the bridge takes us?"

The explorers were all equally horrified at the prospect.

"I believe you can do this, Stella," Felix said. "Remember, you're not just an explorer. You're an ice princess, too."

Stella drew in a deep breath and let it out slowly, trying to accept what had happened. A hand gripped her shoulder, and she looked around to see Ethan standing beside her.

"It's all right," he said in a quiet, steady voice that Stella found immediately soothing. "We can do this. Somehow, we'll figure it out."

She looked at the others, who nodded. There was no choice. If they didn't go on, then they would lose two of their parents as well as Shay. Still, Stella couldn't help thinking it was a terribly bad sign that they had lost two members of their expedition already, before they'd even set foot on the Black Ice Bridge itself.

"All right, Felix," she called back, her heart heavy as a stone. "We're going. But we'll come back for you."

They called their good-byes through the wall. Stella wished with all her soul that she could hug Felix, or at least see him just one more time before she went. After all, they might never lay eyes on each other again. But although the jungle fairies came out to say good-bye, the humans were of course trapped inside.

"Benjamin," Joss called out as they were about to go.

"Yes, Mum?"

"Please promise me that you will come back off that bridge."

Beanie closed his eyes and drew in a deep breath. "I swear it," he said. "I'll come back."

But of course it wasn't a promise he could possibly keep—it wasn't a promise any of them could keep. Beanie's father had promised too, and he had loved his family just as much as they all did, but in the end it hadn't been enough. The bridge had taken him anyway.

And Stella couldn't help being aware, right down to her very bones, that the odds were stacked entirely against them— the chances were that none of them would ever return.

"At the risk of you biting my head off again, don't you think we should take that dragon with us?" Ethan said as they made their way toward the exit.

Stella shook her head. "It's old," she said. "And tired. I

don't think it would get very far. Besides, it's too big to fit through the gap in the wall."

"What about one of these sleighs?" Shay said, gesturing toward them.

They looked over and saw that the gargoyles had already buckled themselves into the harnesses attached to one of the snow-boats and were looking at the explorers expectantly, as if they were waiting for them.

Relieved that something had finally worked in their favor, Stella led the way over to the boat. There was just enough room for the four of them to climb up onto its deck.

CHAPTER NINE

THE GARGOYLES SHOT FROM the mouth of the cave, towing the snow-boat behind them. They came out onto a rocky ledge partway up the cliff. It was wet and slick with salt spray from the ocean, but this seemed to give the sure-footed gargoyles no trouble as they charged up a winding path that was just wide enough for the boat.

The gargoyles stopped when they reached the top, unbuckled their harnesses, and immediately rolled around joyously in the snow. The young explorers climbed out onto the cliff top. The sea sparkled several feet below, and the Black Ice Bridge loomed overhead, but it was the snow-boat they turned their attention to.

It was about the size of a sailing boat, carved from the same shimmering sea crystal they had seen in the caves—a beautiful mixture of white, blue, and green. A carved yeti snarled at the prow, and white and silver sails hung from the mast. A ladder led up to the small deck, where a spoked brass navigation wheel was linked to the gargoyles' reins.

It looked as if it had a lower deck below because there were portholes farther down too.

"This would be perfect for traveling across the Black Ice Bridge," Ethan said. He glanced at Stella. "Do you think you could order the gargoyles to take us?"

She frowned. "They're not slaves, and I'm not ordering them anywhere. But we could try asking them." At that moment, the gargoyles came scampering over. Soon all seven of the strange stone creatures stood on the ledge, bowing in front of Stella. In the sunlight, they could see that the gargoyles had bits of shell and coral embedded in their dark stone bodies, as well as barnacles clinging to their clawed feet and ankles. She wondered how long they'd been in the cave.

Still bent over in a bow, they looked up at Stella expectantly, as if waiting for her to say something.

"Er . . . thank you for trying to warn us about the dragon," she said.

"Can they understand you?" Beanie asked.

"I've got no idea," Stella said, still looking at the gargoyles. "We're actually on a very important expedition. You see, we need to get to the other side of the Black Ice Bridge. It's likely to be extremely dangerous, and of course you're under no obligation to take us, but—"

Stella broke off because the gargoyles were already hurrying to buckle themselves back into their harnesses.

Stella glanced at the others. "I think that's a yes," she said.

They climbed the ladder back onto the little boat, and the moment they were on board there was a lurch as the gargoyles started forward, towing the boat toward the Black Ice Bridge, leaving Queen Portia's castle behind them.

The four explorers went straight to the front of the boat and leaned forward over the railings. They saw that five of the gargoyles were on the ground, leaning into their harnesses and galloping across the snow on all fours. Their faces were screwed up against the cold, but Stella got the impression they were enjoying themselves. The other two gargoyles had spread their wings and risen up high into the sky above them, pulling the boat along from above. Stella could feel the powerful beat of their wings from where she stood, and when she looked down again, she saw that the boat was racing along the snow at a terrific rate.

"Good heavens!" Ethan exclaimed. "They must be immensely strong!"

Stella felt a smile spread over her face. "Just what we need for the Black Ice Bridge," she said. "At this rate, we'll be across to the other side in no time at all."

"And because gargoyles are made of stone, they don't even need to stop to rest or sleep," Beanie said. "Look, we're almost there."

They had indeed finally reached the Black Ice Bridge. This close, it seemed even more looming and forbidding than it had from the ocean. A gigantic, mysterious thing that stretched out over the water as far as the eye could see, until it was eventually swallowed up by the thick sea mist.

But the time for second thoughts and turning back had been and gone. The four junior explorers were racing straight for the infamous bridge that even the bravest of adult explorers only spoke of in hushed tones.

And now that they had such a perfect mode of transportation, Stella felt a small gleam of hope that perhaps they might just succeed after all.

CHAPTER TEN

S TELLA TUGGED GENTLY ON the reins to get the gargoyles to stop and then the explorers climbed down the ladder. They all felt a sense of trepidation as they stepped onto the bridge, but no curse came to strike them and no monster appeared from the fog. The structure must have been at least forty feet wide, but aside from its size it was almost as if it were just any other normal, everyday bridge.

Almost . . . but not quite.

Something felt wrong—Stella sensed it the moment she set foot on it—an unnatural chill that went all the way through her, as if some small, dead hand had just crept into hers, each cold finger trembling as it tried to hold on, and Stella didn't know whether to push it away or try to comfort it.

She shivered as she turned to the others. "Do you feel

it too?" she asked. But she could tell at once from their stricken faces that they did.

"Perhaps it's just the stories about the bridge affecting us?" Beanie suggested hopefully.

Ethan shook his head. "It's the magic," he said. "Evil magic. The bridge is soaked in it."

"I've got a book about evil magic," Beanie announced, surprising everyone by producing a battered old tome from his bag.

"Where the heck did you get that?" Ethan demanded.

"It was one of the books I took from Queen Portia's library."

Ethan stared at the book like it was a dangerous snake that might suddenly strike them.

"Books like that are very dangerous," he said, shaking his head. "You can't just go around collecting them like Easter eggs. If you've got any sense, you'll chuck it away."

Beanie frowned at the book in his hand. "But if evil magic is such a powerful threat, then surely it makes sense to learn as much about it as we can," he said, looking to the others for support.

Shay nodded. "That makes sense, I guess," he said.

"Isn't it against the law to own a book about evil magic?" Stella said. "I think I remember Felix telling me that once."

"I'm only borrowing it," Beanie said, putting it back in his bag. "And we're already breaking a lot of rules. I don't think one book is going to make much difference. Shall we take a proper look on the snow-boat? The gargoyles seem to know where they're going."

They climbed back onto the boat, and the gargoyles continued forward. There wasn't much spare space with the four of them standing on deck. The rest of it was taken up by the spoked wheel at the front, a bench seat at the back, and the mast in the middle.

"Perhaps if we unfurl the sails it'll help the boat move even faster?" Beanie suggested.

None of them really knew much about boats apart from Ethan. As a member of the Ocean Squid Explorers' Club, he had spent a lot of his time on ships, boats, and submarines, and he soon had the sails unfurled. As predicted, the wind quickly caught the billowing fabric and helped propel the snow-boat along the ice even more swiftly.

Stella noticed that there were several silver yeti statues perched along the rails, all holding lanterns with ice candles in them. Normal matches didn't seem to work on them, but remembering that this was a snow queen's boat, Stella reached her hand out toward the nearest one and concentrated on lighting it. Sure enough, a bright white flame burst into life and set off a chain reaction with the other lanterns lighting up too.

"I wonder how you get to the cabin below," Shay said.

They poked around and quickly found a ring handle set

into the deck. When they pulled the hatch open, they found a ladder leading down. The explorers descended cautiously, a little nervous that Queen Portia might have left something dangerous down there, but all they found was a small galley kitchen, long since empty, as well as a couple of hammocks strung up in a cramped little bedroom. Everyone was keen to keep their eyes on the road ahead, so they soon piled back on deck. The bridge really was massive. Not only was it immensely long, but it was also extremely wide. You could have had at least ten sleighs running side by side and there still would have been plenty of room.

Then the sea fog came down thick and fast and they couldn't see more than a little way in front of them, even with the flickering light from the yeti lanterns.

"Perhaps we shouldn't have put those sails up," Ethan said. "I think the gargoyles should slow down. We know there are things on the bridge up ahead. Abandoned camps and whatnot. We might crash into one."

Stella squinted at the gargoyles and wondered whether they could see any better than them. Deciding it was probably a good idea to be cautious, she leaned a little way over the rails and said, "Would you mind slowing down a bit?"

The gargoyles immediately obeyed her command and continued at a more sedate pace as Ethan showed the others how to take the sails back down.

Stella glanced at Beanie and said, "I don't suppose you

brought your father's journal with you? It would be useful to know what to expect."

Adrian Albert Smith's last travel journal contained a log of all that his team had seen and done on the Black Ice Bridge—until the entire expedition mysteriously vanished without a trace.

"I didn't bring it," Beanie said. He took Aubrey from his pocket and began to fiddle with the narwhal. "But I don't need it. I've known every word by heart for years. First we will see a twisted black tree with strange dark fruit you absolutely must not eat because it will set your stomach on fire. Then we will pass a ship graveyard, but we may not see it on account of the fog."

"How will we know it's there, then?" Ethan asked.

"You can hear the ship's bells," Beanie said, sounding glum. "A short while after that we should come across whatever's left of my father's camp. And then . . . we have absolutely no idea."

They continued on across the snow, everyone keeping their eyes strained straight ahead. Stella longed for her telescope. Her compass seemed to be no good on the Black Ice Bridge. When she took it from her pocket and opened the lid, the needle beneath the glass spun wildly, jerking from Shelter, to Yetis, to Angry Gnomes, without ever settling on one particular thing.

"It's probably the evil magic affecting it," Beanie said.

Stella sighed and replaced the compass in her pocket. It had started to snow again. Big fat flakes swirled around the top of the mast, and sea mist rose up so thickly from the ocean that they couldn't even see the water. In fact, it was difficult to see anything much.

The sun was starting to set by the time they reached the black tree mentioned in Beanie's father's journal. Shay spotted its crooked branches poking through the mist like fingers.

"There's the tree," he called, drawing the others' attention. "We should stop and take a look at it."

"It's dangerous to stop," Stella replied.

"It's more dangerous not to," Shay said. "It'll be nightfall soon. We all need to sleep. I don't think we should just carry on hurtling farther over the bridge while we do that. We need to have our wits about us for whatever we encounter. I think we should make camp."

After a brief discussion, they all agreed that perhaps this would be a wise move. So as they reached the tree, Stella gave the command to the gargoyles to stop. They climbed down from the deck and stepped out onto the snow, right into the shadow that the twisted black tree had cast.

It was indeed a strange thing, looming out of the mist, all crooked angles and sticky leaves. Its warped branches drooped in a sickly looking manner, and no wonder, Stella thought. There was nothing for it to live off out here, no

nutritious soil or fresh rain. It was rooted in packed ice filled with evil magic.

As she stepped closer, she was immediately waylaid by one of the gargoyles, who landed in the snow before her and began to point insistently at the dragon charm on her bracelet once again.

"Yes, you were right about the dragon." She sighed. "And I'm sorry we didn't understand your warning back at the castle—"

The gargoyle shook his head with an irritated huff and marched past her to join the other gargoyles, who had taken off their harnesses and were happily rolling around in the snow. Stella led the other explorers over to the tree.

Now that she was close, she could see it seemed to be made entirely from pieces of driftwood all stuck together with a sticky black substance. A salty, seaweedy smell filled the air, perhaps carried in from the ocean by the sea mist. Some odd-looking fruit hung from the bent branches, swollen and shiny.

"That's strange," Beanie said with a frown. "I'm sure Father's journal said the fruit looked like grapes, but these are much bigger. More like melons."

Ethan shuddered and said, "The tree looks like bones that have been broken and then set back at the wrong angle. What kind of idiot would eat its fruit in the first place?"

Beanie looked rather offended, but Shay hurriedly pointed out, "If no one had ever tried the pineapples on Pineapple Island, then they never would have known how delicious they were. And they looked far more dangerous on the face of it. Covered in spikes and things."

The black melons weren't covered in spikes, but Stella didn't think they looked appetizing even so. The moisture glistening on their dark skins had a sweaty sort of sheen.

"It's a good thing the jungle fairies stayed behind," Shay said, and the others immediately agreed. Jungle fairies would eat anything that wasn't nailed down, and even some things that were.

"What's that black stuff?" Ethan asked, peering at the tree.

"Perhaps it's tar?" Beanie suggested.

"I don't think so. It reminds me of something." Ethan frowned. "I just can't remember what. . . ."

"Do you think we should take some of the fruit?" Shay suggested. "As a curiosity for the Polar Bear Explorers' Club?"

Stella found it hard to summon up much enthusiasm for the idea. Not only had she and Felix been expelled, but they didn't know whether they would find a way to cure Shay or make it back alive.

"Come on," Shay chided. "We're still explorers, aren't we? We're aware we can't eat the melons, or whatever they are, but we still don't know what they're made of. And I for one have never seen a tree like this before. If we take some of its fruit back, then perhaps one of the researchers at the club can learn a bit more about it. It might even encourage them to let Stella and Felix back in."

And, with that, he stepped forward, reached up to the nearest branch, and pulled down one of the melons.

"Gosh, it feels awfully strange," he said. "Rather like a water balloon—as if it's full of liquid—"

"That's it!" Ethan exclaimed. The color drained from his face. He groaned and said, "It's not tar—it's ink!" He gestured at the dark melon in Shay's hands and said, "For goodness' sake, put that back, quick! It's not a tree at all. It's a nest!"

Shay looked down at the object in his hands. "What—"

And that was as far as he got before the tree began to scream.

CHAPTER ELEVEN

IT WAS AN APPALLING sound that seemed to slice straight through the air itself.

"It's a screeching red devil squid nest!" Ethan screamed.

"But . . . but I thought they only lived in the Poison Tentacle Sea!" Shay protested, casting a desperate look back at the others.

"They migrate to have their young," Ethan said. "No one ever knew where. For goodness' sake, put that egg back!"

Shay hastily tried to balance the melon—or egg, as he now realized it was—back on the branch, but it was too late. The tree continued to screech so loudly that the ground beneath them trembled—the egg rolled from the branch and landed on the ground, where it burst apart, spraying black splashes of ink onto the snow, as well as Shay's boots.

Writing in the broken skin of the egg was indeed a baby red devil squid. It had bright red tentacles, a cone-shaped head, fearsome horns, and a single staring eye that blinked furiously up at them. It also had a mouth in the center of its tentacles, which it immediately proceeded to open wide and scream as loudly as the tree.

To make matters even worse, the yelling of the baby squid seemed to affect the other eggs because, one by one, they fell from the branches, splattering their ink over the snow as their own sacs burst, exposing more of the baby monsters. Stella recalled how Captain Ajax had told them that a fully grown red devil squid was one of the most dangerous creatures to roam the Poison Tentacle Sea, and it was also the same monster that had killed Ethan's older brother, Julian.

Beanie tugged at his pom-pom hat. "What do we do now?" he cried.

"We get out of here!" Ethan replied, already turning toward the snow-boat. "Before the mother arrives!"

The others were right on his heels. Beyond him, Stella was relieved to see that the gargoyles were already frantically buckling themselves into their harnesses, ready to tow the boat onward. One of the gargoyles beckoned them on impatiently, and they very nearly made it.

They were just a few feet away from the boat when the sea beneath the bridge burst open and a gigantic monster exploded from underneath the surface. A cascade of freezing foam swept up onto the bridge and knocked the explorers off their feet. Tumbling over into the snow, Stella gasped at the shock as the salt water stung her eyes. She wiped them dry with the back of her hand and looked up just in time to see a gigantic red devil squid clinging to the side of the bridge, its tentacles entwining one of the black towers that supported the bridge's cables as it hauled itself up out of the sea.

"Watch out!" Ethan shouted. "If it gets hold of you, it'll drag you straight down into the water!"

Stella *really* didn't want to be taken to her doom by a screeching red devil squid. She rolled to one side and leapt to her feet a second before one of the monster's tentacles came crashing down into the snow right where she'd just been lying. To her dismay, she saw that not only was the tentacle covered in suckers, but it had glistening teeth at the tips as well.

Stella noticed that the others had scrambled up and were scattering in different directions in an attempt to avoid the thrashing tentacles of the great monster. It had to be twenty feet long at least, and in the freezing mist it was hard to tell where it started and ended.

Stella edged away from the tentacle only to crash up against a beak almost as big as she was. To her horror, she realized she had run toward the monster rather than away from it. She had no way of freezing it without her tiara, and the small snow yeti she conjured up out of instinct crumbled itself into snowflakes as soon as it battered its fists against the red devil squid.

The squid's beak opened wide and let out a dreadful scream that was so forceful it blew Stella's hair straight back from her face. The stench of rotten fish and old seaweed had her gagging even as she tried to run from it.

Stella had visions of being bitten completely in half as the huge pointed beak snapped toward her, but then Ethan's hand clamped down on her arm and he yanked her back so forcefully that her shoulder throbbed in its socket.

With a whirr, Shay's boomerang spun out of the mist, flying straight and strong, and hit the squid right in the center of its enormous eye. It let out a bellow of pain as the tentacles thrashed blindly.

Stella saw that Ethan's usually immaculate hair hung over his face and his eyes were wild and desperate. "Run for the boat!" he gasped.

With Shay and Beanie just ahead of them, they turned from the squid and fled, ducking beneath tentacles and leaping over baby squid to get there. Stella felt her breath coming in great gasps that made her chest ache as they raced across the snow, finally climbing up onto the boat.

There was a lurch as the gargoyles pulled them forward, but it was too soon for relief. They'd barely gone more than a few paces before the boat jerked with a horrible juddering sound, and they all fell forward onto the deck.

"Good heavens!" Stella gasped. "It's attacking the boat!"

Indeed, the red devil squid had wrapped its great tentacles around the snow-boat and was dragging it toward the edge of the bridge. Tangled up in its tentacles, the gargoyles were doing their best to unbuckle their harnesses and scramble free into the snow.

"We're done for!" Beanie groaned.

"Quick!" Stella cried. "We'll have to abandon the boat!"

No one wanted to still be on the boat once it got dragged down into the ocean. One by one, they scrambled over the side.

Stella landed in the snow first, followed by Shay and then Beanie. Ethan was the last one on the boat, and when the squid jerked it again, he somehow got tangled in the ropes of the mast. It all happened so quickly there was nothing anyone could do. The squid snapped the mast in half with its tentacles and then pulled it over the edge of the bridge, dragging Ethan with it but leaving the rest of the snow-boat behind.

"Jump!" screamed Stella, but Ethan couldn't free his arm from the rope.

She caught a glimpse of his pale face as the red devil squid slithered over the side, pulling the mast and Ethan down into the sea in a great crash of freezing foam.

CHAPTER TWELVE

STELLA'S EARS RANG WITH the screeches of the baby squid as she stared at the space where Ethan had been moments before. She remembered what he had told them about a screeching red devil squid dragging his brother beneath the surface of the water to drow She couldn't bear the thought of that happening to Et too, and sprinted toward the railings of the bridg others close behind her—ready to leap straigh water after him.

But when they got there, they saw the ten tangled around the rails and broken And to their joy they saw Ethan dang' the rope, several feet above the ripr There was no sign whatsoever c although one of the teeth-tipp Ethan because a line of blo

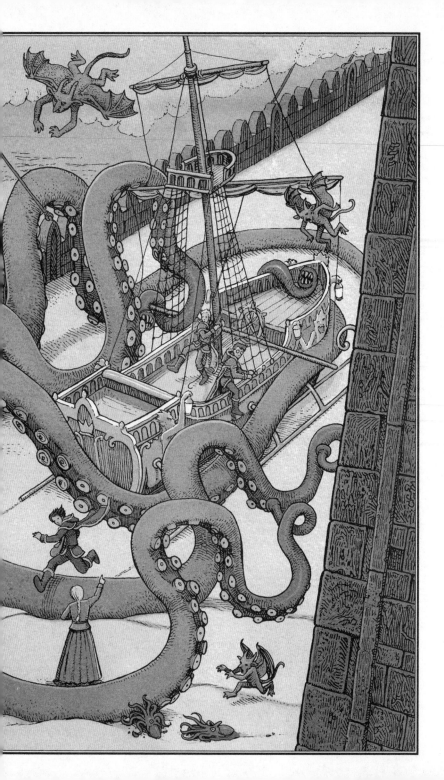

"Oh, thank goodness!" Stella cried. "Help me pull him up."

They all grabbed hold of the rope and heaved.

"Never mind that!" Ethan yelled. "Get the babies! Chuck them over the side! Quick, or else she'll come back!"

They did as he said, rushing around and grabbing the baby squid by their tentacles. Taking care to avoid the teeth on the tips and the frantically snapping beaks, they hurled the squid into the water, where they swiftly sank beneath the surface. Meanwhile, Ethan had struggled up the rope and hauled himself back onto the bridge, panting for breath.

The other explorers hurried over to make sure he was okay and then watched the sea anxiously from the bridge. There was a worryingly large ripple at one point, but no further sign of the monstrous squid and the tree had finally stopped its screaming. Silence seemed to ring around their heads like a bell.

The scene on the bridge was one of carnage. There was black ink everywhere and shards of broken wood. The gargoyles had pulled the snow-boat a short distance away, and Stella saw they were all accounted for and appeared unharmed. Apart from the broken mast, the boat itself seemed to be okay too and the explorers lost no time in climbing back on board.

The gargoyles set off immediately, racing across the snow, and they were all glad to leave the tree behind them.

"I wonder why no squid attacked your father's expedition," Stella said to Beanie.

"Probably because the eggs were smaller," the medic said. "They would have weighed less, so perhaps removing them didn't alert the tree." He looked at Ethan and said, "Let me do something for that scratch."

He walked over to the magician and used his magic to heal the cut.

Ethan thanked him, and Stella noticed that the magician's hands were shaking.

"Are you all right?" she asked.

"Fine," Ethan said. "It was just . . . hard seeing a red devil squid. After what happened to Julian."

"That was truly a ferocious beast," Shay said. He looked at Ethan and said, "Your brother must have been very brave."

"He was." Ethan shuddered. "I'd hoped never to see one of those horrible creatures again."

"Well, it's behind us now," Stella said. "We got away. We were lucky."

She could only hope they would continue to be lucky for whatever might lie ahead.

They traveled on down the bridge for another couple of hours and then stopped to make camp.

Stella asked the gargoyles if they'd like to come into

the magic fort with them, but the stone creatures seemed to prefer to stay on the snow-boat. Night had crept in and colored the fog a dusty gray. And the thicker it grew, the wetter their clothes became.

One of the winged gargoyles pointed at Stella's bracelet again, jabbing at the dragon charm.

"I'm sorry," she said. "I don't know what you want me to do. Is it to use the charm? I'm afraid I can't risk it—it's too dangerous," she added, remembering how Jezzybella had puzzled over the dragon charm at first, then suddenly realized it summoned a huge ice dragon.

"Quite perilous if you're not experienced," the old witch had said. "The dragon is born wild, you see. There've been plenty of snow queens who've lost control and been gobbled up by their own dragon. Perhaps that charm is best left for when you're a bit older, dear."

"Come on," Ethan said, as the gargoyles flew up onto the deck of the snow-boat. "They're made from stone, so they probably don't feel the cold. Whereas *I* feel like there's a frosty trying to chew all my fingers off." The magic fort blanket was already in his hands, and he didn't waste any more time before saying the magic words to open it. "Rattlesnake ragtime!"

The magic fort was one of their best acquisitions from their expedition to Witch Mountain. It looked like any other ordinary blanket, but say the right magic words and it immediately sprang up around them into a wonderful tent. The explorers found it every bit as warm and inviting and comfortable as they remembered, full of silk curtains and overstuffed poufs and gilded ottomans. Stella practically melted at the sight of the fire pit crackling away in the middle of the room, a pot of delicious-smelling stew bubbling on top.

"Good gracious me, where in the blazes are we?" an indignant voice said.

Ruprekt the genie had materialized from his bottle and was wearing his usual colorful robe and cozy slippers. His mustache, Stella noticed, was just as impressive as ever. His eyes, however, had a fearful look in them. "I've got a bad feeling about this place, wherever it is," he said.

"We're on the Black Ice Bridge," Stella told him.

The genie's mouth fell open, and even his mustache seemed to droop. "You're joking with me," he finally said, a little pleadingly.

Stella shook her head.

"Well, I knew it was somewhere cold and forsaken and dangerous, but never in my wildest dreams . . ." He shook his head. "You lot are even more foolhardy than Lord Rupert Benedict Arnold, but far be it from me to try to talk any sense into you. I'm only an expedition genie, after all." He huffed. Ruprekt was somewhat prone to sulking. "I took the liberty of getting your baths ready—"

He didn't get any further, because to the astonishment of the others, Ethan threw his arms around the genie in a hug.

"Oh gods, a bath!" The magician groaned. "A bath is just about the most wonderful thing I can think of in the whole world right now! Thank you, Ruprekt, thank you!"

The genie spluttered a little, looking rather taken aback by the sudden display of affection. "It is my pleasure, Master Rook," he said, disentangling himself from the magician. "Your bath is just through there."

He pointed into the bedroom, and Ethan went straight in.

"I can't think what's come over the boy!" the genie exclaimed, straightening his robe.

Normally, Ethan was quite reserved and didn't care for hugs any more than Beanie did.

"He's had a long day," Stella said.

In fact, they all had, and everyone was glad to take a hot bath and then change into the clean, warm pajamas Ruprekt had laid out for them. They were sand-colored and embossed with the Desert Jackal Explorers' Club crest. The magic fort blanket had once belonged to explorers from that club and a lot of their stuff was still scattered about, from the desert maps pinned on the walls to the pith helmet balanced on top of a snarling stuffed hyena in the corner. There were even some spare telescopes, and Stella selected one to put in her bag for later.

"I don't remember seeing that before," Stella said, waving over at the hyena.

"I found it in the supply cupboard," Ruprekt said, gesturing over to the cupboard in question. "I thought it would spruce the place up a bit."

It was rather a mangy old thing, but Stella patted it on the shoulder anyway. "Ruprekt, I hope you don't mind coming to the Black Ice Bridge," she said, glancing at him. "I know we ought to have asked you first, but you see it all happened in rather a rush and—"

"Nonsense, Miss Stella," Ruprekt replied. He drew himself up to his full height and said, "I'm an expedition genie. Where the adventure goes, I go."

"Well, that's a relief, at least," said Stella.

The genie glanced at the canvas wall of the tent and said, "I'm sure you have your reasons for coming here, but this is a bad place, miss. A bad place indeed. I hear strange voices on the wind, and unnatural echoes, and twisted, tormented things that shouldn't be."

Stella nodded. "I know. But it's our only hope of saving Shay."

The others came out of the bedroom just then, dressed in their pajamas, and the explorers sat down around the fire pit in the main living area to have their stew. Stella recalled how the jungle fairies had sat on the edge of the cooking pot last time, bickering over their one top hat and dipping their toes in the stew. She couldn't help missing their noisy, boisterous company. The thought of them reminded her that Felix and Joss were stuck in the cave beneath Queen Portia's castle, and she hoped they were all right.

Seeing that everyone looked a little glum, Ruprekt cleared away their stew bowls and then brought everyone a steaming mug of hot chocolate with extra marshmallows. Stella thought that hot chocolate could make anyone feel better, no matter what the circumstances, and felt herself relax as the warmth of the drink seeped into her fingers and down to her toes.

"You know, I've been thinking—maybe the bridge isn't as bad as everyone believes," Shay said, blowing froth from the top of his hot chocolate. "Perhaps that screaming squid is responsible for all the explorers who've gone missing. And if people heard the squid and the tree screaming and didn't know what they were, maybe that's how the ghost stories first started."

"Maybe," Stella said, although she didn't really think so. After all, it didn't explain the bad feeling she had on the bridge.

"This is a curious atlas," Beanie piped up.

Stella looked over and saw that her elfin friend had taken out another one of the books that he'd snatched up on their way through Queen Portia's library. It was a large, leather-bound tome, with pleasingly yellowed pages. It looked terribly old, and Stella was sure that it must smell absolutely wonderful.

"Look," Beanie said, holding up the book at an open page to show them the map within.

They all peered closer to get a better look and saw that it was a map of the Jelly Blue Sea.

"There are islands here that I've never heard of," Beanie said, pointing them out. "Like Bobcat Island and Sandy Pearl Archipelago and the Islet of Gentleman Flamingos—"

"Oh, everyone's heard of the Islet of Gentleman Flamingos," Ethan said in a dismissive voice. "It's some balderdash place people used to believe in before they started exploring properly. It doesn't exist."

"But it's right here on the map," Beanie said, peering at the page. "There's even a sketch of a little flamingo wearing a bowler hat and—"

"That atlas looks like it's hundreds of years old," Ethan cut him off. "It won't be accurate. Old maps like that are littered with phantom places that never really existed. I think there's been enough talk today of ghosts and monsters and gentleman flamingos. Who wants to see a magic trick? It's one I've been practicing and I think I've finally got it."

Everybody did, so they put the atlas to one side and Ethan started looking around for a hat.

Beanie tried to offer him his woolly pom-pom hat, but Ethan shook his head.

"No, no, don't be ridiculous. I can't pull a rabbit out of that. It really ought to be a top hat." His eye fell on the hyena over in the corner and he said, "But perhaps that will work."

He took the pith helmet from the snarling stuffed hyena and returned to the others by the fire.

"For ages and ages I kept getting those dratted mongooses," he said. "And they're the most savage things you ever saw—"

"Actually, you know, savage mini-cats are the most savage animals in the world," Beanie said. "And quite dangerous, too, because people often mistake them for kittens on account of their size and—"

"Have you ever seen a savage mini-cat?" Ethan demanded.

"Not personally," Beanie replied.

"Then what I said was accurate."

"Perhaps it's not the best idea to try this trick right now," Shay said. "Not with all this talk about savage mini-cats. It might cause you to create one by accident. Remember that time everyone was talking about the Scorpion Desert and then when you tried to create a polar bean you actually magicked up a scorpion that started scuttling about, clicking its pincers and—"

"Thank you," Ethan snapped. "A reminder of my past failures—that's not the sort of encouragement I need right now. So will you all just shut up and watch before I change my mind?"

Everyone looked as Ethan gazed down at the hat in his hands. Then he drew a deep breath and said, "One, two, three, alakazam!"

There was a little burst of light and a small puff of smoke, which caused everyone to *ooh* and *aah* and also squeak in alarm because they were half expecting a savage mini-cat to climb out of that hat, if they were honest, and Stella noticed Ruprekt even had a butterfly net ready to capture it with.

And then, before their eyes, an animal climbed out of the hat. Only it wasn't a savage mini-cat, or a rabbit, or even a mongoose. It was a bright pink flamingo, and what's more, it was quite clearly a gentleman. They could tell from the fact that it wore a little bowler hat, a smart jacket, and a bow tie, and carried a handsome striped umbrella tucked under one plump wing.

CHAPTER THIRTEEN

THEY SAW THE FLAMINGO for only a brief moment before Ruprekt brought the net down on top of it with a cry of alarm, still believing they had a savage mini-cat problem on their hands.

"Don't worry, Miss Stella!" the genie cried. "I won't let the ferocious beast harm you!"

"Ferocious beast!" a deep, rich, rather refined voice exclaimed from inside the net. "Good heavens, where?"

"He can talk!" Beanie exclaimed. A thought occurred to him, and he looked up at the others in sudden excitement. "Did you all hear that? Or am I a gentleman-flamingo whisperer? Gosh, I do hope it's that!"

"Well, I heard it, sure enough," Shay said.

"And me," Stella agreed. "Ruprekt, it's okay; he's not a savage mini-cat. Let him out of that net."

The genie reluctantly lifted the net, and everyone stared

140

here was just a sort of whiteness over everything. We
when it happened. Three minutes past eleven o'clock.
ow because all the clocks stopped, you see, even my own
andfather clock, which has been passed down through
ily for generations and has never missed a single tick or
nd my pocket watch stopped too, look—oh!"

e flamingo broke off. He'd taken a smart gold pocket
rom his pocket and flipped open the lid. Now he stared
t it and said, "It's started again. It must have happened
s ago, when I got here." He looked up at them. "I
now where my home is—all I know is that it vanished
t a trace and time seemed to stand still. When we all
own to the pebble beach, there were no waves lapping
hore anymore. There was just that strange whiteness
g everything like mist. My brother, Burroughs, set
that mist with a search party to try to find a way
all feared we'd never see them again, but they reap-
from the mist barely five minutes later. If you try to
e island, you just come back to it, you see. So imag-
surprise when I opened my front door this morning
d fetch some strawberries for breakfast, only to find
climbing out of a hat to be here with you fine people.
w there's no time to lose. We must find my home and
he rest of my people at once." He blinked up at them
opeful, earnest expression. "And there's the Island of
wans to be rescued too, of course. Will you help me?"

at the pink flamingo. It was much smaller than an ordinary
one—no more than a foot high—with bright, intelligent
yellow eyes that blinked up at them in alarm, one of which
was magnified in quite a startling way by a monocle.

"Where is this ferocious beast?" the flamingo asked,
staring up at them. "I will drive it back." He brandished
his striped umbrella, clearly intending to use it as a weapon.
"Never fear, madam," he said, to no one in particular.
"You're quite safe now. Melville is here."

"Oh, for heaven's sake!" Ethan exclaimed, staring at
the flamingo in disgust. Then he glared at Beanie and said,
"This is *your* fault. You made me get the spell wrong with
all your nonsense babble about gentleman flamingos!"

"It's all right," Stella said gently to the flamingo. "There's
no ferocious beast here. It was all just a misunderstanding."

The flamingo lowered his umbrella. "Oh, well, in
that case, allow me to properly introduce myself. I am
Melville Montgomery—of the Bayside Montgomerys,
you know." He raised one wing to straighten his bowler
hat and adjust the sleeve of his dinner jacket. "Delighted
to make your acquaintance. Now, please tell me who I
have to thank for saving my life with such bravery and
selflessness?"

"Well, Ethan here pulled you out of a hat," Shay said.
"Although it was a pith helmet, actually."

"A magician!" Melville exclaimed, staring up at Ethan.

"Well, my dear sir, you must be an inordinately talented magician indeed!"

"I am not!" Ethan exclaimed. Unfortunately, he had no idea what "inordinately" meant and assumed he had been told he was an absolutely rubbish magician, since that was how he felt after the rabbit failure. It was a spell he'd been practicing for weeks and weeks, and it was extremely embarrassing to have it all go wrong in front of his friends, even if it *was* Beanie's fault for bringing up gentleman flamingos in the first place.

Fortunately, Stella had a very wide vocabulary, thanks to her lessons with Felix, and quickly put him straight.

"He's paying you a compliment," she said. "'Inordinately' means tremendously."

"Quite right," Melville said. "Yes, you must be tremendously talented to have rescued me the way you did. My dear fellow, I really can't thank you enough. I, and all my people, are forever in your debt."

Ethan stared at the tiny flamingo. "But where did you *come* from?" he demanded.

"Oh." Melville's face fell. "Don't you know?"

"None of the animals I've ever pulled from a hat has been able to talk," Ethan said. "A mongoose will try to take your eyes out and then shoot off looking shifty and hunting about for something—anything, really—to tear to pieces. And a fluffy bunny will just hop around trying to eat the furniture."

"Oh, well, that's a little disapp[...]
don't mean to sound ungrateful, y[...]
that our islet vanished, you see. [...]
Island of Lady Swans. One day it [...]
was just gone." He stabbed the tip[...]
floor for emphasis. "Vanished! Jus[...]
the surrounding ocean high and l[...]
know. My dear sweet Clementine [...]
darling lady swan, the great light[...]
love of my soul. We searched and [...]
no sign of the island. It had just . . [...]

"I saw the Island of Lady Sw[...]
reaching for the atlas again. "It wa[...]
next to the Islet of Gentleman Flar[...]

"But there's no such place," S[...]
for the atlas. "I've studied maps o[...]
Father, and I've never heard of [...]
There's just ocean there."

"That may be so now," Melvi[...]
were there. I'd hoped you'd know [...]

"But . . . but if you've been wh[...]
don't you know?" Stella asked, co[...]

The flamingo shook his head [...]
and looked out the windows of o[...]
find that the sea and sky were gon[...]

"What do you mean?" Shay as[...]

Stella glanced at the others. "I'm afraid that when it comes to rescuing, we have our hands rather full at the moment," she said apologetically. "You see, we're traveling across the Black Ice Bridge."

She expected Melville to exclaim in horror, as most people did, but perhaps the bridge's notoriety hadn't quite reached the Jelly Blue Sea because he just stared up at her politely.

"It's a cursed bridge," she explained. "No one seems to be able to cross it and live to tell the tale. We're in search of a spell that will save my friend here. And once we've done that, we have to go back to rescue two of our parents who are trapped with an ice dragon in a cave beneath a snow queen's castle."

And that wasn't even the half of it. Even if they managed all that, Stella was still wanted for arrest, and Felix was still expelled from the club. It was hard not to feel a bit overwhelmed by it all.

The gentleman flamingo looked suitably impressed and said, "Gracious me, you have taken on rather a lot, haven't you?" He looked at Ethan and said warmly, "And to think you took time out from all of that to rescue me. I'm beyond grateful, sir."

Ethan puffed out his chest and said, "It was nothing."

"Perhaps you could pull the other gentleman flamingos out of the hat?" Shay suggested. "At least then they'd all be free and we could worry about finding their islet later."

"How many of you are there?" Ethan asked.

"Six hundred and seventy-four at the last count," Melville said.

"We'd be here all night," Ethan said. He deflated a little and said, "Besides, I don't know how. The truth is, I wasn't trying to pull *you* out of the hat. I was trying to pull out a fluffy bunny."

"Oh," said Melville, disappointed. "Might you at least try to rescue my brother Burroughs?" he asked. "He's the oldest, you see. He'd know what to do and how to rescue the others. I'm only the useless younger brother and not really cut out for this kind of thing."

"I'm sure you're not useless," Stella said kindly.

Ethan sighed. "Well, I'll try," he said, picking up the pith helmet. "But, you know, I'm not always a very good magician."

"On the contrary, sir! You are an excellent magician," Melville assured him. "Simply capital! One of the best of your generation, I shouldn't wonder."

Ethan's ears turned pink with pleasure, and he stared into the hat with renewed concentration. Finally, he reached in and tugged something out, only this time it wasn't a mongoose, or a fluffy bunny, or another gentleman flamingo.

"Oh, it's a sweet little kitten!" Stella exclaimed, reaching out to stroke it.

Sadly, it was not a sweet little kitten, either, but a savage mini-cat, which flew straight at Stella's face and might very well have scratched her eyes out if it weren't for Melville striking out with his umbrella and blocking its path.

There was some pandemonium while everyone raced around after the savage mini-cat, which tore up the walls, shot under beds, dived into cupboards, and lashed out viciously at anyone who got near it. Ruprekt's net was shredded within seconds, and the genie spent the rest of the chase up on a chair, wringing his hands and wailing.

Finally, after everyone had been thoroughly scratched, they managed to get the savage mini-cat out through one of the canvas walls, where it fled into the snow, and they all breathed a sigh of relief.

"I say." Melville panted. "Perhaps it's better you don't try to pull any more of my kind out of that hat. We'll just have to think of another way. After we've completed your various rescue missions, of course. And if I can help with those in any way, then I'd be only too glad to."

It had been an exhausting couple of days for everyone, and they were pleased to turn in, grateful for a warm bed and clean sheets. Ruprekt set up a little cot for Melville in the bedroom with the others and produced a tiny nightcap for him to wear that looked like it had once belonged to a jungle fairy.

At first Stella was afraid she wouldn't sleep because she was too nervous about being on the Black Ice Bridge. What if something dangerous came along when they were all asleep and gobbled them up? But, in fact, she was so tired that she fell asleep the moment her head touched the pillow.

CHAPTER FOURTEEN

STELLA WOKE UP TO the sound of howling. She jerked upright and scrambled from the bed, half expecting that some dangerous beast had crept into their tent while they slept. But then she took in the scene and saw there was no monster. The howling was coming from Koa.

The shadow wolf hunched in the corner of the tent and, as Stella watched, tipped back her head and let out another howl so full of angst that Stella shuddered. To her dismay, she saw there was far more white fur on the shadow wolf than there had been before. Where it had started out as just a streak, it now took up almost a third of her body. Whatever was happening to her was definitely getting worse.

The sound had woken Ethan, Beanie, and Melville, who were all out of their beds. Shay, however, was tangled up in his sheets, groaning and clutching his hands to his head. Stella hurried over to him, quickly followed by the others, and they crowded around their friend in concern.

"Shay," Stella said, gripping his shoulder. "What's wrong?"

"I can't . . ." The wolf whisperer gasped. "I can't . . ."

"Can't what?" Ethan demanded. "Talk to us."

He took hold of Shay's wrists and dragged them away from his face. The others gasped. One of his eyes had changed from its normal brown to a ghostly silver color, exactly as they remembered the eyes of the witch wolves back on Witch Mountain. And not only was his eye a different color, but it was frozen as well, glittering in a coat of frost that made the light reflect back strangely. It was difficult to look him straight in the eye, and Stella found that her head ached when she tried to.

"I can't see properly," Shay said. "There's something wrong. . . ."

"Let me see if I can help." Beanie raised his hand to Shay's face, and green healing magic fizzed between his fingers.

A moment later, the ice started to melt from Shay's eye and it returned to his usual color.

"You did it," the wolf whisperer said, waving his hands in front of his face. "I can see clearly again. Thank you."

"It's only a temporary fix," Beanie said, looking worried. "Like when Ethan had frostbite, remember? Magic can only slow this down; it can't stop the effects completely."

"It might buy us time, though," Stella said.

She noticed the white streak in Shay's hair had gotten a little wider, even though his eye had returned to normal. And Koa's fur remained white too. It was a reminder to everyone they had no time to lose and no time to make mistakes on the Black Ice Bridge.

"We'd better press on," Stella said.

Shay scrambled from his bed and walked over to Koa. He dropped down into a crouch before the shadow wolf, as Stella had seen him do a hundred times before. Even though she had no physical substance, usually Koa would nuzzle into him affectionately. This time, however, when Shay reached a hand out toward her, she bared her teeth in a snarl.

Shay froze. "Koa," he said softly. "It's all right, girl. Hey, it's okay. It's me."

He moved his hand toward her again, and quick as a flash Koa bit him.

Stella watched in horror as the shadow wolf—who wasn't supposed to have any substance—bit down on Shay's hand. She could tell it was an actual bite by the fact that Shay cried out in pain and a thin trickle of blood ran down his wrist.

Ethan was the first to react—throwing a blast of magic at Koa that caused her to let go of Shay with a whimper.

The magician's attack seemed to shock her back to herself somehow because the next moment she was pressing herself close to Shay with her tail between her legs and a guilty expression on her face.

"Did you see that?" Shay gasped.

"Yes, but how was it possible? I thought Koa was made of shadows—" Stella began.

Shay cut her off. "No, not that. I meant me. I felt like . . . like I disappeared for a moment. Did I?"

Stella stared at him. "I don't think so. No, you were there the whole time."

Shay reached a trembling hand down to touch Koa, but she had gone back to being insubstantial and his hand passed through her like she was made of smoke. The next moment, she disappeared altogether.

Beanie came forward to look at Shay's hand.

"It's not bad," Shay said, as the elf healed it for him. "But she shouldn't have been able to do that."

"We knew that a witch wolf's bite might affect her differently," Stella said, trying to contain her dismay.

No shadow wolf had ever been bitten by a witch wolf before, as far as they were aware, so they couldn't know what the effect would be. But here was proof that, whatever was happening, it wasn't good.

"Look," Beanie said, bending down to the spot where Koa had just been. "Wolf hairs." He held the white hairs up for the others to see. "As if a real wolf had been here."

"We should get on," Shay said quietly.

Ethan nodded, his pale face looking tense. "Let's get dressed," he agreed.

They all returned to their bedsides and drew their curtains to get back into their sweaters, scarves, and cardigans. Once Stella was done, she walked into the main living area to find Shay and Ethan already by the fire.

"How are you feeling now?" Ethan was saying to Shay. "I mean aside from your shadow wolf going mad for a minute and your eye turning weird, do you feel okay?"

Shay sighed. "Well, I feel just about as scared as I can ever remember feeling." He managed a smile and said, "But other than that, I'm fine."

Ethan briefly touched the wolf whisperer's shoulder. "You're not alone," he said. "If there's a way to fix this, we'll find it."

Stella had never wanted something to be true so fiercely, and yet she couldn't help thinking it was an almost impossible task.

She heard Felix's voice inside her head. "A fellow can't turn away from something just because the odds are stacked against him," he'd often told her. "That's the time to really throw yourself into a thing, with every last bit of your might. Marvelous things can happen when you ignore the odds."

They had a quick breakfast. Ruprekt said Melville wouldn't be able to stay in the fort once it had been turned back into a blanket—being a living thing that wasn't a genie he would certainly be pulverized, and since no one wanted that to happen, the gentleman flamingo would have to go with them.

"It's terribly cold out on the ice bridge," Stella had told him, looking at his smart little jacket dubiously. "Perhaps we can fashion something for you to wear."

They hunted around the fort in search of something suitable, and then Ruprekt came up with the idea of cutting holes in the tea cozy.

"It isn't exactly the most elegant ensemble, is it?" the flamingo said, somewhat sulkily. "I look ridiculous."

"You look a bit ridiculous wearing a bowler hat, too, in all honesty," Ethan said. "At least this way you won't freeze to death."

"I shall let that remark pass on account of you saving my life." Melville sniffed. "But I'll have you know that this was my great-great-grand-pappy's hat, and it is superb."

He adjusted it on his pink head.

Ethan rolled his eyes. "Whatever." He picked up the little flamingo and said, "Outsider alert!"

The fort immediately vanished around them as it transformed back into a rather tatty old blanket, which Ethan thrust in his bag. The four explorers and the gentleman flamingo found themselves back on the Black Ice Bridge, and it was every bit as inhospitable as it had been before. The air was thick with swirling snowflakes and freezing fog, and the cold reached right through their skin down into their bones.

"Good gracious!" Melville squeaked. "Aargh, it's so cold! We never had anything like this on the Islet of Gentleman Flamingos, I can tell you. Just sunshine and pineapples all the way. Good grief, this is simply intolerable! My beak is freezing! It feels like it might actually fall off!"

It *was* extremely cold. Even Stella could feel it, and the snow didn't normally bother her. She pulled on her gloves and tried hard not to think of sunshine and pineapples. Ethan stuffed Melville—who was shivering badly—into his sweater before doing up his cloak so that only the little flamingo's head poked out the top.

"Where are the gargoyles?" Shay suddenly said.

Stella turned around on the spot, straining her eyes through the freezing fog. It was so thick they could barely see more than a few feet in front of them. Stella couldn't even make out the rails of the bridge, or the tall towers reaching up into the sky, or the sun itself. Sound seemed strangely muffled too, and she could no longer hear the sea lapping beneath them. Everything was white, and she was hit with the sudden strange feeling that they weren't in a real place at all, but rather inside somebody's shivering dream, or perhaps the cold, dead space inside a broken heart.

But then the gargoyles came clanking through the mist, pulling the snow-boat behind them, its ice candles shining brightly.

Stella was extremely relieved to see them and was just about to walk over to the ladder when she froze.

"What's that noise?" she asked.

"It was just me blowing my nose," Ethan said, stuffing the hankie back in his pocket. "Sorry."

"No." Stella stopped. "It sounded like . . . a heartbeat."

The others stopped too and listened, but there was only the muffled noiselessness of freezing fog cloaking everything.

"You're imagining things," Ethan finally said. "We know the bridge can play tricks on people. We need to keep our heads and not give in to wild fantasies."

Stella frowned as she peered ahead. Her eyes ached with the effort of straining them into the fog. She told herself Ethan was right and they had to remain sensible.

But then, just for a moment, she could have sworn she saw a silhouette.

"There's someone there!" she said quickly to the others, trying to keep her voice low. "I saw them! Just up ahead of us. In the fog."

CHAPTER FIFTEEN

EVERYONE STARED STRAIGHT AHEAD. The fog seemed to swirl around them in ribbons and, as it parted for a moment, Stella dreaded catching a glimpse of a fur-trimmed hood or a lavish ermine coat, a flash of a silken glove or the twinkle of diamonds.

Her mind was full of Queen Portia, who had last been seen fleeing onto the Black Ice Bridge. But that had been over two hundred years ago. Surely she couldn't still be alive out here? How long did snow queens even live? With a lurching feeling, Stella realized she had no idea. She had assumed she would have a normal lifespan like everyone else, but what if she was going to live on and on, long after everyone else was gone? The idea made her feel very tiny and alone.

"I don't see anything," Ethan said.

Stella could no longer see anything either, but the thought of Queen Portia was in her mind now.

"Perhaps it was Koa," Shay suggested. "She's on the bridge somewhere. I can feel her."

Sure enough, the next moment, Koa padded silently out of the fog. She went straight over to Shay and flicked her tongue at his fingers in her old affectionate way.

"There's nobody out here except us." Ethan grunted. "No one else would be so stupid. Let's get a move on."

They climbed up onto the deck of the snow-boat, and the gargoyles set off along the bridge.

Before long the fog had melted, so at least they could see a little way up ahead. They took it in turns keeping watch and spent the rest of the time sheltering belowdecks, browsing the books Beanie had taken from Queen Portia's library or chatting with Melville in order to get to know him better.

"What's that you're reading?" Stella asked, noticing that the little flamingo had a book of his own, bound in smart red leather.

"It's the gentleman's code," Melville replied. "We all endeavor to live our lives according to its rules. Would you care to see it?"

Stella was already shaking her head. "No, thanks," she said. "We've got something similar in the Polar Bear Explorers' Club. I think I know all there is to know about grooming and mustaches and things."

Melville gave her a puzzled look. "What on earth do mustaches have to do with being a gentleman? There isn't a single mustache in this whole book, so far as I can recall—indeed, they're more associated with villains, as I understand it. Here, take a look."

Before Stella could protest again, he'd thrust the book into her hands. Not wanting to seem rude, she opened the cover and flicked through the pages. But then some of the rules started to jump out at her, and she slowed down and started reading them properly. Melville had been right. There was nothing in there about mustaches. Instead, the book was filled with the sort of things Felix had taught her.

Be kind.

Treat others as you would wish to be treated yourself.

Cherish your friends.

To your own self be true.

Stella felt a big smile spread across her face. Here, at last, was a *real* gentleman's code, not the stuffy nonsense peddled by the clubs. She heard President Fogg's insult once again as they stood in the courthouse back at Coldgate:

You, sir, are no gentleman!

Only, when she thought about them this time, the words had lost some of their sting. For Felix *was* a gentleman, right down to his bones, and nothing anyone said could change that.

"How marvelous," Stella said, handing the book back to Melville. "I think everyone should try to live their lives that way." A thought occurred to her, and she said, "Do the ladies of Swan Island have a code too?"

"Naturally," Melville replied. "It's a beautiful book with lots of little pearls encrusted on the cover. Of course, the basic rules are the same as ours, but they have some additional ones as well. Let me see now. . . . Yes, I can remember a few of them. Clementine was particularly fond of number six: 'Laugh as long and as hard as possible, wherever possible, and preferably until tears run down your beak.' And number twelve: 'If you've a choice between turnips and chocolate whoopie pies, always choose chocolate whoopie pies.' Number nine: 'Ward off bullies with firm words and, if necessary, parasols.' And, of course, number twenty-two: 'Make every effort to banish unhealthy envy of others and embrace your own unique weird wonderfulness at every possible turn.'"

"Gosh, how absolutely marvelous!" Stella exclaimed.

She thought, perhaps, that once this was all over and everyone was safe, she might have a go at writing her own lady's code, as a helpful reminder to herself for those times when she lost sight of the person she wanted to be.

After a pause for lunch, they traveled on for an hour or so and then Stella told the gargoyles to stop.

"What are we stopping for?" Ethan asked, poking his head up from belowdecks. "It's too early to make camp."

"Listen," Stella said. "There's that sound again." She

could feel the reverberation throbbing up through her boots, and this time she was sure she wasn't imagining it. "It's definitely a heartbeat," she said.

The others joined her up on the deck, but the next moment the sound faded away.

"It was there," Stella insisted. "I heard it."

Shay frowned. "But if you heard its heartbeat, then whatever it is must be enormous," he said.

"That's another theory about the bridge," Beanie said. "That it was built by giants. And those giants are responsible for all the explorers who've gone missing. They gobble them up, you see. According to the rumors."

"I really hope it's not giants," Ethan said with a shudder. "I'd rather not have my bones ground down for bread."

Stella shook her head. "If giants took the explorers, wouldn't they leave more of a sign? The explorers' camps always look in perfect order, as if they'd just left. Giants would mess the camps up with their huge feet and whatnot."

Stella gave the order to the gargoyles and they continued on their way. The sun was starting to set by the time Beanie—whose turn it was to be on watch—called the others up on deck.

"Is it the heartbeat again?" Stella asked, but immediately had the answer to her question.

She told the gargoyles to stop, and the four explorers

stood and listened to the mournful sound of bells coming from beneath the bridge.

"It's the ship graveyard," said Beanie. "Just like in my father's journal."

The fog had started to draw back in as the sun set, but it wasn't yet so thick that they couldn't see the forest of masts rising up from below.

"Good Lord," Melville said, gawping through his monocle. "How astonishing."

There must have been hundreds of ships. Some of them still carried the tattered remains of flags, while others were little more than hulks of rust—hollowed-out hulls that were already being reclaimed by the sea, covered in strings of seaweed, crusty patches of barnacles, and the odd confused starfish. There were all kinds of vessels down there—smuggler ships, pirate galleons, and whaler boats, clippers and icebreakers, merchant ships and longboats.

Stella saw one mermaid-spotting boat that had clearly been claimed by actual mermaids, for the deck had been turned into a makeshift beauty parlor, with coral combs and shell bras and sea-flower hair accessories scattered all over the deck. In fact, the mermaids seemed to have claimed several of the ships, although there was no sign of the mermaids themselves.

"Looks like they've turned that icebreaker into a seahorse grooming platform," Shay said, pointing. "And the ship next to it is a sunbathing deck, and the one next to that is a manicure boat."

There even seemed to be a few antique explorers' ships down there.

"Look at that one." Ethan pointed at a ship with tall masts and an abundance of shredded sails. "It's got an explorers' crest, but what's the animal on it? A phoenix?" He looked at the others. "There's never been a phoenix club, has there?"

They all looked at Beanie, who easily had the most knowledge about explorers and their history.

He frowned and said, "I've heard of the Sky Phoenix Explorers' Club, but I thought it was just an urban myth. There's this story that once, many years ago, there were five clubs. But the Sky Phoenix Explorers' Club were a bit stupid, always 'discovering' places that didn't really exist. Not very good explorers at all." He scratched the back of his neck. "Plus, it was said they used giant phoenixes to travel, and there's no evidence they ever existed, either. It sounds like they were just an exaggerated version of firebirds, which are extinct now too. I don't think anyone believes the club was ever real. I always thought they were a scapegoat made up by the other clubs to take the blame for mistakes made on maps and errors in log reports and so on."

"If they were never real, then how do you explain that?" Ethan pointed at the ship. The phoenix rising from the flames was still just about visible on the tattered remains of the flags.

Beanie shook his head. "I can't."

"You know, we have a saying on the Islet of Gentleman Flamingos that history is written by the victors," Melville said, squinting through his monocle. "Perhaps your clubs have rewritten history to suit themselves a bit?"

"I hope that's not it," Shay said, frowning. "How did all these ships get here in the first place?"

"Could they have been trying to get to the other side of the bridge?" Stella asked.

"Some of them, maybe," Beanie said. "But not all of them." He pointed out a nearby ship and said, "That's the *Water Witch*. I recognize it from books. It belonged to Captain Conrad Conway Twythe. His expedition was attacked by a giant kraken and the ship sank in Crystal Cove, which is hundreds and hundreds of miles away. Sunken ships from all around the world have turned up here, but it's a mystery as to how or why."

It occurred to Stella that they seemed to be surrounded by mysteries: vanishing islands, materializing shipwrecks, missing explorers, gigantic bridges, ghostly snow queens, and of course, the enigmatic Collector himself, the man responsible for killing Stella's birth parents and stealing the Book of Frost, and they didn't even know what his name was.

There was something indescribably sad about the sight of so many sunken ships, especially as some of them still had their bells, and the melancholy peals carried over to them through the gathering mist. The explorers continued onward, glad to leave the ship graveyard behind them.

The sun was just disappearing below the horizon by the time they reached the ruins of the abandoned camp belonging to Beanie's father.

CHAPTER SIXTEEN

T HE CAMP WAS SHROUDED in ghostly sea mist, almost like a mirage. The rescue party that had gone after Adrian Albert Smith had snatched up some of the explorers' personal possessions to take back with them but otherwise hadn't lingered for too long. No one wanted to test their luck or tempt fate on the Black Ice Bridge.

There were five tents, a couple of which had collapsed, but the other three remained standing, as if a dazed explorer might crawl out of one at any moment. In fact, the whole camp had the air of a place that had only just been left. There were still piles of supplies scattered around, such as rifles, camping mugs, and coils of rope, and the freezing temperatures had kept everything well preserved. There were even still iced gems inside the sacks of unicorn food.

The explorers poked around inside one of the tents to see if there was anything useful they could take with them. They found an entire untouched plate of food, perfectly frozen, as well as a rickety desk with a map and a magnifying glass still set out on it. Some of the stuff outside had been covered up by fresh snowfall, but they could still just about see the outlines.

Stella noticed that Beanie had a pale, pinched look about him, and she knew it must be difficult for him to come here, to the last known place where his father had been.

"Shall we go on a little farther and then set up camp for the night?" she asked.

Beanie shook his head. "We should check all the tents before we leave," he said. "There might be something useful here."

Stella didn't think that was too likely—even the rifles had rusted beyond repair. She suspected Beanie just wanted to search for signs of his father. Nevertheless, they went through the collapsed ruins of the two crumpled tents and found nothing but a few empty cans of Spam.

"There aren't enough tents here," Beanie said with a frown. "There were more expedition members than this."

"Perhaps they fell down and got covered by snow?" Ethan suggested. "Or perhaps they didn't get around to putting all the tents up before whatever happened . . . happened."

"Maybe," Beanie replied, although he still looked dubious.

Finally, they reached the last tent.

"Nothing in this one, either," Beanie said glumly.

"Hang on," Stella said, peering into the corner. "What's that?"

"It's just a stone," Shay replied.

"It's a stone with a hole in it," Stella said. "That means it belongs to fairies. They use them as little bags sometimes—I've seen them do it in the backyard at home. They use the hole in the rock to tie a piece of string through, like a handle." She scooped up the stone. "You just have to know where to press. . . ."

She removed her glove to feel around the stone, and the next second it sprang open with a soft snap.

"I was right!" Stella exclaimed as the others crowded around to get a better look. The stone contained several explorer items, including a pair of tiny binoculars, a perfectly preserved lump of mint cake, and a miniature camera about the size of Stella's thumb. She picked it up and peered at it. "Goodness. How do you think this came to be here?" She looked at Beanie. "Were there any fairies on the expedition?"

He nodded. "One," he said. "He was accompanying Henry Gulliver Rowling, the team fairyologist. These must be his things. I guess the rescue party missed it because they saw it as just a useless stone."

"I wonder what happened to the pictures," Stella said. "They might hold some clue as to what happened to everyone out here."

Before Beanie could reply, Shay said sharply, "What was that noise?"

The others remained silent for a moment.

"I don't hear anything," Ethan finally said. "It was probably just the wind."

Shay shook his head. "No. There's someone out there. I saw their silhouette pass by the canvas."

Stella stuffed the fairy belongings into her dress pocket, and they all hurried from the tent to scan their eyes over the camp.

"You see?" Ethan said. "Nobody."

Shay turned toward the magician, and to Stella's surprise his face was pale with dread.

"Are you joking?" Shay said hoarsely. When everyone stared back at him blankly, he said, "There's a man. Surely you can see him? He's right there."

He pointed to the middle of the camp.

"There's no one there," Stella whispered.

She looked at Shay and saw that one of his eyes had turned that white silvery color once again.

"Who are you?" Shay asked, stepping forward.

The others frowned in concern, wondering whether Shay was having some kind of hallucination.

Then Shay glanced back at them. "He says his name is Henry Gulliver Rowling. The fairyologist."

"Perhaps you'd better sit down," Ethan suggested.

Shay shook off his hand impatiently. "I'm not imagining things, you idiot," he snapped. "He's really there. He says that he hid when the ice lady came, but he froze to death just a few paces from here." Seeing the others still looked unconvinced, Shay turned around again and said, "Why am I the only one who can see you?"

There was a brief silence; then Shay said to the others, "He says he doesn't know. I think perhaps it's something to do with the witch wolf's bite. They feed on souls, don't they? I sensed him before I saw him."

"Your eye has gone silver again," Stella admitted.

"What nonsense!" Ethan exclaimed, while Beanie tugged fearfully at his pom-pom hat. "There's no such thing as ghosts."

"Can you do something?" Shay asked, looking back at the empty space in front of them. "To prove to the others that you're really there?" He was quiet for a moment; then he turned back to the others and said, "He's going to switch the gramophone on."

Ethan shook his head. Melville—who was still stuffed down the front of Ethan's sweater—stared with eyes like saucers. Stella and Beanie waited nervously. They all looked at the gramophone frozen outside one of the tents.

"That thing probably doesn't even work anymore," Ethan said. "Look at it! It's all rusted and—"

He broke off as, before their eyes, the needle started to move and the next moment music drifted out from the machine. It was tinny and crackly, and the record itself was clearly badly scratched, but it was playing just the same.

"There," Shay said, sounding pleased. "Now do you believe me?"

"Ask him if he knows what happened," Beanie said at once. "To the expedition."

Shay looked back at the snow next to the gramophone, listened for a moment, then frowned and turned to the others. "He says he hid when something attacked the camp, but he doesn't want to talk about it. He managed to escape, but froze to death in the blizzard that came later. He just keeps saying that we should get off the bridge and go back while we still can."

"We can't do that," Stella said firmly. "There's something on the other side that we need. More than one person's life is at stake. Please, Mr. Rowling, if you know anything about what lies ahead, then you have to tell us."

They waited while the ghost of the fairyologist gave his response to Shay.

"He says that we should look at the photos inside the fairy's camera—"

Shay broke off as Koa suddenly leapt, snarling, into the space where the ghost must have been. There was a savage, hungry look in her eyes that Stella had never seen before, and it made her blood run cold. But Shay shot out his hand, grabbed the scruff of Koa's neck and thrust her back. A second later, a strange current of air whipped up the snow around them, making everyone shiver.

"He's gone," Shay said to Koa. "It's too late. He's gone."

The shadow wolf growled low in the back of her throat before turning and slinking away into the fog, her newly solid form leaving footprints in the snow.

"Are you okay?" Stella asked, reaching out to Shay.

He gave her a desperate look. "She wanted to consume the ghost," he said. "I think she's turning into a witch wolf. And turning me into . . . I don't even know what. Rowling's gone—she frightened him away. But at least we know the photos are in the fairy's camera."

Hastily, Stella took the camera from her pocket, and the others crowded around her as she prized off the back. The fairyologist had been right. There was indeed a neat little stack of photographs tucked away inside the camera. Stella gently tipped them out on to her palm, taking care that they weren't plucked away by the wind. There were perhaps twenty photos there, but they were so small they could barely make them out.

"There was a magnifying glass in one of the tents," Ethan said.

The magician hurried to fetch it. Even with the aid of the magnifier, the photos were still quite hard to see, but at least they could just about make out the images now.

They could tell they were in chronological order because the photos started with a traditional group shot of all the explorers assembled at the entrance to the Black Ice Bridge beside the Polar Bear Explorers' Club flag. The photos went on to document the screeching red devil squid tree and the ship graveyard.

And then they got to the camp. It seemed as if the fairy had taken the photos from inside the tent because there was a flap of canvas fabric partially obscuring the view. Stella and the others all leaned forward eagerly to get a better look. These must be the last photos ever taken of the expedition. Perhaps they really were about to find out what had happened and finally solve the mystery of why so many people disappeared on the bridge without a trace.

Beanie took the photos from Stella and raised them closer to his face. "Something's already happening in this one," he said. "Look, the explorers aren't just milling around—they've seen something. They're scared."

Stella saw he was right. There were three explorers in the photo: Two were running back toward their tents, while a third had picked up a rifle and was pointing it straight into the fog. The final explorer was Beanie's father. It was impossible to make out their expressions clearly in the tiny photos, but something about their body language made it obvious they were afraid as they faced the mist.

"They can see something we can't," Shay said. "Or else they heard something."

"Perhaps it was the screeching red devil squid?" Stella suggested. "Maybe it pursued them across the bridge?"

Ethan shook his head. "The squid don't hunt like that. They wouldn't travel across land—they're most vulnerable there."

"Go on to the next photo," Shay urged. "Perhaps it will show us something."

Beanie flicked to the next photo. In this one, three other explorers had joined Beanie's father. They stood shoulder to shoulder, all holding rifles aimed in the same direction.

"There!" Ethan cried, pointing at a spot in the photo. "There's something right there."

The others all squinted down at the picture and saw he was right. A shape was emerging from the fog, but it was no tentacled monster or fearsome giant. In fact, it was a woman.

"There's the edge of her skirt," Beanie said. "And that's a hand."

There was indeed a pale, slim hand pointing through the mist at the explorers.

Beanie flicked forward to the next photo and, suddenly, everything was transformed. The explorers were gone and their rifles lay upon the snow, still smoking. A single person now occupied the photo.

"Queen Portia." Stella groaned.

They all stared at the snow queen. It looked as if the fairy had caught her in the act of performing some kind of spell. She was midwhirl, with her long skirts flying around her, one hand stretched out, her beautiful face in profile.

"But . . . but that's not possible," Ethan said. "She looks young—exactly like she did in the paintings back at the castle. But if she was here on the bridge eight years ago, she would have been in her hundreds."

"Perhaps snow queens age differently," Stella said. "Nobody knows for sure, do they?"

"She must have done something to the explorers," Beanie said. "Used magic on them somehow."

He flicked quickly forward to the next photo, which showed Queen Portia standing motionless, hunched protectively over something she seemed to be clasping to her chest. She had her back to them, though, so they couldn't see what it was.

"There's only one photo left," Beanie said, flicking to it.

It was almost identical to the photo before it, except in this one, Queen Portia was looking over her shoulder, directly at the camera. It seemed like she was staring right out of the photo at them, and Stella couldn't help shivering.

"It's like she can see us," Ethan said, echoing her thoughts.

"No," Beanie said. "She saw the fairy who was taking the photos. And then she must have gone after him. There's no more photos after that, and the fairy is gone too."

The explorers all went very still.

"At least now we know," Ethan said.

The mystery had indeed been solved. But no one seemed very much comforted by that.

CHAPTER SEVENTEEN

HOW CAN WE POSSIBLY protect ourselves against a snow queen?" Ethan asked, giving the fire in the pit a bad-tempered jab with the poker. "It's not clear what she even did to the explorers."

They had traveled on a little way from the deserted camp and then put the magic fort blanket up for the night. Ruprekt had been there to greet them with a tray holding four steaming mugs of hot chocolate, as well as a small cup for Melville. Stella could see that the genie was making an extra-special effort because the marshmallows floating in the mugs were polar bear rather than scorpion-shaped.

"Perhaps she turned the explorers to ice?" Beanie suggested, wrapping his hands around his mug.

"But then they would still have been there," Stella pointed out. "Like the people at Blackcastle. And there was no sign of them."

"Perhaps some yeti came along and crunched them up like frozen ice pops?" Ethan suggested.

Beanie winced, and Stella frowned at the magician. "Look, it doesn't really matter exactly *what* she did," she said. "All we need to know was that she used her ice magic to make them disappear somehow."

"But that's precisely my point! How are we going to stop her from—would you stop that fidgeting?" Ethan said to Melville, who was trying to make himself comfortable on the magician's lap and making a fuss about it.

"Sorry, old sport, it's just that your knees are rather bony, you know," Melville said.

"Sit on the chair, then," Ethan grumbled.

"I would, but I want to be as close to the fire as possible. My beak is still frozen solid. I can barely feel it. It's still there, isn't it?" He raised one feathered wing and gave his beak an experimental pat.

"It's still there," Stella reassured him.

"Like I was saying," Ethan went on. "How exactly are we going to stop the snow queen from magically disappearing *us*? We don't have a single rifle."

"Rifles didn't seem to help much last time," Beanie said quietly.

"Nothing has helped that we know of," Shay pointed out. "Expeditions to the Black Ice Bridge have gone armed with all kinds of things."

"And it hasn't helped them one bit." Ethan groaned. "Those were experienced adult explorers, too. We're just four kids. What chance have we got? The snow queen could come storming in here at any second and we'd be absolute goners."

"Giving up before we even start isn't going to help much," Stella said, although she wasn't exactly feeling confident herself at that moment. But she summoned up her last shreds of optimism and said, "Besides which, we do have something the others didn't have. Two things, in fact."

"A genie and a gentleman flamingo?" Ethan sneered. "A lot of use they'll be!"

Stella could feel herself getting annoyed with Ethan, but she tried to remind herself that he sneered the most whenever he was anxious or upset.

"No," she began. "I didn't mean—"

"Ruprekt could offer the snow queen a nice cup of hot chocolate, I suppose," Ethan interrupted. "Perhaps throw a couple of scorpion marshmallows at her. And you," Ethan said to Melville, who'd finally settled on his knee. "What can you do if we come face-to-face with the snow queen?"

"Ethan!" Stella said. "Please listen to me for a moment! When I said we have two things that the other expeditions didn't have, I didn't mean Ruprekt and Melville." She glanced at them and added, "Lovely as it is to have you both along, of course. I was talking about two other things."

"Enlighten us, then," Ethan said, a little sulkily.

"First of all we have an ice princess," Stella said, indicating herself. "And yes, I know I'm not as experienced or as powerful as Queen Portia, but I do have some frost magic of my own, as well as the charm bracelet, so perhaps I might somehow be able to protect us. If we're desperate, I could try the dragon charm the gargoyles seem so keen on."

"And create an ice dragon that may very well devour us all?" Ethan said. "I don't think that would improve our situation much, do you?"

"It's a last resort, definitely," Stella agreed. "But at least it's something."

Ethan sighed. "And what's this second wonderful thing we have that no one else did?"

"Well." Stella glanced at Shay. "We have a shadow wolf who seems to be turning into a witch wolf."

Everyone looked at Shay.

"Koa wants souls, doesn't she?" Stella said. "Well, maybe she will attack the snow queen if she appears. Perhaps you could suggest it to her?"

Shay rubbed the back of his neck. "Perhaps," he said. "But she doesn't seem to want to talk to me much right now. In fact, she's talking to me less and less. And when she does speak, it doesn't always make sense." He sighed and said, "But it's worth a try. She's hungry all the time; I know that. She's looking for souls to devour. Just like the witch wolves. When she saw that fairyologist's ghost, I could feel how starving she was. But perhaps if I tell her there's something on this bridge that she *can* hunt down, it might . . . I don't know . . . be a kind of compensation to her—give her something to focus all this wild energy on." He looked at Stella and said, "It can't hurt. It might even help solve two problems at once."

The others thought it sounded like a sensible idea too, and so Shay called Koa silently inside his head. The shadow wolf appeared almost immediately and sat down close to Shay. They could tell he was talking to her because the whisperer's wolf pendant he wore on a chain around his neck opened its eyes, which sparkled red.

Although Koa was panting slightly, she seemed more her usual self. She gazed calmly at Shay while he talked to her and flicked her tongue at him affectionately a couple of times. She'd lost her solid form, and Shay's hand passed straight through her like it usually did when he tried to stroke her, but Stella noticed that a couple of her white hairs fell to the floor and remained there even after the wolf herself had disappeared.

"I think she'll attack the snow queen if we come across her," Shay said to the others. "But she's changing rapidly, so who knows what will actually happen."

"Well, it's some kind of plan at least," Stella said.

Everyone was tired, so they decided to turn in for the

night. But even though her eyes itched with fatigue, Stella found it hard to sleep. She was worried for Felix and Joss back in the cave, and hoped that the fairies were providing them with enough food.

And she kept seeing the photos of Queen Portia inside her head and recalling the terrified expressions of the frozen people back in Blackcastle. There had seemed to be no reason for the attack on the village or the explorers on the bridge. It was as if the queen had just suddenly turned evil. And Stella was so terribly afraid that one day, no matter how hard she tried to prevent it, the same thing might happen to her.

The explorers set off the next day with a sense of trepidation. This was, after all, unknown territory now that they no longer had Beanie's father's journal to warn them about what was coming up.

"There could be absolutely anything," Ethan complained as they gathered together on the snow-boat's deck. "From rampaging giants to dinosaurs playing hopscotch."

Stella clapped Ethan on the back and said, "That's the spirit. There could be dangerous things up ahead that want to eat us, *or* there could be absolutely wonderful things, like dinosaurs playing hopscotch. At least it's a sunny day today. Hopefully we'll make good time."

The mist had indeed lifted, and they could see a good length down the bridge. It looked clear enough, but they had gone only a short distance before the surface of the bridge changed. Instead of the flat, smooth surface they'd had before, they were now faced with a collection of lumps and large shapes lying beneath the snow. Stella slowed the gargoyles to a halt, and the explorers climbed down from the boat to take a closer look.

"What do you think it could be?" Stella asked.

"I hope it's not bodies," Ethan said. "Or some kind of hibernating monster."

"Well, we'll need to clear a path for the boat, so we'd better find out what we're dealing with before we start digging it up," Stella said, already having visions of them waking up a snoozing dragon.

Cautiously, the explorers started to clear away the snow, and that was when Stella realized that one of the fingers from Ethan's glove was missing so his index finger poked straight through and was rapidly turning blue.

"Oh, what happened to your glove? Did it tear when you fell over the side of the bridge?"

Ethan glanced down at his hand and, to Stella's surprise, blushed. "Oh. No." He paused, then said, "I cut it off."

Stella frowned. "Why on earth would you do that? It's freezing out here."

Before the magician could reply, Melville fluttered up beside them and said, "I say, I'd like to be useful if I can. Perhaps I can dig snow out with my umbrella?"

His posh voice came out slightly muffled, and Stella

glanced at him to see that he was wearing the finger of Ethan's glove around his beak.

She glanced at Ethan, who shrugged and said, "He kept complaining about how cold his beak was."

"You did something nice," Stella said, beaming at him.

"He was getting on my nerves, that's all," Ethan replied.

Stella felt a little burst of affection for her grouchy friend and said, "You should have mentioned it before. I've got a spare pair in my pocket."

She pulled out the gloves and handed them to Ethan, who gave her a grateful look as he slipped the new glove on.

They continued to dig and quickly revealed an object.

"It's a flag," Beanie said, pulling it free.

"Which club?" Ethan asked.

Beanie brushed away a layer of frost to reveal a fiery-red emblem. He looked up at the others. "The Sky Phoenix Explorers' Club," he said quietly.

"I think this is the remains of a hot-air balloon," Shay said. "It must have crash-landed here. Look, this is the basket, and this is the balloon itself."

The others saw that he was right. They were indeed standing upon the ruins of a crashed balloon. As they brushed away more snow, they saw it was unmistakably a Sky Phoenix Explorers' Club vessel. The balloon itself was striped red and white and painted with yellow and orange flames. A second Sky Phoenix Club flag hung down from the basket.

Inside, they also found explorers' bags made from red fabric and stamped with the phoenix emblem. Some of them had the individual explorer's names stitched onto them.

"Percy Leeroy Vane," Ethan read from one of the bags before going on to the next. "And Theodore Franklin Goudge."

"This one says Harkam Peewee Lewis," Beanie said, indicating another bag.

When they opened the backpacks, they found broken compasses, battered telescopes, and antique sextants, along with balls of string and emergency whistles.

"But this means there really *was* a Sky Phoenix Explorers' Club," Shay said, peering into an open bag. "These were the actual names of some of the explorers, and this is their stuff, and they really were here. They're not a myth at all."

It felt very strange to the four junior explorers to learn that there had once been a fifth club. There had only been four for as long as anyone could remember.

"Incredible," Stella said. "Felix will be so excited to learn about this. We should take the flag back with us as proof."

They carefully removed the flag from the basket, folded it up, and put it in Stella's bag.

"There are no bodies," Ethan said, as they continued to clear a path through the ruins of the balloon, the gargoyles following along with the snow-boat behind them.

"Well, I guess there wouldn't be after all this time," Shay said. "This balloon must have crashed here hundreds of years ago."

"You'd still expect skeletons, though," Ethan said. "Maybe the snow queen got to them?"

There were in fact several crashed balloons on the bridge, all belonging to the Sky Phoenix Explorers' Club. They saw bags, and supplies, and more flags, but there was no sign of the explorers themselves.

To make matters worse, when they got past the balloons, they found themselves confronted with a sinister sign:

GO BACK! LAND END GIANT AHEAD!

Alongside this were several other signs, all reading things like DANGER! or BEWARE! or DO NOT ENTER!

Stella saw another one that read TRESPASSERS WILL BE MUNCHED BY GIANTS.

While another read DO NOT DISTRACT, TICKLE, OR AGGRAVATE A LAND END GIANT UNDER ANY CIRCUMSTANCES. SUCH ACTION MAY LEAD TO CATASTROPHIC LOSS OF PLANET.

And another: GIANTS ARE DUMB-WITTED CREATURES, EASILY DISTRACTED BY MANY THINGS, INCLUDING:

EXPLORERS AND ADVENTURERS

SHADOWS AND WHISPERING

TIPTOEING AND CHEWING

BREATHING AND BLINKING

There must have been fifty or so signs altogether, and they all seemed to contain the same basic message: There was a Land End Giant up ahead of them, and if the giant so much as caught a whiff of their presence, then it was very likely to become distracted, which may lead to it dropping its corner of the world, which would, in turn, lead to the destruction of their entire planet.

"Good heavens," Shay breathed. He turned to the others with a worried look. "Do you really think that could be what's on the other side of the bridge?"

"Look at what we're standing in!" Beanie exclaimed. "I didn't notice at first, but look!"

The others glanced down and saw that what they had at

first taken for a shallower area of snow was, in fact, a footprint. An impossibly huge footprint.

"Only a giant could have made this!" Beanie exclaimed. "It's got to be six feet long at least!"

"Perhaps it's a yeti footprint?" Stella suggested, but even as she spoke she realized that couldn't be true because yetis were always barefoot—whereas the owner of this foot had clearly been wearing a shoe.

"If this is true, we should go back," Shay said. "We can't risk destroying the entire world. Not for anything."

"But it can't be true," Stella said. "Jezzybella said the Collector lives on the other side of the bridge."

"No offense, Stella, but Jezzybella doesn't exactly have all of her marbles, does she?" Ethan said. "I mean, for all we know, the Collector might not even exist. Besides which, even if he did come from the other side of the bridge all those years ago, there's no guarantee he's still there now."

"I know all that," Stella replied, clenching her hands into fists. "We all knew this was a long shot. But anyone could have put those signs and this footprint there. It might have even been the Collector himself, trying to keep people away."

"Maybe," Shay admitted. "But it's still a risk."

"Look, if we see a Land End Giant, we'll be very quiet and careful not to distract him, and we'll turn back," Stella said. "But there's no proof that's actually what is on the other side."

"Except for the footprint," Beanie said. "That's proof, isn't it?"

Stella frowned down at it. "Is it?" she said. "It seems very convenient to me."

"How do you mean?" Beanie asked.

"Well, it's very clearly defined, for a start," Stella said. "There's no blurred edges or anything. It's almost like someone put it here deliberately. Plus, how come there's only one print? Where are all the others? I mean, the giant must have gotten here somehow. Even if it only has one foot and hopped all the way down the bridge, there ought to be more footprints, and there aren't."

"You're right," Ethan said, gazing down the bridge. "The rest of it is just clean snow."

"Exactly," Stella said. "I don't think there is a giant. I think those signs are nothing more than a trick."

They decided to keep going, but on foot so they could keep their eyes open for any sign of giants.

CHAPTER EIGHTEEN

THEY HADN'T BEEN TRAVELING long before Beanie said, "What are those things up ahead?"

They squinted through the mist that had started to drift back in and saw that the path before them was blocked with bulky, circular objects.

"Hopefully they're nothing to do with giants," Shay said. "They could be huge bouncy balls, or something like that."

"I just hope they're not more screeching red devil squid nests," Ethan said with a shudder.

"They're not," Stella said. "They're too bulky for that."

She paused to take her telescope from her bag, training it on the mystery objects.

"Good heavens!" she exclaimed.

Ethan sighed. "Go on, then. Let's have it," he said. "I suppose they're poisonous rocks, or spiky eggs, or barbed—"

"No," Stella replied. "Nothing like that. It looks like they're tiny submarines."

"Nonsense," Ethan said dismissively. "They're far too small to be subs."

"But I can see the big glass dome," Stella said. "And the propeller at the back and—"

"I tell you, it's not possible," Ethan said. "The smallest submarine in the world is ten times as big as those things."

When they reached the objects, though, it looked as if Stella was right. The gargoyles hung back with the snow-boat while the explorers took a closer look.

"These are definitely submarines," Shay said, peering down at the nearest one. "This one even has the word 'submarine' painted on its side."

"Well, it's not a functional one," Ethan pointed out. "There's a great big hole in it."

There must have been twenty of the little submarines scattered around the bridge. Each one was extremely small—barely large enough for a single adult human to fit into. It looked as if they had all once been green in color, but the paint was rusting and peeling away. They were also, Stella noticed, slightly different designs. Some were round and bubble-shaped, while others were long and sleek, like the nose of a swordfish.

"They must have belonged to an Ocean Squid Explorers' Club expedition," Stella said.

"I tell you, there's never been a submarine like this in our club," Ethan replied. "Our subs are all large enough to carry an entire expedition, for a start. Plus they all have the Ocean Squid Explorers' Club crest stamped on the side and a waterproof flag flying from them somewhere. These look as if they've been designed to carry just one person and nothing else." He gave a derisive snort. "You wouldn't get far in that. Submarines need to have a galley for storing food, and bathroom facilities, and harpoon cannons to ward off kraken. These things are useless. No wonder they're all damaged."

Stella had to admit he had a point. It certainly didn't look as if these submarines were designed for traveling long distances. Most of them seemed to consist only of a seat for the pilot to sit in.

"There's *something* written here, though," Shay said, rubbing frost from the side of the nearest sub.

"Perhaps it's something else from the Sky Phoenix Explorers' Club?" Beanie suggested as they gathered around.

But the image on the submarine wasn't a crest at all. Instead it was an image of the world, with four words curving around it.

"The Phantom Atlas Society," Stella read. She frowned and looked at the others. "Has anyone ever heard of that?"

But the others all shook their heads.

"There's no such thing as a phantom atlas," Ethan said with a shrug. "Perhaps they belong to some half-crazy maverick explorer. He obviously wasn't a member of any of the clubs or there'd be a crest and a flag. And he clearly didn't know anything about geography because the world in that crest is a globe. He probably got snatched up by the snow queen."

"Hmm." Stella frowned at the submarines. "But then why are there so many of them?"

No one had an answer to that.

But before anyone could comment upon it further, there was the startling sound of a long, loud, extremely smelly burp from inside one of the nearby submarines.

The junior explorers all spun around on the spot in time to see a small creature, about the size of a large cat, crawl from the wreckage of the submarine. It was pale blue in color, with webbed feet and hands, bat-shaped ears, and large golf-ball-size eyes that seemed to bulge right out of its head. Its skin was lumpy and bumpy, with a leathery sort of texture, and it had sharp pointed teeth that poked down over its lip.

Stella had never seen anything like it before, but Ethan recognized the creature immediately.

"Good heavens, it's a sea-gremlin!" he cried. Moving quickly, he snatched it up by its skinny ankle and held it firmly at arm's length. The gremlin didn't like this much and thrashed around in Ethan's grip, but it was a bony thing without much muscle and didn't seem able to free itself.

"Don't hurt it!" Stella said, immediately concerned for the creature, which she couldn't help thinking was rather sweet in a crooked sort of way.

Ethan rolled his eyes. "Stella, I know you're probably thinking it's cute and that you'd like to cuddle it or knit it a hat or something, but sea-gremlins are a terrible menace. They get into the inner workings of submarines and meddle with the machinery—cutting wires and biting through cables and poking things into the propellers and goodness knows what else. They're responsible for dozens of Ocean Squid explorer deaths every year."

"He's right, you know," Beanie said. "It's estimated that two hundred and thirty-nine deaths of explorers from the Ocean Squid Explorers' Club are attributable to sea-gremlins meddling with the machinery inside submarines. They're even more dangerous than frosties."

"Normally they're extremely fast," Ethan said. "This one must be old or I wouldn't have been able to catch it so easily."

Now that Stella looked more closely, she saw that the gremlin did indeed have tufts of white hair sticking out of its ears and a rather wrinkled look about its face and body, as if its skin were a little bit too big for it. It curled its hand into a knobbly fist and shook it angrily at Ethan.

The magician ignored it and said, "I bet gremlins were responsible for all these damaged submarines."

"Can they talk?" Stella asked.

"When it suits them," Ethan replied. "But then it's normally just to swear at you."

Stella moved a little closer to the gremlin, but Ethan drew it away. "Careful," he warned. "They go for the eyes and, trust me, you really don't want it poking at your eyeballs with its dirty fingernails. Julian got a terrible eye infection that way when he tried to remove a sea-gremlin from a submarine engine once."

Stella didn't want an eye infection, so she kept a careful distance and said to the gremlin, "Hello, I'm Stella Starflake Pearl. What's your name?"

Ethan rolled his eyes at her polite tone. The gremlin blinked up at Stella, then opened its mouth. For a moment she thought it was about to reply, but instead it gave a great yawn before sticking its bony finger straight up its nostril and extracting a blue booger which it deftly rolled up into a ball and flicked at her.

The slimy lump was flying straight toward her face, but with lightning-fast speed Shay shot out his hand and the booger landed in his palm with a splat.

"I say, that was well done, old man!" Melville said. He looked up at Stella and said, "You know you've got a true friend when they catch gremlin boogers for you. Probably the most effective test for true friendship there is."

Stella couldn't help thinking the gentleman flamingo

was right about that and gave Shay a grateful look. The wolf whisperer grinned back at her and shrugged. "You touch far worse things looking after wolves," he said, before leaning down to wipe the snot off in the snow.

The gargoyles had all clearly decided they were in the line of fire and had moved back a little distance, taking the snow-boat with them.

"Don't be so disgusting!" Ethan said to the gremlin, giving it a shake.

"Let me go!" the gremlin said, speaking for the first time in a croaky voice. "Or it'll be boogers to the face for you!"

"Ethan, just let him go," Stella said. "We don't have any submarines or machinery, so he isn't a threat to us."

"Don't call me a he!" the gremlin spluttered. "You wanted to know my name? Well, it's Daphne!"

"Oh, I'm sorry," Stella said. "But really it's your own fault. If you'd introduced yourself nicely rather than throwing a booger at me, then I wouldn't have made that mistake."

"Fortunately, I know a thing or two about sea-gremlins," Ethan said. He glanced at Stella and said, "Including the fact that if you question one while dangling it by its ankle, it has to answer your questions truthfully." He looked down at the gremlin. "So, where did you come from?"

The gremlin scowled up at him. "If you must know, I came with Harkam Peewee Lewis."

Stella frowned, recalling the name she'd seen written on the bag in the wreckage of the balloons. "From the Sky Phoenix Explorers' Club?" she asked.

"Duh!" Still dangling upside down, the gremlin crossed her arms over her bony chest and said, "I don't know of any other Harkam Peewee Lewises around here—do you?"

"But no one has had contact with that club for years and years," Shay said. "How old *are* you?"

"It's rude to ask a lady that question!" Daphne snarled. Her large nostrils flared. "But it was my two hundred and fourth birthday yesterday."

"Happy birthday for yesterday," Beanie immediately said.

"Two hundred and four!" Ethan exclaimed. "Good grief, no wonder you're as wrinkly as an old prune!"

"Ethan," Stella said in a warning voice.

"What?" the magician demanded. "She is." He glanced back down at the gremlin. "I thought sea-gremlins only traveled in submarines."

"Harkam Peewee Lewis came from his home by submarine and set a trap for us in the engine room. He was going to take us back to the Sky Phoenix Explorers' Club and present us as curiosities to be stuffed. But then my brother, Bobby, got free. First he bit a hole in that horrid explorer's trousers—right on the bum!—and then he bit a hole in the balloon."

"Causing them to crash-land here?"

"Yep."

"Do you know what's on the other side of this bridge?" Ethan asked.

The gremlin exposed her teeth in a grin. "Yes," she said. "But you won't get the chance to ask me what it is."

Ethan frowned at her. "Why not?"

The gremlin snarled up at him. "Because, while you've been jabbering away, my friends have got you surrounded!"

Ethan narrowed his eyes. "What friends?"

But before anyone could say another word, about fifty sea-gremlins erupted from beneath the snow.

CHAPTER NINETEEN

THE SEA-GREMLINS WERE, AS Ethan had said, extremely fast. They showered snow everywhere as they flew at the explorers, landing on their heads, and backs, and legs. One of them even tucked Melville under his arm and tried to run off with him, but Ethan lunged after them, snatching the flamingo back and stuffing him down his cloak. The action forced him to drop Daphne, who scampered off to a safe distance and perched on top of one of the wrecked submarines. The gremlin plonked her bony bottom down on the roof, dangled her webbed feet over the edge, and then proceeded to let loose a volley of swear words at them.

"Hey, that's my hat!" Beanie cried as one of the gremlins snatched his pom-pom hat and ran off with it, snickering.

Meanwhile, Stella had to fight off a pair who seemed determined to rip her charm bracelet straight from her wrist. Shay was having the same problem with his whisperer's wolf pendant, and Ethan was having to keep a tight grip on Melville.

"They're scavengers!" the magician called out as he batted another gremlin away. "Watch your pockets, or they'll empty them!"

The gremlins seemed quite determined to go after their clothes, too, and had already started dragging Beanie's cloak off him.

There were too many of them and they seemed to be swarming everywhere.

"How do we stop them?" Stella cried as three more gremlins scrambled up the back of her dress.

"I don't know!" Ethan groaned. "They don't like bright light. Has anyone got a flashlight? They'll scurry off if you shine a light on them."

Unfortunately, no one had a flashlight with them.

"How many of you did Harkam Peewee Lewis capture?" Ethan exclaimed.

"Just me and Bobby," Daphne said, pointing at another wrinkled old gremlin who was in the process of sticking his bony arm down Shay's boot. "The others are here for the school."

"What school?"

Daphne snapped her fingers, and all the gremlins fell off the explorers and turned toward her, waiting to see what she would do.

"Didn't you see the sign?" Daphne demanded, glaring at the explorers.

She waved her skinny arm at one of the signs behind them. They'd walked straight past it, assuming it was another sign warning of the Land End Giant, but now Stella saw that it read DAPHNE'S GREMLIN SCHOOL.

"Gremlins come here to learn how to be gremlins," she said with a nasty grin. "I teach 'em, using these old subs."

"But where did the submarines come from in the first place?" Stella asked. "And why do you want to sabotage us? What have explorers ever done to you?"

"Explorers poke their noses in where they have no right to be poking," Daphne said. "They'd ruin the world if we let them."

"What are you talking about?" said Stella.

"Nosy explorers poking in their nosy noses!" Daphne replied. "Just like now. You're not allowed on this bridge. Can't you read? Didn't you see the signs about the giant? You've got to turn back."

"We can't turn back," Stella replied. "We're looking for someone who lives on the other side of the bridge. He's known as the Collector. Do you know anything about him?"

Daphne was silent for a moment. Then she said, "The Collector doesn't want to see you. The Collector doesn't want to see anyone."

"So, he *does* exist, then?" Stella said, excited.

"You go back," Daphne insisted, pointing at the bridge stretching out behind them. "Or else these gremlins will poke their bony fingers into your eyeballs. Eye infections for everybody. And then we'll flick you with more boogers."

"We're not turning back," Stella said. "So please get out of our way."

Daphne turned around, shaking her head. She raised her hand into the air and snapped her fingers. The gremlins sprang into action once again, tearing and clawing at the explorers' clothes and lunging at their eyes with their long fingers. It was pandemonium and they were completely outnumbered, making it very difficult to keep the gremlins at bay. One of them succeeded in climbing up onto Stella's shoulder, where it raked its nails across her face hard enough to draw blood, just narrowly missing her eye.

She was aware that Ethan was throwing magic arrows at the gremlins, but the little creatures were so fast they just snatched them straight out of the air and threw them right back at the magician. The first time Shay threw his boomerang, a gremlin grabbed it and ran off with it. And when Beanie chased after the one who'd taken his hat, he got ambushed by seven other gremlins who all fell on him at once.

Feeling desperate, Stella reached her hand down toward the sleigh charm, hoping she might be able to summon it once again and that the two wild polar bears might frighten away the gremlins. But one of the little creatures yanked at her bracelet at the last moment, causing Stella's fingers to close around a different charm instead—the unicorn.

Sparkling light immediately burst from the charm, and the gremlin hanging on to Stella's wrist let go with a howl of pain, shielding its large eyes from the sudden blazing brightness. The other gremlins stopped what they were doing and dropped back too.

Out of thin air a unicorn appeared, snorting and stamping. At least, Stella thought it was a unicorn, but then it unfurled its wings and she realized it was actually a horned Pegasus. There were wings engraved upon the charm that she had overlooked, and the real Pegasus now spread these out wide against the sky, light gleaming from every feather.

The creature seemed to be made entirely from starlight, flashing diamond twinkles with every movement. It had a half-wild look, with an untamed mane and sparking eyes and nostrils that flared as it tossed its head. From the very tip of its horn there shone a beam of white light so bright that it was hard for even the humans to look directly at it.

The gremlins howled, shielding their eyes and faces, and staggered over themselves in their attempts to get away. Before long, they had all turned and bolted for the edge of the bridge, leaping over the side and tucking their knobbly knees up to their chins to make little cannonball shapes, plunging down into the water with a splash.

Even Daphne fled when the starlight Pegasus cantered toward her. Squealing, the gremlin leapt up onto the railings and looked back at the explorers just long enough to shriek, "No one's allowed on the bridge! I'm telling on you!"

"There's nobody out here," Ethan pointed out. "Who are you going to tell?"

The gremlin grinned. "The boss," she said.

Then, without another word, she leapt from the side and cannonballed down to the water with a splash, leaving the explorers alone.

The Pegasus was trotting around in agitated circles, so Stella stepped forward and put her hand out. The Pegasus stopped, snorting puffs of frosty breath into the air as Stella gently brushed her fingers over its neck. Stella had thought that perhaps the Pegasus might not have any substance and that her hand would pass through it, just like with Koa, but in fact she was able to touch the creature, who felt as cold and smooth as glass.

"It's okay," Stella said quietly. "The gremlins have all gone. You frightened them away. Well done."

"Wow," Ethan said. "That bracelet comes in handy, doesn't it?"

He scooped up Beanie's pom-pom hat, which the gremlin had dropped in its haste to get into the sea. Beanie immediately put it back on his head so that he could tug at it in consternation.

"How marvelous," Shay said, joining Stella beside the Pegasus.

It was such a beautiful, magical creature that Stella would have liked to keep it there, especially as its light pushed away the sea mist and made it easier for them to see what was coming up ahead. But she could already start to feel a slight itch behind her eyes and recalled how exhausted the polar-bear sleigh had made her feel. The gremlins had left, so it seemed sensible to save the magic for when it was really needed.

Stella, therefore, said good-bye to the Pegasus, released her concentration on the spell, and let the magical creature fade away into the fog.

"Will the gremlins come back?" Beanie asked, gazing around in concern.

But Ethan shook his head. "Not quickly," he said. "They can't fly, so they'll need to fashion some kind of seaweed rope or something to—oh!"

He had leaned out over the side of the bridge as he spoke but now quickly drew back.

"They're all sitting down there," he whispered, gesturing back toward the bridge. "There's a little floating platform attached to a rope ladder. I suppose Daphne's students need some way to get up to the bridge from the ocean. They can come back up here anytime they want. I guess they haven't realized the Pegasus has gone."

"Well, let's get moving before they do," Stella said. "It looks like the bridge is fairly flat up ahead. If we just shift some of these submarines to clear a path, then we can get back in the snow-boat and put some distance between us."

They grouped together to roll some of the subs out of the way; then Stella beckoned the gargoyles, who were still keeping back. They came straight over, the explorers got back into the boat, and soon they were speeding along the bridge once again, keeping a lookout for gremlins following behind them.

"Any sign?" Shay asked, joining Stella at the back of the boat after about half an hour.

She lowered her telescope and shook her head. "Nothing," she said. "They must have stayed behind. Let's head back inside."

"What do you suppose that gremlin meant about telling the boss?" Shay asked as they went belowdecks. Beanie was poring over a book in one corner of the galley, while Ethan sat at the table with Melville, playing dominoes.

Stella shrugged. "Perhaps she meant the snow queen? Or the Collector, I suppose. She seemed to know of him."

"Stella, this doesn't make sense," Beanie said, looking up from his book with a frown. "This is one of the books I took from Queen Portia's library. There's a lot of information in it about snow queens. Look."

He stood up and handed her the open book. One page

depicted a painting of a snow queen, while the other contained facts. Stella ran her eye down them with a shudder. She didn't particularly want to be reminded of frozen hearts and evil spells right now.

"We already know all this," she said, trying to hand the book back.

But Beanie shook his head and said, "Look there." He pointed at a box in the top corner of the page. "It's got some facts and figures about snow queens," he said. "Including their life span."

"Seventy years," Stella read.

"So what?" Ethan said, glancing up from his dominoes game. "That sounds about normal."

"But when we saw Queen Portia in those fairy photos, she looked exactly the same as she did in her portrait," Beanie said. "And even eight years ago, she would have been in her hundreds."

"You're right," Stella said. "I wondered about that myself."

"The book must be wrong," Shay said, frowning. "I mean, we all saw her in that photo, so what other explanation is there? Books are wrong sometimes."

"I suppose that must be it," Stella said, handing the book back to Beanie. "It seems strange, though."

"Aha!" Melville cried, laying down a domino. "I win!" He extended his wing out to Ethan, who shook it, albeit with a bit of a grumpy expression.

"Better luck next time, old crumpet," Melville said.

"Best out of three?" Ethan said.

"Hang on," Shay said, walking over to them. "Where did those dominoes come from?"

"Melville found them somewhere," Ethan said. He glanced at the flamingo and asked, "Where did they come from?"

"I took them from one of those little submarines," Melville said. Then he looked up with an alarmed expression. "Gosh, you don't think anyone will mind, do you? It's just that no one seemed to be using them, but that was before we found the gremlins. Perhaps they might be peeved?"

"Who cares about the gremlins?" Ethan replied, flipping the dominoes facedown to shuffle them up.

Stella saw that they were marked with something on the back and leaned down to pick one up.

"It's the Phantom Atlas Society again," she said, frowning. It was quite a handsome set—all the dominoes were made from glossy wood with what looked like mother-of-pearl dots. She handed the domino back to Ethan. "It's so strange that no one's ever heard of them," she said.

"Perhaps it's a dead society that existed hundreds of years ago," Shay suggested.

"Or it could be a secret one," Beanie said. "That's another theory about the bridge, you know—that it leads to some ancient secret society."

"And what's this society supposed to do?" Stella asked.

"No one knows," Beanie said. "It's a secret."

After they'd put some distance between themselves and the gremlins, they stopped to put up the magic blanket fort and have a late lunch on the bridge before carrying on with their journey. They didn't come across anything else of any interest for the rest of the afternoon, except for a few more signs warning them of the Land End Giant. The needle of Stella's compass was still spinning around uselessly, but it didn't really matter because they knew they simply had to keep on going across the bridge.

Indeed, the gargoyles seemed very eager to get there. The morning after the gremlin episode, the explorers were still eating the breakfast Ruprekt had prepared for them when one of the gargoyles lifted the canvas and stuck his stone head through the gap, grumbling away at them in his own gravelly language. When Stella went out to see what he wanted, the gargoyles were already buckled into their harnesses, gesturing at the snow-boat and eager to be away.

"Why are they so excited?" Ethan wondered.

"Who knows?" Shay replied. "Perhaps they're a bit like wolves and just need to run sometimes."

They traveled on for the next two days, seeing nothing of any note except for another conspicuous giant footprint. There was the sound of some sea monster splashing unseen in the mist beneath the bridge on the second day, and also a huge, dark, unidentifiable bird that flapped over their heads, creating such a wind rush with its wingspan that it blew their hoods back from their heads.

And then, early that afternoon, Stella was on the deck of the snow-boat, training her telescope on the bridge, when she saw something that made her breath catch in her throat. "Stop!" she cried out to the gargoyles.

"What's up?" Shay asked, straining his eyes through the mist.

She looked at her friend. "I can't be sure, now that the fog is coming back," she said. "But it looks like the bridge runs out up ahead."

"Runs out?" Shay repeated. "You mean, there's no other side?"

He looked dismayed, and Stella couldn't blame him. After everything they'd faced and all the effort they'd made to get here, it would be terrible to find there was no other side to the bridge—and no Collector, no Book of Frost. It would mean they'd come all this way for nothing and had no way of saving Shay and Koa or releasing Felix and Joss from their ice cave.

"Let's walk the rest of the way on foot and see," Stella said. "If it does run out, we don't want to go hurtling over the side in the boat."

The gargoyles had slowed to a stop, so the explorers made their way out into the snow. The sea fog was rolling in fast, and before long they could barely see more than a few feet in front of them. The bridge itself was utterly silent. There was no splashing of sea monsters below, or flapping of monstrous birds above. It was like the five of them were the only living things there.

They went slowly forward, with the gargoyles trudging through the snow pulling the boat behind them, everyone straining their eyes through the swirling mist.

"Just remember," Shay whispered. "If we come across one of the Land End Giants holding up one of the four corners of the world, then we just back away as silently as we can. No one can even so much as sneeze. There could be disastrous consequences if we were to—"

He broke off then because Koa had appeared at his side and started to growl. Almost half of her fur was now white, and Stella could tell that she had a physical substance again from the way she brushed against Shay's leg. Her ears were pressed flat against her head as she stared into the looming fog, and the growl rumbled too loudly in the back of her throat. Usually snow muffled noise, but the bridge seemed to echo the sound back at them.

"Shhh, Koa!"

Shay tried to quiet her, but this only made her growl more urgently, and the next second she lunged forward. Shay tried to grab her, his hand closing on the scruff of her neck, but Koa twisted free and bolted into the mist, barking ferociously.

"Well, that's really ruined things," Ethan exclaimed. "We'd better hope it's not a Land End Giant out there, for all our sakes. If a tadpole burping is enough to distract them, then a shadow-wolf/witch-wolf hybrid is definitely going to do the trick, isn't it? The giant will drop its corner of the world, we'll all roll off into space, and it will be our fault for single-handedly destroying the whole entire—"

"It's not a Land End Giant," Shay said. The whisper-er's wolf pendant at his throat had opened its eyes, which gleamed red in the dimness and meant that he was talking to the shadow wolf inside his head. "Koa says it's the snow queen."

"Use the Pegasus charm again, Stella," Beanie urged. "At least then we'll be able to see."

Stella thought this was a good idea and was just reaching for her bracelet when Koa's bark was suddenly cut off short. It was a strange, unnatural, abrupt end to the noise, as if the shadow wolf had suddenly ceased to exist altogether.

And Stella could sense something else, too—a presence that was surely very close to them in the mist. Her fingers closed around the cold silver Pegasus charm, and the magical creature immediately exploded into life in flashes of starlight, the light from its horn cutting through the fog and illuminating the bridge up ahead.

And there, right before them, was Queen Portia herself.

CHAPTER TWENTY

THE MIST DRIFTED APART in ribbons to expose the snow queen, standing just a few paces ahead of them in the middle of the bridge, which did indeed come to an abrupt end. It just . . . stopped, with nothing but fog and a great drop swirling beyond it.

The snow queen looked exactly as she had in the paintings back in her castle, and in the fairy's photographs. Her lustrous velvet dress was royal purple, edged in soft white fur. Her black hair was pulled back into intricate plaits, and her skin seemed even paler and whiter in comparison.

There was no sign of Koa, but Stella's eyes went straight to the snow queen's gloved hands, and she saw that they held a snow globe. It had a beautiful silver base encrusted with snowflakes and whirls of pale blue ice. And trapped within the snow globe was a wolf. Not a wolf made from glass, as Stella had seen inside the snow globes at Coldgate, but a real miniature wolf that moved around inside, pacing back and forth as it tried to find a way out. Even from this distance, Stella could see that the wolf was half white and half black.

"It's Koa!" Shay gasped. "She's captured her!" He turned his furious gaze on the snow queen. "What have you done to my wolf?"

"Saved her life, probably," Queen Portia replied in a smooth, cool voice. "She was going to turn into a witch wolf at any second, but time is frozen inside the globe. Do not worry. It won't hurt her."

The snow queen reached into the pocket of her cloak and pulled out another snow globe. This one was empty, but Stella realized that Queen Portia meant to trap them in it. This surely was how she had attacked the other explorers on the bridge, and the reason why so many explorers had gone missing over the years. Their hope that Koa might be able to stop her had failed, and Stella knew she had to act immediately or else they could all be done for too. Certainly boomerangs and magic arrows and jelly beans would be no use against a snow queen. It was all up to her.

Felix and Jezzybella had both warned her against using the dragon charm, saying it was too dangerous and that she'd be just as likely to summon a dragon that would immediately gobble her up, but what choice did she have? If she didn't act now, the snow queen would definitely take them.

Stella reached for her charm bracelet just as the gargoyles pushed past the explorers and gathered together in front of the snow queen. Queen Portia paused in the act of unscrewing the glass dome from the base of the snow globe. The gargoyles were all jumping up and down and waving their arms, as if trying to tell Stella something. She got the sense they didn't want her to attack Queen Portia, but what choice did she have? It was her or them, and Stella was determined to protect her friends if she possibly could.

So she took a deep breath and closed her fingers around the dragon charm, concentrating with all her might. She fully expected an ice dragon to burst into life, just as the Pegasus had done. She thought it would be huge and spectacular, rather like the ice dragon they had encountered in the caves beneath Queen Portia's castle. But instead there was a flash of silver light and then . . . nothing.

Stella thought the spell hadn't worked at first. That perhaps she hadn't been strong enough to create the dragon, or maybe she could use only one charm at a time and needed to send the Pegasus away. But then something tickled over her wrist, and she looked down to see the world's tiniest dragon clinging there. Silver from snout to tail, it was no bigger than her little finger and pattered back and forth over her hand, its tiny scales sparkling in the light that blazed from the Pegasus. It was flesh-and-blood rather than ice, but its small body was still cool to the touch.

Suddenly it looked up at Stella, and its bright eyes were like little beads in its face. Then it spread out its spindly wings and flapped up into the air, snorting icy breath in little puffs. Normally, Stella would have been utterly delighted by the cutest, smallest dragon she had ever seen, but now she felt only despair. It was no wonder the gargoyles were clapping—for this tiny dragon was not going to be any help to them whatsoever.

She thought it was going to fly off into the fog, but to her surprise it flapped up to her shoulder and from there flew right to her left ear, where it attached itself like an extremely beautiful ear cuff. Its small feet curled gently around her lobe and its spiny tail trailed down her neck as it rested its small snout against her ear and whispered to her in a peculiar voice that was as soft and smooth as smoke.

"It is an honor to serve you, Majesty," it said. "Who would you like me to translate?"

"Translate?" Stella repeated, frowning. "What do you mean?"

"I'm a translator, Majesty," the dragon said, its small tongue tickling Stella's skin. Her ear tingled with cold as well as something else—a fizz of magic. "Just tell me which language you wish to speak and then when they speak you will understand them through me."

"Oh. I . . . I'm sorry, it's just that I thought you'd be a magnificent fighting dragon, you see."

"No, I'm definitely not a fighting dragon," it replied. "Translations only."

"What's going on?" Ethan demanded. "Who are you talking to?"

Stella realized the others couldn't hear anything the dragon was saying. Her mind was racing as she tried to work out what was happening. Queen Portia looked just as perplexed and was still frozen in the act of whatever she'd been about to do with the snow globe. In fact, she was no longer looking at Stella and the others, but at the gargoyles, who were still jabbering fiercely at Stella. There was a strange expression in the snow queen's emerald-green eyes—not the murderous rage Stella had expected, but a sad, sorrowful look.

"The gargoyles seem rather keen to communicate with you," the little dragon hinted. "Perhaps you might like to understand what they have to say?"

"Yes," Stella replied, mostly because she didn't know what else to do. "Yes, please translate them for me."

The moment the words were out of her mouth, her left ear tingled more than ever and suddenly it was as if she could hear two different versions of the gargoyles. Through her right ear, their voices had the same incomprehensible gravelly chatter that they always had. But through her left, where the dragon clung, she could suddenly make out words. She had to concentrate on them, especially since her right ear was still hearing them as she had before, but there were definitely words there now. Unfortunately, though, it was even more difficult to follow because of the fact that all seven gargoyles were talking at once, and Stella could only catch snatches of their sentences, which were all muddled up.

"Queen Portia is not who you think."

"The magic spilled out everywhere—"

"The Collector took it—"

"—wasn't her fault."

"All right, all right!" Stella said, waving her hands at them. "I can understand you."

"You can?" Shay asked, staring at her.

"Yes, just about." She looked at the gargoyles. "But not if you all talk together like that. One at a time."

The gargoyles fell silent, and then one stepped forward, heaving a great sigh. "About time," he grumbled, his voice like a bunch of stones being jumbled together. "We kept telling you to use the dragon charm."

"I thought it would create a wild, dangerous monster," Stella said. "I had no idea it was a translator charm."

"Well, why didn't you study your Book of Frost?" the gargoyle asked testily.

"That's kind of a long story—" she began.

The gargoyle cut her off. "Never mind. Listen, you may not have been able to understand us, but we could understand you, and you've got it all muddled up about Queen Portia. She isn't evil and she didn't freeze the village. Or at least she didn't mean to. It was Jared—or the Collector, as you seem to call him. There was a magical protection on the Book of Frost. He managed to break through the spell and steal it, but it caused broken magic to leak from the castle, and that's how the village was frozen."

Stella looked at Queen Portia, who had knelt down in the snow and set the snow globes to one side in order to gather some of the gargoyles into her arms, like they were long-lost pets, her eyes sparkling with tears.

"I don't understand," Stella said.

The gargoyle went over to Queen Portia and whispered something to her. The snow queen nodded and reached behind her neck to unclasp her dragon locket. She passed it to the gargoyle, who returned to Stella's side.

"Jared Aligheri was a sorcerer," the gargoyle explained, holding out the locket. It was just as Stella remembered it from the painting—a silver dragon curled around a golden disc with a twinkling starflake held in one clawed foot. Now that she saw it up close, Stella realized there was an inscription engraved in the middle of the disc. It read *Love you to the stars.*

"He was one of the last sorcerers of his kind," the gargoyle went on. "Even two hundred years ago." Carefully prying open the locket, he held it up so Stella could see the tiny oil painting hidden inside. It depicted a handsome man with a neat, pointed beard, blond hair, and magnetic eyes.

So this was the Collector—the man who had murdered Stella's birth parents and stolen her Book of Frost. She couldn't help shuddering as she gazed into his cold dark eyes.

"But . . . but if he was an evil sorcerer, why does Queen Portia have a painting of him inside her locket?" Stella asked. She glanced at the snow queen, who still knelt on the ground before her. She'd made no attempt to join the conversation in any way and didn't seem as if she was even listening to it. There was a faraway look in her eyes, and

one solitary tear was making its way slowly down her face.

"Because he was her soul mate and she loved him," the gargoyle said simply. "He wasn't evil to begin with. He made her happy. He gave her this locket. He loved her."

"So what happened?" Stella asked.

"Well, they started to disagree about something very important to them both," the gargoyle said. "Their difference of opinion got bigger and bigger until eventually it fractured their love right down the middle."

Stella frowned. "What was the disagreement about?"

The gargoyle sighed and glanced back at the snow queen. "That is a long story," he said. "And I will explain, but right now what you need to know is that Jared stole the Book of Frost from Queen Portia. And in doing so he released a dangerous magic on Blackcastle. The neighboring village thought Queen Portia must be responsible and came banging on the castle doors with their flaming torches and their pitchforks. Everything was in chaos. Queen Portia told us to wait for her in the cave, but she never came back."

"According to the ancient accounts, the mob chased her out onto the Black Ice Bridge," Stella said.

"They didn't chase her out here!" The gargoyle sneered. "Maybe that's what they thought they were doing, but she'd intended to come here all along. To confront Jared and take back what was rightfully hers. When she didn't come back, we knew something must have gone wrong—that Jared had won the fight instead of her. And we could do nothing but stay in our cave and grieve. We couldn't even try to go after her because she had sealed us inside to keep us safe. Only an ice princess could open the doors and wake up the castle."

"Well, what *did* happen?" Stella asked, looking at the snow queen. "What's wrong with her? And how is she still alive after all this time? She looks exactly the same age as when she left, but that was more than two hundred years ago." She recalled Beanie's father's expedition and said, "And we know she's been attacking explorer expeditions that come onto the bridge. If she really isn't evil, why has she been doing that?"

"I haven't had a chance to ask her yet, because I've been standing here jabbering with you!" the gargoyle replied, a little peevishly. "But now that you're not determined to attack the queen, perhaps we can attempt a civilized conversation." He paused and narrowed his eyes at Stella. "You *have* changed your mind about attacking the queen, I hope?"

"We never wanted to attack anyone," Stella protested. "That's not why we came here. We're simply trying to get to the other side of the bridge, to find the Collector." Her eyes went past the queen to the vast emptiness beyond. She sighed and said, "Although it doesn't look as if there *is* another side to the bridge. It doesn't look like there's anything there at all."

It was a crushing disappointment to the young explorers, but the gargoyle's focus was solely on Queen Portia and he turned away from Stella and bowed to his mistress before handing her the locket. She clasped the necklace back around her neck.

"My queen," the winged gargoyle said in a gentle voice. "We waited for you, but you never came back. What happened?"

The snow queen raised her head to look at him, and finally she spoke. "We were friends once, a very long time ago," she said, frowning as if trying to remember.

"Oh yes, Majesty," the gargoyle said, reaching for her hand and clasping it in both of his own. "Very dear friends."

The Pegasus still stood at Stella's side, and in the light from its horn something glinted at the snow queen's wrist. Her charm bracelet was there, looking just as it had in the portrait except for the golden heart charm, which had badly rusted. But something else flickered there next to the bracelet, and Stella realized it was a handcuff. It was a pearly white color—strangely beautiful—but a handcuff nonetheless. Stella could clearly see that the snow queen's skin was red and raw where the cuff pressed into it.

Stella pointed at it now and said, "Are you a prisoner?"

The snow queen let go of the gargoyle's hand and rose

slowly to her feet. She gazed at her handcuff for a long moment before saying, "A prisoner. Yes. He took my heart, you see. I caught up with him—here on the bridge, I think. We fought. . . ." She frowned again. "It is hard to remember." She looked down at the cuff again. "But I suppose he must have won. His magic was stronger and fiercer than mine in the end. So I have been here for all these years, forced to do his bidding."

"You attack people who come onto the bridge?" Stella said. "Make them disappear? In those snow globe things?"

Her eyes went to the empty snow globe the queen had placed on the ground. A dull pain had started up behind her eyes from the effort of keeping both magic charms going at once, so she allowed the Pegasus to melt away into nothing.

"The Collector doesn't want to be disturbed," Queen Portia replied. "There is important work to do, you see. Even I have not seen him in years. The signs about the Land End Giants were not enough to keep people away, so I'm cursed to roam the bridge, looking for trespassers. No one has come for such a long time that I have not been patrolling the bridge as I should. But also I am so very tired." She looked at Stella and said, "I am sorry about the explorers. Truly." Her free hand fiddled with the white handcuff. "But the enchantment he put on me is a powerful one. If I see trespassers on the bridge, I must capture them. . . ."

She trailed off, her eyes fixed on Stella as if she were

only just seeing her. Both her hands began to tremble, and she seemed to turn even paler.

"Oh!" she gasped. "You . . . you're an ice princess!"

"My name is Stella Starflake Pearl," Stella replied, a little warily. The snow queen was staring at her with a very intense expression all of a sudden.

The explorers all flinched as Queen Portia suddenly moved, but it was only to drop to her knees in the snow before Stella and grab hold of her skirts. "Please set me free!" she cried.

"What?" Stella stared at her. "What do you mean? I have no idea how."

"He used a spell from my own Book of Frost to make this cuff," the snow queen replied. "Only ice magic can unlock it."

"Then why can't you do it?" Stella asked.

"I lost my powers when he took my heart," she replied. "Only another magical person can free me from the enchantment." She looked up at Stella and said, "It would be in your own interest to help me. With every moment that goes by, the urge to trap you all inside a snow globe becomes harder for me to resist."

"It's not that I don't want to," Stella replied. "It's that I have no idea how."

Queen Portia gave her a disbelieving look. "But there the charm hangs right before my eyes," she said.

Stella glanced down at her charm bracelet. "Which

charm do you mean?" she asked. "Look, I didn't grow up as an ice princess, so I don't know everything about this stuff. You'll have to explain it to me."

"The key," Queen Portia said, indicating the silver charm. "Using it creates an ice key that can open any lock."

"Oh. And it works like the other charms? I just touch it and think of what I want it to do?"

"Yes. Concentrate upon it really hard and it will happen."

"Is that such a great idea?" Shay said to her quietly. "You've already used two of the charms in the last five minutes."

The snow queen groaned and seemed to grab on to the snow globe on the ground almost against her will. "Do it quickly!" she gasped. "Or else you'll all end up trapped within this globe."

"What choice do I have?" Stella said, glancing at her friends. "We know what will happen if I don't. Besides, it's the right thing to do. No one should be enslaved like this."

So she pressed her fingertips to the key and concentrated as hard as she could, even though the effort caused her head to pound. A moment later, a small ice key glittered in the palm of her hand. Stella didn't hesitate, and reached out to insert the key into Queen Portia's cuff.

The key went straight in, but to Stella's surprise it wouldn't turn.

"What's wrong?" she asked, looking down at the queen.

Queen Portia was staring at the cuff in dismay. "It must be because he has my heart," she said. "He took it right here on the bridge." She gazed up at the forbidding black structure. "Some evil magic soaked into the marble when he attacked me, and made the bridge go a little strange. But he took my heart with him. Locked away inside one of his snow globes. The key can't set me free because part of me isn't here." She slipped the key into her pocket and looked at Stella. "You're going to have to fetch my heart from the Collector. And you're going to have to be quick. I'll stay here for as long as I can, but sooner or later I'll have to go after you and deliver you to the Collector."

"But . . ." Stella's head was spinning. "But where is the Collector? The bridge runs out. There's nothing here."

They had come so far and risked so much to make this journey. All along, she had believed there would be *something* on the other side of the bridge. She had thought they would win in the end, and save Shay, and Felix, and Joss. The alternative was too terrible to think of. But perhaps it was simply a fact that not all stories could have happy endings. . . .

"The Collector is here," Queen Portia replied. "But not on the other side of the bridge. Beneath it."

"What do you mean, *beneath it*?"

Stella's head was pounding and she couldn't seem to think straight. She could feel the magic slipping rapidly away from her as the tiny dragon whispered good-bye in her ear. She swayed slightly and Shay immediately took hold of her arm.

"There's no more time!" Queen Portia gasped. She grabbed the snow globe with Koa trapped inside it from her pocket and threw it to Shay. "You must go at once!"

"But—" Stella began.

"I can't resist the spell anymore!" the queen cried. "You must go *now* or else it will be too—"

But it was already too late. As Queen Portia spoke, her hand unscrewed the top of the snow globe and a great hurricane of ice seemed to burst out of it, heading straight toward them.

The explorers tried to run, but the ice magic followed them until they were trapped right at the edge of the bridge. Stella couldn't prevent herself from looking down, and saw that the ocean had run out as well—the bridge seemed to be suspended above a great, vast, black emptiness that stretched on and on. It looked as if they really were at the very edge of the world, with nothing but outer space surrounding them. Stella even thought she caught the faint twinkle of distant stars down there. . . .

The queen's ice magic tugged at her dress, and Stella knew that it meant to suck them all up in its grasp and whip them away into the snow globe, where they would be trapped forever. And this time there would be no hope of any rescue party coming to their aid, no hope of Felix risking everything to save them. It would be the end of everything. If Stella had had her ice tiara she could have tried to fight back against the hurricane, but without it she had no idea what to do.

Fortunately, Ethan leapt in front of the blast and threw up his hands to produce a large magic shield that hung suspended in the air before them. It was a magnificent shiny black object, stamped with the crest of the Ocean Squid Explorers' Club. But it wasn't strong enough to withstand Queen Portia's ice magic for long, and multiple cracks raced out across its surface.

The next moment, the shield had been smashed apart. But it had given just enough time for the gargoyles to race toward the explorers, barreling into them with their full weight—which was easily enough to send them all hurtling straight off the end of the Black Ice Bridge, plummeting into the vast, endless nothingness below.

CHAPTER TWENTY-ONE

A S SHE WENT HURTLING over the edge of the bridge, Stella wondered if the gargoyles had suddenly turned on them. What other explanation could there be? One of them was yelling something, but Stella could no longer understand now that her dragon charm had disappeared.

They were free-falling—plunging into nothing with icy air racing around them, tugging at their clothes and hair. It was so fast and terrifying that Stella couldn't get enough air to scream, and being forced to fall in silent horror was somehow worse. It must have been the same for the others—even Beanie wasn't reciting his usual explorer death facts.

Stella could see nothing up ahead but blackness and thought they were probably just going to fly right out among the stars, where they would most likely freeze or suffocate to death. No one knew for sure what would happen to a person in space because no one had ever been there, but everyone agreed that no human could possibly survive.

Stella's mind flew to Felix, and as she tried to prepare herself for the cold vast terror of space, she thought of how much she loved him and desperately wished she could have hugged him again just one last time. . . .

But then she hit the top of a tree—crashing through its branches and scattering leaves and fruit until she landed on the ground hard. All the breath was squeezed out of her with an *oof*!

She was vaguely aware of her friends and the gargoyles hitting the ground beside her, groaning and gasping for air as more leaves showered down around them. Stella noticed the leaves were bright pink and wondered whether perhaps she might be hallucinating.

The next moment there was a hand on her shoulder. "You okay, Sparky?" Shay said.

Stella let him help her sit up, her head spinning as she tried to work out what on earth was happening.

"I . . . I think so," she said. "What about the others?"

She gazed around and was relieved to see Ethan and Beanie picking themselves up beside her. Apart from a couple of bumps and scrapes, they seemed okay, although everyone's cloaks were looking a little worse for wear. Not only were they snagged and ripped, but they had bright purple stains on them too.

Beanie was deathly pale, but nodded and said, "Six hundred and thirty-three explorers have died falling from bridges."

"I've been better," Ethan grunted, pulling twigs—and a wonky squish-squish frog—from his collar. "But I'll live."

"Why do you have a wonky squish-squish frog?" Shay asked, staring.

"What? Oh, it's Melville," Ethan said. "I changed him on the way down just in case." He held up the frog so the others could see that it had been squashed completely flat when Ethan landed on it. Fortunately, as they knew from their previous expedition, this type of frog could be bounced, squashed, and even set on fire without any harm coming to it.

Ethan quickly pulled the frog back into a frog shape, put it down on the ground, and then threw a magic spell at it to turn it back into Melville. The gentleman flamingo tottered around rather unsteadily on his long legs, his eyes huge inside his head.

"You okay?" Ethan asked, leaning down to poke him.

"Good heavens, that was a shocking experience!" Melville replied. He patted himself down and said, "But I appear to be all in one piece, thanks to you, kind sir."

"Koa seems to be okay too," Shay said, peering into the snow globe where the shadow wolf still paced around. He thrust it into his pocket and said, "Nice work with the shield back there, Prawn."

"Fat lot of good it did," Ethan replied tersely. "The

snow queen ripped right through it like it was made of paper! For weeks I've been practicing that!"

"Well, it gave us enough time to escape," Shay said. "So the hard work definitely paid off."

"But where have we escaped *to*?" Ethan said.

"Your guess is as good as mine."

Shay offered a hand down to Stella, who scrambled to her feet and finally took in her surroundings. Her mouth fell open in astonishment, and she could see that the others—including the gargoyles—were equally stunned.

They appeared to have landed in an orchard. Sunlight dappled through the leaves of tall silver trees, which were indeed bright pink. Clusters of purple fruit about the size of oranges hung from the branches. The ground beneath their feet consisted of lush soil, with a winding white marble path curling through the trees. There was no snow to be seen, and it was no longer very cold. In fact, the sunshine made it practically balmy.

Stella looked up and saw that the Black Ice Bridge towered some way above them, and thin silver chains attached the orchard to the bridge.

"I think we fell through some kind of canopy," Ethan said, peering upward. "You can see the tattered remains of it—look!"

He pointed, and Stella saw that he was right. Shreds of a large canvas hung from ropes attached to the bridge.

"Perhaps it was a magic-disguise painting," Ethan said. "Made to look like space and hiding all this from view."

The trees made it hard to see beyond their immediate surroundings, although Stella could hear water falling somewhere close by, as well as the most beautiful birdsong.

"Let's get out of the orchard," she suggested. "Perhaps we'll be able to see around us a bit better then."

"Good idea," Shay said. He peered closely at her. "You know, you're very pale, even for you. And that was a lot of magic back there. Are you feeling okay?"

In fact, Stella felt absolutely exhausted—like she'd just run a marathon or something. What she wanted most of all was to crawl into bed and have a good long rest. But there was no time for that now. Queen Portia had said she wouldn't be able to hold off alerting the Collector to their presence for very long. So although Stella's fingers itched to erect the magic fort blanket and recuperate for a while, she shook her head and said, "I'm fine. Let's keep moving."

The snow-boat had been left on the bridge, so they would have to walk. Ethan scooped Melville up and tucked him back into the front of his cloak as the explorers stepped on to the white path. But the second they began to walk down it, something extraordinary happened. Every purple fruit in the orchard started to sing a lilting, lovely song that caused the trees themselves to shiver and their leaves to turn from bright pink to sky blue.

"Good heavens!" Ethan exclaimed. "What in the blazes is happening? Are we under attack?"

They all stopped on the path, and the fruit immediately fell silent.

"Oh my goodness!" Beanie whispered, a look of wonder shining in his eyes. "Could it be . . . ? But no. Surely not . . . ?"

"What are you babbling about?" Ethan demanded.

Beanie shook his head and said, "I have a theory. Everyone start walking again."

They all did as he said, and immediately the fruit began to sing to them once more. Stella couldn't understand their language so had no idea what they were singing *about*, but the song was utterly beautiful nevertheless and it made her heart soar to hear it.

"These are the singing blue trees!" Beanie exclaimed.

At that moment a bird landed on a nearby branch, tilting its head this way and that as it looked at them with a curious expression. It looked a little bit like a peacock except that it was smaller and its feathers were a glorious red and yellow and orange. The next second, it disappeared in a little burst of flames, before reappearing on the ground at Stella's feet.

"Gracious!" she gasped. "Isn't that a firebird?"

"I thought firebirds were extinct," Ethan said with a frown.

"The orchard of singing blue trees and the aviary of firebirds," Beanie muttered under his breath before looking up at the others. "I think I know where we are! These might very well be the Hanging Gardens of Amadon!"

Everyone stared at him for a moment.

"Impossible!" Ethan finally replied. "The hanging gardens are just a myth. They never existed."

"But this is exactly how they were described by explorers in the ancient accounts," Beanie said.

Shay frowned. "I thought that Amadon was somewhere on the other side of the Exotic South Sea. That's at the other end of the world from where we are now. If these really are the hanging gardens, how could they have gotten all the way over here?"

No one had an answer to that, so they continued walking through the orchard—serenaded all the way by the fruit—until they came out on the other side, where they stood and gawped. For Beanie had been quite right. These really were the Hanging Gardens of Amadon, dangling beneath the Black Ice Bridge on individual islands that each hung from their own silver chains. Some of the gardens looked tiny—no larger than Stella's bedroom back home—while others seemed to be big, sprawling places, large enough to accommodate an entire forest.

Swaying rope bridges connected one island to another in a circle, and Stella could see that on their right-hand side was the aviary of firebirds that Beanie had mentioned. The air above this island was all lit up with orange and yellow flames as the birds flitted to and fro, curling and diving through the air, leaving dancing fire in their wake. And on their left-hand side was a large island that consisted of tiers upon tiers of cascading waterfalls—the sapphire-blue water edged with lacy foam. A cool clean smell wafted across the gap to Stella and the others.

She could make out a few of the other islands, and they all seemed to consist of some unique botanical marvel. She glimpsed trees with zebra stripes on one of them, golden parrots swooping through the air on another, and trickling fountains whose water seemed to run the wrong way—up toward the sky rather than down to the ground—on yet another.

But even more extraordinary than the gardens themselves was the fact that someone clearly lived here. In the middle of the circle was another island, which contained a beautiful mansion with a white-pillared facade and a fantastically huge globe adorning its front garden.

Beanie nudged Stella and pointed at the wrought-iron gates at the edge of the road. She noticed that these, too, were engraved with an image of a globe, surrounded by words picked out in curling ironwork: *The Phantom Atlas Society.*

The explorers gazed at one another.

"That must be where the Collector lives," said Shay.

Stella frowned. "It's not what I imagined," she said. "I thought an evil sorcerer would live in a dungeon or something."

She glanced back the way they had come. There was no

sign of Queen Portia following them yet. She looked around for another way down to the gardens from the bridge but couldn't see one. Perhaps the snow queen had some other means of communicating with the Collector? Either way, if they hoped to retain the element of surprise, they would have to move immediately.

It was the moment they had all been building up to, and yet now that they were here, Stella found herself hesitating. She was so very afraid of the Collector—or Jared Aligheri, as she now knew him to be—the man who had murdered her birth parents and changed her life forever. And the thought of coming face-to-face with him filled her with dread. Suddenly, this felt like the last place in the world she wanted to be. But the Collector had taken the Book of Frost from her, and she needed it back.

She straightened her shoulders and turned to the others. "Well, then," she said. "That central island must be where we need to go. How do you think we get there?"

"It's too far to jump," Ethan said. "Shame we don't still have that magic carpet—then we could fly across and make a speedy escape later too. Goodness knows how we'll ever get back up to the bridge."

"Let's worry about that later," Stella said hurriedly. "There must be some way; otherwise the Collector would be trapped too."

"The rope bridges seem to lead from one outer garden

to the next," Beanie said. "And it looks like some of them lead to the central garden. That one over there is probably the nearest one to us."

He pointed at the garden on the other side of the water-fall one. They could only see the edge, so it wasn't clear what the garden contained.

"Right," Shay said, shouldering his bag. "Let's head there, then."

They made their way around the outside of the orchard to the rope bridge leading to the waterfall garden. It was very narrow and seemed to stretch a long way, but it looked strong and stable enough, and the explorers began to walk across it in single file. The gargoyles followed them—Stella supposed they were eager to try to recover Queen Portia's stolen heart. She briefly considered using the dragon to talk to them again, but her head still throbbed and she didn't dare use another magic charm again so soon.

"So, let's have it, then," Ethan said to Beanie when they were about halfway across the bridge.

The elfin boy looked back at him in confusion. "Have what?"

"You love those death facts. Aren't you going to tell us how many awful, dangerous things there are in the hang-ing gardens that can kill you dead? You must be gagging to educate us about how many people have been poisoned, incinerated, pulverized—"

"None," Beanie replied promptly. "No one has ever died here, that we know of. The hanging gardens were designed to be a paradise by the emperor of Amadon, as a birthday gift for the empress. They are full of natural wonders and priceless artifacts and beautiful things."

"Oh," Ethan replied, taken aback. "Well. That's a pleasant surprise, I must say. It's about time we had some luck."

"The gardens themselves may not be dangerous," Shay said quietly. "But we know that the Collector is."

They carried on across the bridge. A blue sea spread out beneath them, dotted with sparkling white ice slabs. They soon reached the other side and began their winding ascent up the path that ran alongside the tiers of waterfalls. Each one cascaded into a pool, which then led to another waterfall. Stella peered into one of these pools on the way up and saw it was full of small orange fish with red fins.

"Fortune-telling fish," said Beanie. "They can see the future."

"Gracious," Stella said, peering at them.

The temperature was so pleasant that the explorers were forced to remove their cloaks as they ascended the waterfalls.

"How is it so warm here?" Stella asked. Of them all, she was the most uncomfortable in the heat. "We're still in a very cold part of the world, after all. There was even ice floating in the sea back there."

"The gardens probably have a magic weather charm placed on them," Beanie said. "So they have their own climate."

The explorers and gargoyles finally reached the top of the waterfall pyramid and began to make their way back down the other side. Instead of fortune-telling fish, the pools in this part were home to water sprites—a kind of blue fairy with shimmering dragonfly wings. Stella saw them flitting about the water or sitting on the edge to dangle their slim feet into the pools. They waved at the explorers but made no move to interact with them in any way.

Stella would have liked to speak to them and indeed to explore all of the hanging gardens properly, and Beanie clearly felt the same because he sighed and said, "It would have been wonderful to find the singing harp that's meant to be here somewhere. And the candy urns and the cartwheeling roses."

But there was no time for that, so they pressed on to the rope bridge that led across to the other garden. When they first arrived it appeared to be just a pretty manicured space, but then Beanie gasped and said, "Look! It's the ornamental pears!"

He pointed at a row of five plinths up ahead. On each one there rested a vibrant green pear.

"What are they made from?" Stella asked, peering at them. "Are they jade or emerald or something?"

"Oh no," Beanie said. "They're much rarer than that. These pears are made from ogre boogers."

"Gross!" Ethan exclaimed. "Why the heck would anyone put ogre boogers on display in a garden? Let alone shape them into pears in the first place?"

"Most peculiar," Melville agreed.

"Well, they're fantastic barometers," Beanie explained.

"They're what?" Ethan snapped.

"A barometer is a kind of weather predictor," Stella explained. "It measures changes in atmospheric pressure."

"That's right," Beanie said. "An ornamental pear will

be green if good weather is expected, but it'll turn black if a storm is coming, or blue if there's to be snow. Then there's purple for hurricanes, red for typhoons, silver for tornadoes—"

"Sounds like a very useful thing to have at sea!" Ethan exclaimed. "Perhaps I ought to take one back to the Ocean Squid Explorers' Club."

"I don't know if you should remove anything from the gardens," Stella said, uncertain.

"Why ever not?" Ethan replied. "They belonged to the empress of Amadon, who's long dead, and it's not like there's anyone left to enjoy them around here. Except maybe the Collector."

Before anyone else could protest further, Ethan snatched up one of the ornamental pears. Stella half expected a trap of some kind to spring up around them, but nothing happened as Ethan stuffed the pear into his bag. Stella frowned at the now empty plinth but didn't say anything more. They continued through the garden and out the other side, where they found themselves standing at the start of the rope bridge that led straight to what seemed to be the Phantom Atlas Society's headquarters.

CHAPTER TWENTY-TWO

NOW THAT THEY WERE on the other side of the central island, they could see things that had been hidden before. They appeared to be looking at the back of the house, which had a large wraparound porch with several comfortable-looking rocking chairs. A rope ladder led down to the ocean below, where there was a little floating pier. Docked there was a tiny submarine, very similar to the ruined ones they had seen up on the bridge. Only this one was shiny and new and they could clearly see the black Phantom Atlas Society symbol painted on the side.

The submarine wasn't the only interesting transport by the house, however. A hot-air balloon floated gently off the side of the island—a handsome thing with gray and white stripes and a large wooden basket.

But most incredible of all was the strange contraption

parked on the sweeping back lawn. It had a long body, with a tail at the end and great wings spreading out from either side. There was also a shining propeller at the front, as well as a cockpit in the middle that looked just large enough to seat one or two people.

"What in the world is that?" Ethan asked, staring at it.

"I think it might be some kind of flying machine," Stella said. "I read an article about them in one of Felix's journals the other day. There are lots of people around the world who've been working on trying to invent one. The idea is that they'd be faster than balloons and dirigibles, easier to control, and more fuel efficient."

"No one's perfected it yet, though," Beanie said. "Although there have been thirteen deaths and a further twenty-four injuries in the attempts."

"Look!" Stella said, suddenly noticing something. "There's a door open on the patio there."

"The Collector could be in there for all we know," Ethan pointed out. "If the four of us just go strolling into the house, he'll probably turn us all into lizards. Or whatever it is that sorcerers do."

Stella recalled the vague memory she had of blood on the snow when the Collector had gone to her home all those years ago and had to suppress a shudder.

"Well, what choice do we have?" she asked. "If he still has the Book of Frost, then it's most likely to be in there somewhere. So we need to go inside and look for it. *And* Queen Portia's heart, if we can." She studied her friends' faces. "Maybe you should all stay here? I can go across and search for the book. There's no sense in everyone risking it."

But the others were all shaking their heads at her before she'd even finished the sentence.

"Not a chance," Shay said.

"We go together," Ethan agreed.

Beanie nodded as well.

"All right," Stella said, pleased she wouldn't be going in alone after all. She glanced at the gargoyles and said, "Why don't we split up? The four of us can try to find the Book of Frost while the gargoyles search for Queen Portia's heart."

One of the horned gargoyles nodded its agreement. They walked over the rope bridge and a few moments later their little group was hurrying across the lawn. There was no cover, and Stella was painfully aware they might be spotted from one of the mansion's windows at any moment, so they ran as quickly as they could, finally reaching the relative cover of the porch area, where they avoided the windows and pressed their backs up against the wall.

Stella was nearest to the open door and she tiptoed over, pausing to listen for a moment. She could hear the faint scratch of a gramophone playing a violin record from within, but when she peeked around the doorway she saw that the room was empty. It was a library paneled with dark wood, and bookcases lined the walls. In one corner, a green globe stood beside the gramophone on a walnut table.

Stella beckoned to the others. With their hearts racing, they slipped into the room and hastily perused the bookshelves in the hopes that the Book of Frost might be there somewhere. But all the books in the library were related to travel. They saw atlases and almanacs and expedition logs, but nothing magical like the Book of Frost.

Fortunately, there was no sign of the Collector, either. They breathed a sigh of relief before cautiously making their way to the door on the other side. Stella pulled it open, and they all tumbled out into a darkened corridor. Other doors led off it, and at the end was a grand staircase that led up to the second floor. The gargoyles immediately scampered toward this—moving surprisingly quietly on their stone feet—while the explorers went the opposite way, down the hall. The tiles on the floor looked like they belonged in an explorers' club—they each depicted a mode of transport, such as a hot-air balloon or a train, or an exotic location such as an island, or a volcano, or a jungle. Framed maps adorned the walls, only they were for places that Stella had never heard of before.

"Look," Beanie whispered to Stella. "The doors have names on them."

Stella saw he was right. Each door had a brass plaque on it. As none of them had any idea where the Book of

Frost might be kept, especially given that they had already searched the library, they crept along to the nearest door, which contained a plaque reading ISLAND ROOM.

The junior explorers frowned at one another.

"There can't really be islands in there, surely?" Shay whispered.

"Let's find out," Stella replied. She pressed her ear to the door, listening for any sign of the Collector. There was no sign of him, so she carefully turned the knob and pushed open the door.

It was unlocked and swung forward easily beneath her hand. They stepped inside, and Stella thought they were in another library at first. It had the same polished wooden floorboards and shelves lining the walls, but it was a much larger, taller room, and these shelves weren't filled with books—instead they contained snow globes. There was row after row of them, with ornate silver bases sparkling with silver snowflakes, just like the one Queen Portia had used to trap Koa. The shelves reached up so high that there was even a ladder to get to the top ones.

Stella walked over to the nearest shelf.

"Popping Peanut Island," she read from the label carefully stuck to the snow globe's base.

Next to it was Elephant Island, the Island of Dancing Flowers, and Hopscotch Island, and they all seemed to contain real, living things. When Stella peered closely, she could see the water lapping at the shore of Hopscotch Island and the breeze ruffling the palm fronds in Elephant Island, and on Popping Peanut Island she could just about make out a bored-looking monkey sitting on the beach tossing peanut shells into the water in a morose fashion.

She frowned down at the snow globes as her mind raced with thoughts. She remembered what Melville had told them about how the Island of Lady Swans had simply vanished one day and how soon after that everyone on the Islet of Gentleman Flamingos had woken up to find that the ocean had disappeared and they were surrounded instead by a strange white mist that they had been unable to find their way out of.

She recalled what Felix had said after they'd fled from Coldgate on the polar-bear sleigh, about the Land of the Pyramids and how he'd seen it himself. Then there was the Lost Island of Muja-Muja, which no one had seen for centuries, and the mysteriously vanished Sky Phoenix Explorers' Club. Stella also recalled something she had overheard when they had broken into the Polar Bear Explorers' Club to reclaim the tiara—two explorers bickering about the disappearance of Frogfoot Island.

And then of course there was the name of this society itself—the Phantom Atlas Society.

"Do you think this is what the Collector is collecting?" she asked, turning to the others. "Islands and distant lands and wonders like the Hanging Gardens of Amadon? All those things we thought might just have been myths, mistakes on maps, or stories that explorers had made up to impress their clubs? Maybe those places really *were* there until the Collector came and trapped them inside these snow globes?"

The words were barely out of her mouth before Melville let out a great, shocked squawk from across the room—clearly forgetting the need for stealth. The others quickly hurried over to shush him, but he was practically hopping up and down.

"It's right there, by Jove!" he exclaimed. "Right there!"

"*What's* right there?" Ethan hissed. "And keep it down, you fool, or we'll all be captured and probably murdered!"

Melville pointed at one of the nearby shelves with his striped umbrella, and they all saw the snow globe that had caused him to react like that. The island trapped inside it seemed to be full of flower blossoms and bright blue ponds on which elegant swans in big sun hats glided back and forth.

"It's the Island of Lady Swans!" Stella breathed, reading the label attached to its base.

"Oh, Clementine!" Melville groaned, pressing his face to the glass. "Oh, my darling, she must be in there somewhere! Clementine, can you hear me?"

"Stop that!" Ethan said, pulling the little flamingo back.

"If the lady swans see your giant beak filling the sky, they'll probably all have heart attacks."

"I'm not sure they *can* see out," Stella said, peering more closely at it. "They don't seem to be reacting to us anyway—"

She broke off as something banged somewhere inside the house. The explorers all jumped, wondering what on earth it could be.

"The Book of Frost isn't here," Ethan said, glancing toward the door. "Let's move on."

"But we can't just *leave* them!" Melville wailed. "My own island is probably around here somewhere too."

The junior explorers did a quick search of the shelves, but no one could see the Islet of Gentleman Flamingos.

"I'm sorry, Melville, but we can't afford to linger—it's too dangerous," Stella said. "But we'll take this with us and see if we can work out how to free them later."

She snatched up the snow globe containing the Island of Lady Swans and put it into her bag. The others all grabbed up some snow globes at random, stuffing them into their own bags before hurrying back to the door.

"What do you think that bang was?" Beanie whispered as they crept out to the still empty corridor.

"Hopefully it was the gargoyles ambushing the Collector," Ethan replied.

They made their way down the rest of the corridor,

poking their heads into the various rooms as they went. The brass plaques on the doors all had names like VOLCANO ROOM or JUNGLE ROOM or WATERFALLS ROOM or RARE SPE-CIES ROOM on them. And they all contained shelf after shelf of snow globes.

"This is terrible!" Stella said as they crept out of the Mountains Room. "I wonder how many pieces of the world he's managed to steal. And why on earth would someone do such a thing in the first place?"

"I'm more concerned about where he is," Ethan replied, glancing over his shoulder. "This is his house, isn't it?"

"Maybe he moves slowly now on account of being so old?" Beanie suggested. "He must be over two hundred, after all."

"We still need to speed this up," Ethan said.

They opened the door to the last room at the end of the corridor, which was oddly named the Explorer Room. When they stepped inside, they found there were nowhere near as many snow globes as there had been in the other rooms. It was barely larger than a storage cupboard, and there was only one shelf with snow globes on it.

Stella's eyes went immediately to the one on the end. "Good heavens!" she breathed. "Would you look at that? It's the Sky Phoenix Explorers' Club!"

Everyone stared at the white building trapped inside the globe. It perched on the edge of a cliff, like a bird's nest, with several hot-air balloons floating beside it all striped in the same red and yellow colors as the crashed balloons they'd seen on the bridge. The Sky Phoenix Explorers' Club crest was clearly emblazoned on their sides.

"It's real after all!" Stella said. "The Collector must have stolen it and that's why no one's heard of them in so many years." She picked the snow globe up. "We'd better take this one back with us too. There might be explorers still trapped inside there."

"Could they really be alive after all this time?" Ethan asked.

"Queen Portia said that time was frozen inside the snow globes," Stella said. "So they might be. We'll just have to—"

She broke off because Beanie suddenly let out a cry and lunged to snatch up one of the snow globes farther along the shelf.

"What is it?" Stella asked, shoving the Sky Phoenix globe in her bag before hurrying to her friend's side.

Beanie wordlessly held up the snow globe in shaking hands so that they could see the label attached to its base. It simply read EXPLORER EXPEDITION. Added beneath this was a date from eight years ago.

"This is the date my father's expedition went missing," Beanie said. "At least, it overlaps with when they think it got lost. And it's on the Black Ice Bridge—look."

The scene inside the globe was indeed of an explorer

camp—there were even a couple of tents and a few explorer supplies scattered about.

"There's no sign of any explorers," Ethan pointed out.

"People can move around inside the globe, can't they?" Beanie said. "Perhaps they're inside the tents. My father could be in there right now!"

He gripped the base of the snow globe, as if to unscrew it, but Stella put out her hand to stop him. "Don't," she said. "We don't know what will happen, exactly. And we can't afford to do it here. We need to find the Book of Frost and Queen Portia's heart and then get out before the Collector catches us."

Beanie looked momentarily stricken, and his hand clenched the globe's base even tighter for a moment before he sighed and said, "You're right. But we should take all of these." He gestured at the remaining snow globes on the shelf. "There's seven of them. And they could all have explorers trapped inside. We've got to find room for them."

"Quite right," Ethan said promptly. "Explorers don't leave other explorers behind."

The four of them gathered up the snow globes and shared them between their bags, which were now completely full.

Stella just about managed to close hers—and was leading the way toward the door when suddenly a wailing, piercing alarm began to ring throughout the house.

CHAPTER TWENTY-THREE

THE SILENCE SHATTERED AROUND them like broken glass as the alarm wailed deafeningly. Stella supposed one of the gargoyles must have done something that had tripped it, but either way their cover was blown. They hurried toward the door, and Stella tumbled out into the corridor first, moments before an iron grille slid down from the ceiling, trapping the other three inside.

"Oh no!" she groaned, gazing back at her friends in dismay.

"Darn it!" Ethan exclaimed, grabbing hold of the metal bars and tugging at them ineffectually. "I knew we shouldn't have brought those gargoyles!"

"Could you try using the key charm?" Beanie asked Stella.

Her heart sank at the thought of using magic again so soon and how exhausting it was sure to be, but she wasn't about to leave her friends trapped in there like that. She was already reaching for her charm bracelet when Shay pointed at the gate and said, "There's no keyhole."

Stella saw he was right. Even if she managed to create another key, there was no lock to use it on.

"The gate came down from the ceiling," Beanie said, squinting up at it. "There must be some central mechanism controlling it somewhere."

The last thing Stella wanted was to leave her friends trapped there, but there was no way of freeing them if she stayed. Their only chance was for her to venture into the house on her own and try to find some way of raising the gate.

She clenched her hands into fists. "This isn't going well, is it?"

The others gazed back at her with the same worried expressions.

But standing around wasn't going to achieve anything, so Stella tried to sound as confident as possible as she said, "If there's some way of raising the gate, then I'll find it."

"Be careful," Shay called after her.

"Good luck," Melville added.

Stella nodded and set off quickly down the corridor. She saw that all of the doors had similar iron bars across them and that the library also had a number panel on the wall outside it. She paused by this, wondering whether it might be some kind of lock, but with no way of knowing what the combination was, it didn't really help her.

She had just reached the end of the corridor when a loud clattering announced that something was coming down the staircase. She quickly tucked herself into the corner in case it was the Collector, but a few seconds later the gargoyles came into view, falling over one another as they tumbled down the last stairs. One of them was clutching a snow globe, and Stella realized it must have been taking this that had set off the alarm.

She came out to intercept them, and they startled at the sight of her before relaxing when they saw who it was. They had found the snow queen's heart—it took up most of the space inside the snow globe and looked like a normal heart except for the fact that it was frozen and little particles of ice sparkled all across its surface.

"That's great," Stella said with a sigh. "But you set off the alarm, and now the others are trapped in one of the rooms down there."

She waved back the way she had come, but the gargoyles didn't seem to care, and Stella supposed it was no surprise. The only thing they had come here for was Queen Portia's heart, and now that they had it they didn't seem too keen to hang around. One of them even grabbed hold of Stella's hands and gave her a little tug toward the library door.

"Absolutely not!" she cried, pulling her hand free. "Not without my friends."

The gargoyle shrugged, and they continued on without her.

"You won't be able to get through that way," Stella called. "The doors have all got iron—oh!"

She broke off as one of the gargoyles marched right up to the gate and pulled the iron bars apart with his bare hands, creating a gap just large enough that they could all scamper through it.

Stella called out for them to stop in the hopes that they might come back and help free her friends, but they disappeared into the library. She hurried in their footsteps in time to see them break through the iron gate that had appeared at the terrace doors and then disappear into the garden. Stella shook her head as she turned back to the staircase.

There was another corridor stretching away from the staircase, but the gargoyles had come from the floor above and Stella had the feeling she was more likely to find what she was looking for up there. So she put her hand on the banister and cautiously began to climb up to the second floor of the house, keeping her eyes peeled for the Collector.

She half expected to find the murderous old man waiting for her in the shadows at the top of the stairs. Indeed, when she reached the circular landing, a tall figure loomed there and several faces peered down at her from the walls, making her jump.

But it was only a suit of armor and some paintings. They were all portraits of different men, and Stella immediately recognized Jared Aligheri, with his good looks and ruthless expression. There were several other men there too, and from the fashion of their dress it looked as if they were from various time periods throughout the last two hundred years. One of them in particular—a man with black hair and a widow's peak—looked as if his portrait had been painted only twenty years ago or so. The name-plate beneath the painting read ELI SAUVAGE. There was a cold, soulless look in the man's eyes that chilled Stella to her bones.

She frowned at the paintings, trying to work out what they might mean. But before she had time to puzzle over it any further, there was a flash of movement down the cor-ridor leading away from the landing. A few seconds later, something moved in the shadows again, and Stella realized it was a sea-gremlin, scampering across the hallway before disappearing into the nearest room.

Light spilled from the doorway, and there was the faint patter of small footsteps from within. Perhaps the Collector was in there with the sea-gremlins? Stella could see several rooms in the corridor, but unlike downstairs, these didn't seem to have plaques labeling them. She would just have to search at random, and to do that she would have to walk right past the open doorway. If the Collector was in there, then he was bound to notice her—unless he was so old he could barely see or hear anymore.

Stella's eyes fell on the suit of armor standing against

the wall on the landing. It had a beautiful sword gripped in its gauntleted hands, which gleamed even in the dim light. An idea came into her head, and Stella went over and slid the sword free. It was extremely heavy and she could barely carry it. Certainly she had no intention of trying to stab anyone with it—not even the Collector himself. He may have murdered Stella's birth parents, but Stella was not a killer, no matter what anyone said. Still, it might be useful to walk in armed as a form of self-defense.

And if the Collector rushed at her, she might be able to knock him on the head with the handle or something. Most of her frost magic wasn't much good for launching attacks. She had the charm bracelet, but Stella thought one more spell might finish her off. She felt like she needed to sleep for a week as it was, and her legs wobbled a little as she crept toward the open door.

If the Collector was in there, then she might get lucky and he'd be snoozing in an armchair or something and she would be able to simply tiptoe past him. Perhaps he might even be dead, she thought. Maybe that was why he hadn't come running at the alarm—which was still wailing away downstairs. After all, he had to die sometime, didn't he? Even sorcerers didn't live forever.

She could no longer hear anything from inside the room, although strangely she thought she could detect a faint smell of paint. . . .

She risked a peek around the doorframe, and what she saw almost made her drop her sword in shock. The room beyond was a sort of parlor, with cabinets lining the walls, and there were several sea-gremlins in there, most of whom seemed to be clustered around an easel set up in one corner. They all held paintbrushes and kept shoving one another out of the way to daub at the canvas set up on the easel. Clutching their paintbrushes, scratching their blue heads, and scowling, they were all peering at a person on the opposite side of the room, who was sitting on an elegant chaise longue.

Only it wasn't the bent old man Stella had been expecting, but a young woman. She had long dark hair that tumbled down to the small of her back and she wore men's clothing—a pair of straight brown trousers tucked into tall boots, paired with a dark leather jacket that was far too big for her. On her knee rested a sheepskin hat with a pair of goggles attached to it—a bit like the sort Stella had seen hot-air-balloon pilots wear when they took to the sky.

She was looking toward the gremlins, but she must have known Stella was there, because without turning her head she spoke in a voice that was low and slightly husky.

"Well, Miss Pearl, are you just going to stand there? Or are you going to come in?"

CHAPTER TWENTY-FOUR

STILL KEEPING A TIGHT grip on the sword, Stella walked slowly into the room.

The dark-haired woman turned her head to look at her, and Stella realized, to her surprise, that she was even younger than she'd first thought—probably no more than twenty-one. There was something striking about her magnetic green eyes, large nose, and full, dark eyebrows, which gave her a stern look. Her skin had an unhealthy pallor, and she had a widow's peak that reminded Stella of the portrait she'd seen out on the landing.

"Who are you?" Stella blurted. "How do you know who I am?"

The woman raised an eyebrow. "Surely *I* should be asking *you* the questions given that you have broken into my home and are in the process of stealing my possessions."

Stella was about to deny stealing anything, but then she

heard the clink of the snow globes knocking together inside her bag.

"If I've taken anything it's because it doesn't belong here," she replied. "I'm looking for the Collector."

"Well, you've found her." The woman took a cigar from her pocket, lit it, and drew on the end so that the tip glowed red-hot. "Scarlett Sauvage," she said, exhaling smoke, "at your service."

The sea-gremlins began to grumble. "We can't capture you if you keep moving, Miss Sauvage," one of them said.

"Oh, you must have finished that blasted thing by now!" Scarlett responded. "I've been sitting here for hours. You'll just have to fill in the blanks with your imagination." She glanced at Stella. "It's a stupid tradition, so far as I'm concerned, but every member of the Phantom Atlas Society has had their portrait hung on the wall of this house, and sea-gremlins do love their traditions. So here we are." She waved her cigar, leaving a trail of vanilla-scented smoke in its wake.

"But I . . . I don't understand," Stella said, trying to think through the pulse of her headache.

"Why don't you take a seat and I can explain it to you?" Scarlett suggested, waving toward a table over in the corner that had been set for afternoon tea. "We're both ladies," Scarlett went on. "So I assume we can do this in a civilized manner. What happened to your friends, anyway? Daphne told me there were four of you."

"They're trapped in a room downstairs," Stella said. "An alarm went off—"

"Oh yes, when the gargoyles took the heart snow globe. It's one of the few that's alarmed. Not that I give two hoots about it either way, but a few of my predecessors were rather preoccupied with the snow queen. I suppose in the early days she was necessary to stop explorers from wandering over the bridge and poking their noses in where they didn't belong, but people seem to know to leave the bridge well enough alone now, and the ones who somehow miss Queen Portia come upon the sea-gremlins or those warning signs about the giant." She gave Stella a close look and said, "You're the first visitors we've had for ages. Don't worry about the alarm—I entered the deactivation code a few minutes ago. It will stop anytime now."

Indeed, the alarm ceased to wail before she'd even finished the sentence.

"There," Scarlett said. "The gates will open automatically after fifteen minutes or so."

She walked over to the table, pulled out a seat, and sat down. Not sure what else to do, Stella followed her. Scarlett didn't *seem* as if she meant any harm, but there was something in her eyes that Stella didn't much like. It wasn't quite the soulless look she'd seen in Eli Sauvage's portrait, but it was a hard sort of ruthlessness that made Stella think this was a woman who didn't allow anything to get in her way.

"If you've come to murder my father, then I'm afraid you're too late," Scarlett went on. "But I can offer you tea and cake. Is tea all right? I'm afraid I'm not too sure what children normally drink, and I could hardly offer you firewater."

As she spoke, she reached for the bottle of firewater at her elbow and filled her teacup to the brim. Felix kept a bottle of firewater in the liquor cabinet back home. He never drank it himself, but it was brought out sometimes when other explorers were staying with them and wanted to toast the success of their next expedition. Stella had once tried a sip when none of the grown-ups were looking, and the amber-colored drink had almost blown her head off. Yet Scarlett took a deep glug of it like it was no stronger than fairy-water.

She raised her dark eyebrows over her teacup at Stella. The teacup was a beautiful object—dark green and black, painted with the crest of the Phantom Atlas Society. "Well?" she said.

"I'm sorry—I've forgotten the question," Stella replied.

"Dear me, you are on your last legs, aren't you?" Scarlett replied. "I don't think a fight to the death would have gone in your favor, if I'm honest. I was asking if you would like tea?"

"Oh. Yes, please," Stella said. "And I really don't want to fight anyone to the death. I've only come here to take back something that was rightfully mine all along."

"The Book of Frost, I suppose?" Scarlett asked, reaching over for a tall green teapot and pouring tea into Stella's cup. It didn't steam, and Stella heard the clink of ice cubes from within the teapot.

"I thought you'd prefer iced," Scarlett said. "Being an ice princess."

Stella frowned. "How come you were expecting me? And knew who I was?"

"Daphne told me you were coming," Scarlett replied. "You met her on the bridge, I believe? And made quite an impression too, from the sounds of it. As for knowing who you are—well, everyone knows, don't they?" Her eyes gleamed slightly. "The first female explorer in history. You know, I'm the first female Collector, so we actually have something in common. Do help yourself to sandwiches. Or would you prefer cake?"

The cake *did* look good, but Stella waited until she'd seen Scarlett bite into one before she took one of her own. The mixture of cream, jam, and sugar was delicious, and she could feel some of her energy returning after eating just a few bites.

Then she looked at Scarlett and said, "Why would you think I'd come here to hurt your father?"

"Oh, well, he was an absolute villain, you see," Scarlett said. "And you're an ice princess, so I expect he murdered your parents, or your auntie, or your granny or something.

He picked off quite a few of your kind while stealing all those Books of Frost."

Stella frowned. "But what did he want with them in the first place?"

"There was a particular spell he was looking for," Scarlett said. "He never did find it, though he hurt a lot of people in the search."

"Your father was Eli Sauvage, wasn't he?" Stella asked. "I saw his portrait out on the landing."

"That's right."

"But I thought Jared Aligheri lived here. I thought *he* was the Collector."

"He was," Scarlett said. "Two hundred years or so ago. He was the first Collector, but he's long since dead. Nobody lives for two hundred years, not even a sorcerer. He had to find someone else to hand his magic down to. Someone sympathetic to his cause. And it's gone on in a chain like that ever since."

"So . . . does that mean *you're* a sorcerer, then?" Stella asked.

Scarlett frowned. "Technically speaking," she said. "I have the staff."

She flicked a hand in a lazy gesture toward a staff in the nearby bay window. It was made from twisted white wood, with a glowing red stone set at the top, and it had the unmistakable air of something magical and powerful. Stella couldn't help noticing that for all Scarlett's apparent relaxed civility, she had left the staff in a place where it would be easy to grab.

"But I'm also an inventor," Scarlett went on. "In fact, I've finally succeeded in creating a one-person submarine that's actually serviceable—after many failed attempts. I'm also an aviator. And a scientist. We can be more than one thing, can't we? I imagine you would know all about that yourself."

She looked closely at Stella, and just for a moment it seemed like here was someone who might actually be able to understand how it felt to be seen only as an ice princess—a villainous caricature rather than an entire person made up of a whole bunch of strengths and weaknesses, dreams and talents, faults and idiosyncrasies, yearnings, hopes, and fears.

"Oh, yes," Scarlett said, perhaps reading Stella's thoughts on her face. "I understand how it feels. That's why I thought perhaps you might like to become partners?"

"Partners?"

"How much do you know about the Collector and the Phantom Atlas Society?"

"Hardly anything."

"Just as I thought. The society is meant to be secret, you see. It's easier to carry out our work that way."

"What is it exactly that you do?" Stella asked.

Scarlett rested her elbows on the table and steepled her long fingers together. "We're conservationists."

"What's a conservationist?"

"Someone who dedicates themselves to protecting the planet," Scarlett replied. "Someone who concerns themselves with the greater good. Jared Aligheri and Queen Portia were the first. It began with endangered species, I believe. Queen Portia noticed that the snuffle bear was dwindling to dangerously low numbers, so she created these magical snow globes to contain a few of them and keep them safe. Then there was the occasional island where a volcano was about to erupt and destroy everything. Imminent natural disasters and catastrophes—that sort of thing. They saved those places by putting them inside snow globes, where they would be protected until some solution could be found. Animals, and people, go on living inside the snow globes, you see, but time stands still, so they don't age. For a while, Jared and Queen Portia worked together harmoniously on this."

"And then they had some kind of disagreement?" Stella said, remembering what the gargoyles had asked.

"Indeed," Scarlett replied. "Queen Portia's view was that their collecting should be kept to a bare minimum, whereas Jared felt that their responsibility to the world exceeded that. He began to collect places that weren't being cared for properly. The Hanging Gardens of Amadon, for example. People didn't respect it. They left rubbish. They polluted the waterfalls. They disturbed the wish-fish in their greedy desperation to have all their selfish wishes granted. Jared felt that if people couldn't look after a place, then they didn't deserve to keep it."

"So . . . he just took it?" Stella asked. "But he had no right to do that. The wonders of the world belong to everybody."

"Do they?" Scarlett replied. "Even if no one cares about them? People are lazy, and selfish, and stupid. Sooner or later, they spoil everything."

"That's not true," Stella protested. "Some people might be like that, but not many. And not everyone."

"It's certainly the case that some people are not stupid," Scarlett replied. "But then they're clever, and violent, and cruel, and that's even worse." She met Stella's eyes. "I think that's a lesson my dear departed father taught us both. But he was right about one thing, and that's that people don't deserve the world and it's our duty to collect as much of it as we can before it can be spoiled. That's why we moved on to places that hadn't actually been corrupted yet—like the Islet of Gentleman Flamingos."

"You took it even though there was nothing wrong with it?" Stella asked, thinking of Melville.

"There was nothing wrong with it *yet*," Scarlett replied. "But why wait? If we're going to try to preserve and protect the world, then surely it makes more sense to do so before it can inevitably be spoiled or tarnished in some way. There is less value in saving a broken thing, after all. So, yes, for some years now the various Collectors have been trying to collect our most treasured places and natural wonders. But there was a problem—there was only a finite number of snow globes because Queen Portia refused to make any more when she and Jared fell out. And those were all filled a long time ago. If we wanted to collect a new place, then we had to put somewhere else back. For years we've been trying to work out how to make new snow globes."

"Couldn't the Collector have just forced Queen Portia to do it?" Stella asked, recalling how the queen had been compelled to guard the bridge.

"Not without giving her heart, and therefore her powers, back," Scarlett replied. "And then they would have been right back to where they were before—trying to kill each other on the bridge. No, the Collector thought it was safer to try to track down the spell and perform it himself."

"That's why he took the Book of Frost," Stella realized.

"That's right."

"And did he find it?"

Scarlett shook her head. "Unfortunately not. None of the books contained the spell. The books are all slightly different, you see, but all quite worthless to us. You're welcome to have yours back, with my sincerest apologies."

She got up and walked over to one of the lacquered cabinets. When she pulled open the door, Stella saw it was filled with more than a dozen different Books of Frost, their icy spines turned out toward them. Scarlett picked up a thick pair of gloves lying on the nearby shelf and peered at the volumes.

"Let me see . . . which one was it?" she murmured. "Ah, yes. Here it is. Queen Jessamine's."

She selected the book, which was so large that she had to carry it over to Stella using both hands.

"The book is freezing cold to the touch," she explained as she set it down in front of Stella. "If an ordinary person touches it, it gives a nasty ice-burn."

Stella gazed down at the book in front of her. It was a majestic tome with intricate ice swirls adorning its cover, along with detailed, complex snowflakes. The entire volume glittered in a coat of sparkling frost that was indeed icy cold to the touch, although it didn't burn Stella when she rested her fingertips against it.

When she flipped the book open, she found the inside cover inscribed with her birth mother's name.

"I am sorry for what my father took from you," Scarlett said quietly. "He was an evil man, and that's all there really is to say about him."

Stella looked up. "Do you . . . do you know how he managed to kill my biological parents?" she asked.

It was a question that had always been there in the back of her mind. She did not know much about snow kings and so had no idea whether her birth father had possessed any powers of his own, but Queen Jessamine certainly should have been able to defend herself with ice magic.

"Well, sorcerers derive their power from fire," Scarlett replied. "Rather like snow queens use ice." She gave a small shrug. "And fire melts ice."

"Are you . . . are you saying that he burned them?"

"I wasn't there, so I don't know for sure," Scarlett replied. "Although I saw him use fire magic to kill people with that staff at various other times. It was not a pretty sight, and not something I would recommend you dwell on."

"It doesn't matter now," Stella said. "He's gone, and so are they, and my life has been the better for it. My biological parents were cruel people that I never knew, and I don't mourn them."

"Well, then," Scarlett replied. "That's another thing we have in common."

Stella looked back down at the book and turned the thick creamy pages. Inside were dozens and dozens of spells describing how to perform various types of magic, from making poisonous snow cookies to freezing someone's heart. Or unfreezing it. Stella saw that this was the spell she had come all this way for—the one that might be able to save Shay. It clearly described what she needed to do, and she felt her breath catch in her throat with excitement. She and the other explorers had risked so much and come such a long way to get this book back, and now that it was really in front of her, she could hardly believe it.

"I'd happily return the other books," Scarlett said, glancing at the cabinet, "but most of them were stolen years ago and I have no idea where to take them. None of them were any good to us. The only book that contained the snow globe spell was Queen Portia's."

"But I thought Jared stole her book from her," Stella asked, recalling what the gargoyles had said.

"Oh, he did," Scarlett replied. "It's over there in the case. But I suppose Queen Portia must have suspected that Jared might do something like that because she ripped out the page containing the snow globe spell and destroyed it." The Collector looked at Stella and said, "I mentioned a partnership earlier and I meant it. With an ice princess on board, we could really do extraordinary things. If you could find some way to re-create the snow globe spell, then we could save the whole world."

"But we wouldn't be saving it!" Stella exclaimed. "We'd be stealing it from everyone else. And that's not right! The world belongs to us all."

Scarlett raised an eyebrow slightly. "If you really feel that way," she said coolly, "then why on earth did you march straight past those signs warning about the Land End Giant?"

Stella felt like she had walked into a trap. "Well, I . . . I didn't know for sure that there actually *was* a Land End Giant there—" she began.

"You didn't know there *wasn't*, either," Scarlett pointed out. "We always want right and wrong to be clearly defined, but that's not the way of things, is it?"

Stella couldn't think of a defense. Her desperation to save both Felix and Shay had made her behave recklessly, but she couldn't regret it—not now when the Book of Frost was sitting in front of her, containing the spell she needed.

"I suppose being an explorer has rather corrupted your perspective," Scarlett went on. "Explorers have always been the most terrible bother to the Phantom Atlas Society, you know, bringing the world's attention to places that did not need to be discovered—places that should have been left alone. That's why we have, historically, been enemies, even if you have been unaware of us. Nothing seems to keep you away. We even gathered together all those shipwrecks—in order to block the path beneath the bridge as much as we could and hope that it would put off any explorers thinking of sailing farther. And the sea-gremlins have come in handy too. They do an excellent job meddling with machinery and thereby stopping anyone foolish enough to try to venture past the wrecks."

"That's been done on *your* orders?" Stella couldn't hide her dismay. "But it's so dangerous! Many people have *died* as a result, and many more have been hurt."

"Boo-hoo," Scarlett replied coldly. "Sometimes you have to make sacrifices for the greater good. Hopefully you will appreciate that one day when you're older—once your heart has frozen over—and then you might think of what I've said and reconsider."

"I'm never joining you," Stella said, standing up. "I think what you're doing is wrong. Even if I knew how to do the snow globe spell, I'd never help. The idea of it . . . It's against everything the explorers' clubs stand for."

"That is a pity," Scarlett said with a sigh. "I had hoped, as an ice princess, you might see things more reasonably. But if it's not to be the case, then you must understand, of course, that I can't possibly permit you to leave. The Phantom Atlas Society has to remain secret, and you know far too much."

Stella snatched up the Book of Frost and took a few steps back. "So, what are you saying? That you'll take us prisoner?"

Scarlett slowly shook her head. "This is no prison," she said. "And I'm no warden. Prisoners require care and attention and time that I simply don't have. I'll make an exception for you on account of the fact that you may be useful to me later. No human can understand a gargoyle, so they're irrelevant. But your companions will have to be destroyed, I'm afraid."

Stella could see in the other woman's eyes that she meant what she said, and what's more, she didn't feel any uncertainty or guilt about the idea of hurting young explorers.

She recalled the soulless look in Eli Sauvage's portrait out in the hall and thought Scarlett must have had a very strange upbringing, living with only her murderous father for company in this lovely house. Really, it was no wonder she saw the world in such a peculiar way.

Her eyes went to the staff and she made a desperate lunge for it, but Scarlett was much quicker. Moments later, the Collector had the sorcerer's staff gripped in her long-fingered hands, and the stone at the top glowed a deep, bloody red as she pointed it straight at Stella.

CHAPTER TWENTY-FIVE

Y OU MAY NOT APPRECIATE it yet, but this is the defining moment of your life," Scarlett said, still pointing the staff at Stella with a calm, steady hand. "It's also the biggest mistake you've ever made. One day you will look back on this and wish desperately that you had joined me when I gave you the chance."

Stella tightened her grip on the book, raised her chin, and said, "You've got it all backward. Threatening my friends is the biggest mistake *you've* ever made."

"Friends!" Scarlett scoffed. Her lip twisted into a look of contempt. "You can't really imagine that they're truly your friends? That they care about you in any way? People like you and I are the villains in the story. We don't have friends. That's why we have to look out for ourselves. The gates downstairs will have opened by now. I expect they're already fleeing."

Stella shook her head. There had been a time once when she'd worried the four of them weren't really friends. She'd mistakenly thought that Shay, Ethan, and Beanie had left her at the ice castle, the captive of stone trolls and a magic mirror. But actually they had been trying to save her all along. And since then they had been through so much together—first in the Icelands, then on Witch Mountain, and now on the Black Ice Bridge. And Stella felt so sure of the love and friendship from the three young explorers—and she knew with such certainty that Scarlett was wrong— that it made her heart glow warmer than it ever had before.

Her hands tightened around the Book of Frost. "You're wrong," she said. "They would never leave without me."

Scarlett's eyes narrowed. "How are you doing that?"

Stella followed her gaze down to the Book of Frost clutched in her hands. She saw little ribbons of gold were spreading from her fingers across the front cover, blazing brightly beside the ice.

Scarlett shook her head impatiently. "No matter." She reached into the pocket of her flight jacket and drew out a snow globe. Stella saw that it was empty, and suddenly she knew what the Collector meant to do.

Everything seemed to slow down as Stella spun on her heel, running for the open door, which looked impossibly far away. At the same time, she drew a great breath and gave a shout for help, as loud as she could, hoping it would reach the boys on the ground floor. Scarlett had said their gates would open soon and Stella knew they would race to her aid as soon as they were free.

She had time to scream for help only once, however, before Scarlett Sauvage spoke her full name in a clear, quiet voice.

And then the doorway before her vanished. And so did the room itself.

Stella staggered, trying to keep her balance on the pale white floor that was suddenly beneath her feet rather than the tiles of the Collector's house. She turned around and saw that Scarlett was gone. Everything was gone. There was just a white space about the size of a room, and beyond that an ivory-colored fog. Stella recalled what Melville had said about a fog pressing in around his island and that they couldn't get through it or see anything except for the occasional blur of movement from the other side. Then Stella knew, with a shiver of dread, that she had been trapped inside a snow globe.

She felt her heart speed up in her chest as she turned around in the empty white space, looking for a way out that didn't exist. Her breath came in quick gasps as she saw a cold, lonely future stretched before her as a prisoner inside a magical snow globe, frozen there for years and years, like Melville had been. But the gentleman flamingo *had* escaped. Ethan's magic had somehow plucked him right out of his prison. Which meant that it had to be possible to get out.

Stella closed her eyes, held tightly to the Book of Frost, and concentrated on slowing her breathing. She couldn't think if she was panicking, and she *really* needed to think right now.

"I will not be a prisoner here in this snow globe," she whispered to herself. "I will *not*!"

She opened her eyes and tried to peer through the fog swirling at the edges of the room, but she couldn't see past it. When she reached out her hand, the fog felt cool to her touch. She took a step back and looked down at the Book of Frost. Perhaps there was a spell in there that might break her free. She dropped down to her knees, put the book on the ground, and opened it, riffling desperately through the pages. But she couldn't see anything that might be helpful for breaking out of magical prisons, and at the back of her mind she couldn't help thinking that Scarlett was too smart to have given her the book if there was a spell in it that would get her out of the snow globe.

Stella closed the book and sat back, frustrated. Then her eyes fell on the front cover, and she saw that the gold ribbons she'd noticed earlier were still there, and in fact they were twisting and spooling together until finally they froze into a small, solid shape no bigger than her little fingernail.

Stella leaned forward, staring down at the gold object that had solidified on the cover of the Book of Frost. It was quite clearly a heart—shining and bright amid the sparkling ice. It looked just like the gold heart charm Stella had seen in the paintings of Queen Portia back at her castle.

The thought had just occurred to her when something brushed against her wrist, making her look down at her

own bracelet. The silver fairy charm was moving. Its wings fluttered gently as the fairy's delicate silver fingers reached into the pocket of its dress and drew out a tiny gold object attached to a thin silver chain. It was so small it just looked like a little ball to Stella, but then the fairy deftly clipped it to her charm bracelet and the golden thing grew bigger and bigger until it was the same size as all the other charms. And now Stella could see that it was a golden heart, exactly the same as the one on the Book of Frost.

The silver fairy charm had frozen once again, so still and lifeless it was hard to believe it had ever moved. And yet there was the golden charm on Stella's wrist, exactly the same as the one Queen Portia had worn in her paintings. Stella touched the charm and found that, unlike the others, it was warm to the touch, and the heart on the Book of Frost was the same.

She pulled the book into her lap and noticed that suddenly it felt heavier. She saw there were pages at the back that hadn't been there before, edged with gold rather than frost. Opening the book, she flicked to the first golden page and saw that it contained a title:

The Warm-Hearted Volume

And beneath this there was a paragraph that read:

Herein lies the warm-hearted volume, which will reveal itself only to the snow queen who possesses a warm heart. This section will appear when the book senses that warmth but

will disappear again at any time should the
queen's heart become frozen.

Stella eagerly flipped through the golden pages and saw that they contained more magic spells. And they were indeed different from the others—softer and lovelier. There was one for healing frostbite, another for creating an ice-cream forest, and another for making frost fireworks. She carried on flicking through the pages, and her eyes suddenly fell on a drawing of a snow globe.

She stared down at the page. The snow globe looked exactly like the one she was trapped in, with its ornate frozen base. The only difference was the one in the book held a single blue rose instead of a human prisoner. There was writing beneath the picture, describing how to create a snow globe, which it seemed had originally been meant as a kind of vase in which to store and preserve flowers.

The elegant script explained that unscrewing the glass from the base would enable a person to change the flower inside whenever one wished, but there was also a brief postscript at the end:

If one should accidentally become trapped inside a snow globe, it is a simple enough matter to free oneself. Simply touch the golden heart charm on one's bracelet and count to three in order to release the safety mechanism.

Stella looked back down at her bracelet and felt hope

rising like a balloon inflating inside her chest. She could get herself out of this! She hadn't lost quite yet.

Without delay, she scrambled to her feet.

"One," she said, hugging the book close to her chest.

"Two." She made sure her feet were planted firmly on the floor, ready to run or fight.

A small glow of triumph rushed through her. The president of the Jungle Cat Explorers' Club, and the newspapers, and Gideon Galahad Smythe, and all those others had been wrong. She did not have a frozen heart, and this proved it.

She closed her eyes briefly, and the final number came out as a whisper.

"Three."

There was a faint *pop* and a showering of broken glass and the white space inside the snow globe disappeared. Stella was back in the Collector's house once again. Only she was no longer in the same room as before. Now it was darker, and she could hear shouting, and the floor wasn't flat. She staggered as she tried to keep her footing and heard Scarlett let out a shout somewhere close by, and then she was falling.

Falling back and back as she saw too late that she was on the staircase. During the time she had been in the snow globe, Scarlett must have started to make her way downstairs. Luckily, she'd been almost at the bottom, and Stella fell only the last couple of steps before hitting the wooden floorboards with a thump that knocked the wind out of her.

"What in the world?" Scarlett exclaimed.

Stella propped herself up on her elbows and saw that the Collector was standing a few steps above, a shower of broken glass at her feet and trails of blood running down her free hand. Stella realized the snow globe must have been in her hand and had cut her when Stella escaped. The Collector's other hand, though, was still tightly wrapped around the sorcerer's staff as she stared down at Stella.

"There's no way you should have been able to do that!" Scarlett hissed. For the first time, she looked uncertain. "What *are* you?"

Stella's eyes went to the fiery-red tip of the magic staff and she knew her troubles weren't over yet; there was still plenty of danger and no obvious way out of it, yet she couldn't help a tiny burst of pride as she looked up at the Collector from where she lay sprawled on the floor and said, "I'm an ice princess with a warm heart."

She could hear her friends calling out to her from down the corridor, obviously still trapped within the Explorer Room. She couldn't make out what they were saying because they were all shouting at once, but amid the noise she distinctly heard Shay call out Koa's name. And the next moment, the shadow wolf appeared at the top of the staircase behind Scarlett.

Stella guessed Shay must have released Koa from the

snow globe in the hopes that she would be able to help. She was still partly a shadow wolf after all, even if she was rapidly becoming a witch wolf as well. Indeed, she seemed to have more white fur than black now, and Stella felt a thrill of worry about what that might mean for Shay.

But the wolf was there now and was baring her teeth at Scarlett in a way that made her look quite terrifying.

"Warm heart?" Scarlett repeated, her lip twisting into an expression of disgust. "Then what use are you?"

She began to raise the staff as Stella scrambled to her feet, wondering what on earth she could do. Scarlett had been right, after all—fire melted ice, and Stella didn't even have her magic tiara. She began to raise the Book of Frost, hoping that it might act as a shield somehow. At the same time, Koa leapt from the top of the staircase, her sleek body flying through the air straight toward the Collector.

The wolf moved silently, but Scarlett must have sensed her somehow because she spun around at the last moment, raising the staff. There wasn't time for her to point it at Koa, although it still succeeded in protecting her because the shadow wolf bit down on the staff rather than Scarlett herself.

Stella heard the crunch of wood, and Scarlett cried out as the weight of the wolf knocked them both from the staircase. They landed on the floor at Stella's feet, and a blast of fire shot from the red tip of the staff, scorching the opposite wall.

Koa released the staff with a yelp, and Scarlett scrambled to her feet. Her hair was tangled and her eyes were wild as she pointed the staff straight at Koa.

"What trickery is this?" she gasped. "Is that . . . a shadow wolf or a witch wolf?"

"Right now, she's kind of both," Shay called.

Stella looked behind her and saw that the grating must have finally risen, because Shay, Ethan, and Beanie were all hurrying down the corridor toward her, with Melville bundled into Ethan's sweater.

"Are you hurt?" Beanie asked, gasping for breath as he stopped beside her.

Stella shook her head, relief flooding through her that she was no longer facing the Collector alone.

"Enough of this," Scarlett said. "You should never have come here. You have only yourselves to blame."

She raised her staff, and dancing fire shot from the end of it once again, but Koa's bite had clearly damaged the staff because the fire didn't shoot in a clean, straight line. Instead it blasted out sporadically, first in one direction, then another, randomly scorching floorboards and maps and even the ceiling. It was obvious that Scarlett wasn't in control of the staff at all.

"Get back!" Ethan cried as a ball of fire burst straight toward them.

The other three dived sideways and the magician threw up his hands to re-create the shield they'd seen on the Black

Ice Bridge. It hovered in the air before them, proudly displaying the crest of the Ocean Squid Explorers' Club, and it seemed it was more effective against flame than ice because although Scarlett's fire blasted straight into it, the shield stood firm, barely scorched.

The next moment, Scarlett let out a shriek of pain, and when Stella peered around the edge of the shield, she saw the Collector's sleeve was on fire. The staff fell to the floor as she frantically struggled out of the jacket, dropping it in a heap, where it extinguished itself. But Scarlett must have hurt her hand because she hunched over it protectively as she snatched up the staff from the floor and then dashed into the library's open doorway.

Ethan collapsed the shield. "Should we follow her?" he asked, glancing around at the others.

But before anyone could reply, Shay reeled back, clutching both hands to his head, and Stella saw that both his eyes had turned silver colored this time.

"Let her go," Stella said. "We've got more important things to worry about."

Koa had shrunk back when fire was going off everywhere, but now she was pacing toward them and she didn't look at all friendly. In fact, her teeth were still bared, and Stella didn't think she even recognized them as friends. Shay must have sensed her mood too because he tried to speak soothingly to her, but the wolf hardly seemed to be aware of him and the next moment she leapt straight at Beanie, who was nearest to her. She clearly meant to sink her fangs into him, but Shay jumped in front of her and the wolf slammed into him instead, sending them both to the floor.

"Koa, *no!*" he gasped, but more of the shadow wolf's fur was turning white by the second, and Shay was forced to wrap his hands around her snout to prevent her from biting him.

Stella dropped to her knees, slammed the Book of Frost on the floor, and began riffling desperately through its pages, trying to find the spell for unfreezing a heart that she had seen earlier.

"Come on, come on," she muttered.

Koa seemed so enraged by Shay's attempt to restrain her that Stella was afraid she might break free at any moment. She also knew that the more of a witch wolf she became, the harder it would be to do the spell. In fact, it may not even be possible at all. They were running out of time, and fast.

Finally, Stella found the page she was looking for. Most of it focused on freezing a heart, but there was a short spell there for if you changed your mind or froze the wrong person by mistake and wanted to undo it. The page also suggested you should touch the star charm for extra power, so Stella squeezed her fist around the cold, spiky charm and read the spell in the book aloud.

"This shard of ice shall be no more,

"Revert to how it was before."

A surge of icy, crackling power raced down her arm to her fingers, leaving a tingling feeling like pins and needles. She opened her hand just as a beam of silver light shot from her fingertip and hit Koa directly in the middle of her shoulders.

The shadow wolf immediately ceased struggling in Shay's arms. He let her go, and she took a couple of paces back, shaking herself as if not quite sure what had just happened.

"Look!" Beanie cried, pointing at Koa's back. They saw that the spot where Stella's magic had hit was now back to its usual dark color, and the fur around it was turning black too. Not only that, but the wolf was becoming a little softer around the edges as she lost her physical form. Eventually she was dark once again from head to toe, except for a few white hairs on her chest, and when Shay reached out his hand, it passed right through her like it always had before.

The shadow wolf sniffed at his fingers for a moment before flicking her tongue out at him in an affectionate gesture. Her dark eyes had lost their wild look and were calm and steady once again.

"It worked!" Shay breathed. He looked at Stella. "You did it."

Stella felt a great glow of happiness mixed with relief when she looked at her friend and saw that his eyes were no longer silver and his hair had almost all returned to its usual color, with only a small streak of white remaining.

She opened her mouth to say something, but then a great weight of exhaustion seemed to press down on top of her, so profoundly heavy she could barely think, let alone speak.

She realized Ethan was on his knees beside her. "It's okay," he said, and it sounded to Stella as if he were speaking from the end of a tunnel. "You did it."

His arm went around her, warm and reassuring. Stella could no longer keep her eyes open, and it was a relief to let Ethan take her weight as she crumpled into him, her head dropping down on his shoulder as the world faded away.

CHAPTER TWENTY-SIX

STELLA OPENED HER EYES just a few minutes later to find herself outside in the sunshine. She was leaning against the base of a marble gazebo and for a moment couldn't remember where she was. But then a firebird swooped by and she realized she was in the Hanging Gardens of Amadon. And Beanie was right there beside her.

"Do you feel any better?" he asked. His fingers still fizzed with green sparks, and Stella figured he must have used some of his healing magic on her.

"Yes, a bit," she said, surprised. She still felt extremely tired, but at least she was awake.

Shay and Ethan stood nearby, both holding a hand over their eyes to shield them from the sun while they gazed up into the sky. Stella let Beanie pull her to her feet, and then she joined them.

"What are you looking at?" she asked.

"Scarlett Sauvage is up there," Ethan said, pointing. "She flew off in that flying machine with the gremlins."

"Oh." Stella would very much have liked to see the flying machine in action and was disappointed to have missed it.

"How are you doing, Sparky?" Shay asked, turning to look at her.

"Better," Stella replied. "Just a bit tired."

Shay brushed his hand against her arm. "Thanks a million for what you did," he said. "I'll never forget it."

"Very brave," Melville agreed, tapping the tip of his parasol against the ground for emphasis.

Stella shook her head. "It was the least I could do."

"We were thinking we should go back into the house," Beanie said, "and gather up some more snow globes. I don't think we'll be able to carry them all, but it seems wrong to leave them here."

"We should take the hot-air balloon, too, if we can," Stella said, eyeing the gray-and-white-striped balloon tethered to the house.

"There she is," Ethan suddenly cried, pointing. "She's coming back this way!"

Stella followed his gaze and quickly spotted the flying machine. It was astonishing seeing such a large piece of machinery suspended in the air like that, but there was something very graceful about the way it swooped through the clouds.

"Gracious!" Stella exclaimed. "Isn't it marvelous? It looks like it goes much faster than a dirigible."

"Much," Ethan agreed. Then he frowned and said, "It looked like she was flying away, but now she seems to be turning back." He looked at the others. "You don't suppose she has a rifle or anything like that, do you? Perhaps she's about to take a shot at us!"

"I hope not," Shay replied. "Though seems to me it'd be difficult trying to fly that thing and shoot a gun at the same time, and with an injured hand, too."

"Probably not impossible, though," Beanie said. "Captain Yancy Tuckerton Trotter once navigated a raft over the side of a waterfall with one hand while shooting a pistol at some pursuing poachers with the other."

"And what happened to him?" Ethan said.

"He was never seen or heard from again," Beanie replied. "Presumed dead," as if that were obvious.

"Whatever she's doing, she's getting very close," Stella said, watching the plane warily.

Scarlett was flying it straight toward them, and so low that they could see she was wearing her leather cap and goggles, with her long, dark hair trailing loose behind her.

"I think we should take cover," Stella said. "Just in case."

They piled into the gazebo, crouching down low against the wall as the plane swooped toward them.

"You'd better get ready to do that shield again,"

valked across the bridge, past the ornamental
egan to make their way back up through the tiers
. In one of them they noticed a shoal of blue fish.
ess!" Beanie exclaimed. "They look like wish-

ish?" Ethan replied eagerly. "Should we make
?"

er to make a wish, you have to give the fish one
memories," Beanie said.

that doesn't sound so bad," Ethan said. "I
ind losing a bad memory or two. The fish are
them."

nie shook his head. "I want all mine," he said
hey help make me who I am. I'd be a little bit
a little more afraid without them."

ouldn't help thinking he was right. Whatever
ey each possessed had been hard earned, and it
terrible shame to have to go through those les-
So they left the fish as they were and continued
gardens.

they got to the rope bridge they had crossed
y noticed a garden they hadn't seen properly
d been facing the other way. And the first thing
as the flag.

right at the edge of the island and flapped gen-
reeze. It displayed the same crest they had seen

Beanie said to Ethan. "Just in case she does have a pistol."

"It's pretty tiring, you know," Ethan said, a bit peevishly. "I'm not sure I *can* do it again so quickly."

"*I'll* protect us," Melville said, leaping up onto the wall and opening his striped parasol.

Ethan rolled his eyes. "That little thing won't do any good at all," he said.

"My dear boy, it most certainly will," Melville replied. "It's bulletproof. All gentleman flamingos carry bulletproof umbrellas with them at all times. It's because sometimes we like to—"

He broke off as the plane swooped past them so close that they could feel the force of air from the propellers. But Scarlett's plan wasn't to fire at them with a rifle. As she flew by, the entire columned white mansion suddenly vanished before their eyes, along with the hot-air balloon tethered next to it. They were simply gone, leaving nothing but a big circle of dried earth behind.

Everyone gasped, and the next moment Scarlett pointed the nose of the plane high into the sky and shot away from them, quickly lost in the clouds.

"Good heavens!" Ethan exclaimed. "How on earth did she manage to do that?"

"I bet she put it in a snow globe," Stella said. "She must have had one more with her. All she has to do is say the name of whatever she wants to go inside it, I think."

"She's taken all those snow globes that were inside the mansion," Beanie said, sounding crestfallen. "We lost them."

"Well, at least we managed to save some of them," Stella said, giving her friend a sympathetic smile. "And we know about her now and can tell the world what she's been doing."

Beanie nodded. "Yes," he said. "And we have the Phantom Atlas, too."

"The what?"

Everyone crowded around Beanie as he produced a large, handsome leather-bound book from his bag.

"It was in a case in the library," he said. He looked at Stella. "I took it while Shay and Ethan were carrying you outside."

He opened the cover and they saw it contained a record of all the places the various Collectors had stolen over the years, from the Lost City of Muja-Muja to the Hanging Gardens of Amadon.

"At least now we'll know what's missing," Beanie said.

"So many places," Ethan said, gazing down at the book. He shook his head. "It's incredible that it's managed to go on for so many years without anyone noticing."

"Well, people *did* notice that lands that were once reported as being there were missing when they went back," Shay pointed out. "But I guess it just seemed more likely that the original explorers who discovered them had made a mistake or made the whole thing up for credit or funding."

"At least now we know the truth," Stella said. "And

that's a start. But it won't he
bridge. The balloon is gone.

"We'll just have to make
Shay said, sounding worri
across something that migh

Since Scarlett Sauvage
to return, the four explorers
blanket in the gardens. Eve
of a good meal, a decent nigl
Stella told the others about th
lett Sauvage and the Book of
taken the stolen heart back
cally fell into her bed and d
next day, when Beanie came

"Sorry, Stella," he said.
but it's the afternoon now a
to find a way back to the B

Stella sat up. She felt n
was ready to get up and sta
They set off through the g

"Are you going to try
your father's expedition in
they made their way across

He shook his head. "I
get back to civilization," he
home, and it will be dange

Th
pears, a
of wate
"G
fish."
"W
wishes.
"In
of your
"We
wouldn
welcom
But
quietly.
weaker
Stell
strength
would b
sons aga
through
Whe
before, t
when the
they saw
It sto
tly in the

on the crashed hot-air balloons back on the bridge—the crest of the Sky Phoenix Explorers' Club.

The junior explorers stared at it, all feeling the same tug toward the flag.

"Perhaps we should take just a quick look?" Stella said.

The others immediately agreed, and so they made their way around the side of the waterfall garden to the rope bridge leading to the Sky Phoenix hanging garden. It was very large compared to most of the other islands. It was also, they quickly saw, a cage. Once they crossed the bridge, they found a locked gate that was set into a thick iron mesh that spread all the way up into the air to form a dome at the top . . . like an aviary.

Stella glanced at the others, trying to control her excitement. "Do you think there really could be phoenixes in here?"

"They're just a myth," Ethan said, although he sounded uncertain. "Aren't they? Pretty much everyone agrees they never existed."

"We thought the Sky Phoenix Explorers' Club never existed, either," Stella pointed out. "And we know that isn't the case because I'm carrying it around in my bag."

"That's true, but even if a Collector took the club all that time ago, wouldn't the birds have died out by now?" Ethan asked.

Beanie shook his head and said, "Phoenixes can live for many hundreds of years. And, even then, once they die, they're reborn from fire."

"So, if they're in there, they could be the very same birds that once belonged to the Sky Phoenix Explorers' Club?" Shay said.

"It's definitely possible."

They tried to peer through the mesh, but the large leaves from the trees were pressed up against the sides, making it impossible for them to see.

"If they're in there, we can't just leave them cooped up like this," Stella said.

"But the gate is locked," Beanie said.

"I can make a key, remember?" she replied, already searching for the correct charm on her bracelet.

Stella concentrated on the spell, and a moment later a small ice key appeared. But the effort of creating it seemed to make the world spin around her, and she would have fallen forward onto her knees if Shay hadn't grabbed her arm. For a horrible moment, she feared she was going to be sick.

"You really shouldn't do any more magic for a while," Ethan said, taking the key from her hand before she dropped it. "One good night's sleep isn't enough to be back to normal, and you're not used to it, either."

"I know," Stella replied. "But I'm not leaving phoenixes locked up in there."

Ethan sighed but didn't say anything more as he put the key in the lock and turned it. It clicked back and the gate swung open. Ethan picked up Melville and put him back in his sweater, just in case a small gentleman flamingo was a snack to a giant phoenix, and then the four of them walked in through the gate.

A path wound its way into the garden, and they followed this past various trees and bushes. It was extremely quiet, and Stella was beginning to think that perhaps there was nothing there after all.

"This certainly looks like it was once part of the Sky Phoenix Explorers' Club," Beanie said. "The crest keeps coming up on the path tiles. And the stone benches are in the shape of phoenixes. And the lanterns hung in the trees are shaped like phoenixes too, look."

Stella saw he was right. Ornate brass lanterns hung from the trees at regular intervals, each one fashioned in the shape of a phoenix, clinging to the lantern with its great claws.

"Those trees over there are sizzling chili trees, and the chilies that grow on them are supposed to be a phoenix's favorite food. And the air smells of bonfires, which is a sure sign of phoenixes."

"And, you know, there *was* famed to be a giant Sky Phoenix stable on the grounds of the club," Beanie went on, "although I don't think it had a cage around it then. It's one of the more far-fetched stories, because it's said to be built in the shape of a—"

They turned a corner of the path, and Beanie fell suddenly silent as they all stared in wonder.

"Were you about to say a giant feather, by any chance?" Ethan asked.

Beanie nodded wordlessly. In fact, they were all speechless at the extraordinary sight. Before them rose a gigantic stable in the shape of an orange and red feather, which reached hundreds of feet into the air. Every strand formed a long perch on which the phoenixes rested. There were perhaps fifty of them altogether, boasting the most spectacular fiery plumage. This was obvious to the explorers even from a distance, but then one of the birds noticed them and flew down to land directly in front of them.

It was bigger even than the vultures at Witch Mountain had been, easily reaching a height of ten feet or more. It gazed down at them with fierce, intelligent eyes for a moment before suddenly spreading out its magnificent wings, which seemed to glow like embers in the sunshine—a glorious mixture of orange and ruby and even the odd flash of blue.

Beanie jumped, startled by the sudden movement, but Stella didn't think the bird meant them any harm. Indeed, it lowered its head and shoulders and knelt to the ground, as if expecting to be mounted. Stella looked into the bird's gleaming yellow eye and felt that there was something beseeching in its expression, as if it was urging them to fly far away on it. Moments later, the other phoenixes noticed what was happening and came down to them in a flurry of fire-colored feathers. The air was thick with the scent of smoke and ash.

"They want us to fly them," Shay said.

Stella looked up into the sky and saw the mesh of the cage suspended above them.

"But how?" she said. "They're far too big to fit through the door we came in by."

They looked at each other hopelessly.

But then Beanie squinted back up at the mesh stretching above them and said, "It looks like there's an opening mechanism up there. I can see the hinge."

"Well, how do we open it?" Ethan asked.

"There must be a lever around here somewhere," Beanie replied. "Perhaps it's in the stable? Let's take a look."

The four explorers walked to the ornate wooden door, carved with the crest of the Sky Phoenix Explorers' Club. It was set in the stem of the feather, which formed a circular turret. They found the ground floor full of books detailing the care, feeding, and training of phoenixes. Many of them were inscribed with explorers' names.

"Look at this one," Shay said, holding up a book. "There's a handwritten note that says 'Property of the Sky Phoenix Explorers' Club. If lost, please return to the club library.'"

There was no longer any doubt about it. There certainly

had once been a fifth explorers' club. The four children continued up to the second floor of the turret, where they discovered leather tack, including a range of saddles and reins.

The third floor contained a sort of bar, which didn't surprise Stella very much because explorers were fond of a drink, without exception. This one contained mostly dusty whiskey glasses, as well as a few remaining bottles of firewater. It looked like mice had attacked the once elegant red furniture, and there was also an empty humidor there, once used for storing cigars. It was stamped with the club's crest and still smelled faintly of tobacco.

The other rooms contained more paraphernalia belonging to the lost club, and the four explorers had to make their way all the way up to the very top floor before they finally found what they were looking for. In the middle of the otherwise bare room was a stand containing a single red lever, illuminated with the light flooding in from the panoramic windows. It is almost impossible for any young explorer to resist the allure of a big red lever, but this one was even more thrilling because, printed neatly beneath it, were the words AVIARY ROOF.

They rushed over to it, and Beanie pulled the lever triumphantly. They immediately heard the groan and clank of machinery and raced to the windows in time to see the top of the aviary winding back, leaving a vast gap for the phoenixes to fly through.

The great birds took to the sky immediately, and for the next few minutes the view from the turret window was a nonstop flurry of red and orange wings as they soared to freedom like fiery little rockets. Stella felt her heart swell with the sight and grinned at the others in delight.

Finally, there were no more birds in the air, so they made their way back down. When they opened the door and stepped back outside, however, they saw that not all of the phoenixes had left after all. Two of them remained. One was the phoenix that had first knelt before them, and it had been joined by another bird, which had taken up a similar stance. They looked right at the explorers with fierce, wise eyes.

Stella's hands flew to her mouth. "They waited for us!" she exclaimed. She looked at the others. "Do you think we might actually be able to ride them?"

"It could be a way back to the bridge!" Shay exclaimed. "None of us have been trained to ride phoenixes, though. . . ."

He trailed off. Everyone was grinning. There was no way they weren't going to ride those magnificent birds, and everybody knew it.

"I'll fetch the tack," Shay said, already turning back to the stable.

CHAPTER TWENTY-SEVEN

THE TWO PHOENIXES EXPLODED into the sky in a riot of glorious feathers. They were both singing in delight, and their song was as strong and golden and glorious as fire, covering Stella's skin with a feeling of warmth, every note like melted butter. She gripped the phoenix's feathers and found it quite impossible not to let out a cry of delight. Behind her, Shay tightened his hold around her waist and laughed in her ear.

The Hanging Gardens of Amadon spread below them in colorful bursts of extraordinary flowers, interspersed with glittering blue pools and waterfalls. But the sight was there for only a moment before the phoenixes soared up through the clouds, past the torn magic-disguise painting, and finally burst out into the sky.

"They're all here!" Stella exclaimed.

And, indeed, the phoenixes were all there above the

clouds, wheeling and swooping and stretching out their great wings to catch the sun's rays, singing their delight at finally being free in the sky, like they were meant to be.

Stella glanced over and saw Beanie and Ethan marveling at the display, just as they were. The magic-disguise painting hanging from the bridge hid the gardens once again so you would never know they were there if it weren't for the rip in the fabric. Apart from that, the view consisted only of the sparkling stars of space. Above them, the Black Ice Bridge stretched back across the surface of the ocean, its black stone glittering in the sunlight.

"Now we just have to hope that they listen to our instructions," Shay said to Stella. "And that they don't take it into their heads to fly off wherever they fancy."

"I guess it depends how well trained they are," Stella replied. She glanced back at Shay. "Let's hope they're like Polar Bear Explorers' Club expedition wolves rather than those untrained ones the Ocean Squid Explorers' Club brought on our first expedition."

"One way to find out," Shay replied.

Stella nodded and turned back to the phoenix. "Beautiful bird, I have no idea whether you can understand me," she said. "But we need to cross the Black Ice Bridge to get back to Queen Portia's caves in Blackcastle."

The bird gave no indication of having understood Stella, but when she gently tugged on the reins to direct it

up toward the bridge, the phoenix responded instantly and all the other phoenixes followed, rising into the sky together like a great golden cloud.

In all the excitement of the escape, Stella had completely forgotten about Queen Portia. When the phoenixes flew up over the side of the bridge, she saw the snow queen at once, surrounded by her gargoyles, who must have flown straight up from the gardens. She was standing right at the edge of the bridge, gazing out as if looking for something.

Stella looked back at Shay. "I suppose we'd better land and make sure she's all right."

She guided her phoenix down, and Ethan and Beanie did the same. The snow queen's eyes widened at the sight of the two magnificent birds, and the gargoyles shrank back in fear, clutching at the queen's skirts like children.

"Shhh," Queen Portia soothed them, reaching down her hand to rest upon one of their stone heads. "They won't harm you."

She seemed different from before—there was a clarity in her eyes that hadn't been there previously. She still looked exhausted, but she also looked as if she fully understood where she was and what was happening.

"Are you all right?" Stella asked, leaning down from the saddle to speak to the snow queen. She saw she held an empty snow globe in one hand, but the cuff was still fastened around her wrist. "Didn't the key work?" she said.

"I'm sure it will work now that I have my heart back," Queen Portia said. "Here, you'd better take this."

She handed the snow globe up to Stella, then took the ice key from her pocket.

"I just wanted to thank you first," she said. "And to say I'm sorry."

"For what?" Stella replied.

"For creating those snow globes in the first place. I remember it all now. I remember the horror of understanding the Collector would take the whole entire world if he could. The gargoyles tell me there's another Collector there now, but she sounds every bit as bad as Jared Aligheri."

"It's okay," said Stella. "At least now that we know what's happening, we'll be able to fight back against the Collector and the Phantom Atlas Society. And that's something."

"The collecting started off as a noble endeavor," Queen Portia said. "We really were trying to do good. I hope you can believe that."

"I do," Stella replied. "It's okay. You don't have to worry about it anymore."

Queen Portia closed her eyes briefly. "Thank you," she said. "And good luck."

She lifted the sparkling ice key to her handcuff and once again it slid in smoothly. But this time the lock clicked back and the cuff fell to the floor. The ice queen took in a great gasp of air, as if she'd been holding her breath underwater for a really long time and had finally broken the surface.

A big smile spread over her face as she looked at Stella and silently mouthed her thanks once again. And then she was fading from view, melting away into dozens and dozens of starflakes, which hung for a moment, glittering in the air, before they too vanished into the sea mist sweeping in across the bridge.

The gargoyles looked both sad and relieved as they watched her go. The seven of them nodded their thanks to Stella and then took a running leap into the sky, spreading their wings and disappearing into the fog. The snow-boat was left abandoned on the bridge behind them, but luckily the young explorers didn't need it anymore.

Stella let out a sigh. "Right," she said. "Let's go."

She tugged gently on the reins to urge her phoenix up to join the other birds in the sky, with Ethan and Beanie right behind her. They turned in the direction of the castle and began their journey back across the bridge.

It turned out that the phoenixes could fly incredibly quickly, forcing Shay, Beanie, and Ethan to wrap their cloaks and scarves tightly around themselves as protection from the icy wind racing past. But they made good progress through the air, where there was nothing to hinder them. They passed a couple of abandoned gremlin crow's nests situated on top of the bridge's towers, and Ethan remarked on these when they stopped to put up their fort for the night.

"I bet that's how they brought down those hot-air balloons," he said. "The gremlins would have catapulted themselves on board and interfered with the inner workings of the balloon."

"They can do that?" Stella asked. "That must have been a pretty powerful catapult."

"Oh yes," Ethan replied. "Gremlins can catapult themselves for miles and miles if they want to."

Despite the iciness of the wind and the cramps they developed in their legs, the four explorers all agreed that traveling by phoenix was absolutely marvelous, especially with the other phoenixes swooping and wheeling around them in a colorful flock.

They made good progress, stopping only to eat and to sleep as they raced back toward Blackcastle, and Stella was delighted that after a couple of days Shay and Koa seemed to have made a complete recovery. Koa was back to her usual self, and Shay appeared to be too—with no more nightmares, or voices, or headaches.

Although when they flew back over the abandoned expedition camp Stella felt Shay startle behind her. When she looked back to ask what was wrong, he said, "It's probably nothing. . . . But just for a moment I thought I saw the ghost of that fairyologist waving at us from the ground."

Stella frowned. "You don't think that you're still able to see ghosts somehow?"

Shay shrugged. "I hope not," he said.

They continued on, and after just one more day, suddenly they were there. They could see the end of the bridge, and the craggy cliff top, and the castle clinging to the side of it.

"We made it," Stella said, hardly believing it was true.

They landed their phoenixes outside the castle and scrambled to the ground.

"Time to rescue our parents," Stella said, grinning at Beanie.

She ached to see Felix again and hoped that the two of them had been okay down in the ice cave with only the jungle fairies to look after them. She'd deliberately done no magic whatsoever during the journey back so that she'd be ready to melt the ice wall the moment they returned.

Stella and the other two were already heading for the door when Beanie said, "Wait."

They turned back to see that Beanie had a snow globe in his hand—the one containing his father's lost expedition.

"I need to do this first," he said, looking paler than usual. "If it doesn't work . . . If my dad isn't there, then at least my mum won't ever have to know. I don't want her to get her hopes up."

Stella nodded. "Of course," she said.

She could see Aubrey poking out of the top of Beanie's pocket, and the moment seemed suddenly charged with an unbearable hope for all of them.

Stella held her breath and crossed all of her fingers. Beside her, she was aware of Ethan and Shay doing the same. Even Melville somehow managed to cross his wings.

Beanie looked down at the snow globe and slowly started to unscrew it.

CHAPTER TWENTY-EIGHT

A FEW MINUTES LATER, STELLA was hurrying down the stone staircase into the cave with the others close behind her. It looked exactly as they had left it—water was steadily dripping into the rock pools from the stalactites, and the ice dragon was snoozing peacefully on her shining bed of shells. Below, the ice wall trapping Felix and Joss inside remained thick and solid, and Stella's fingers were already itching to perform the spell that would melt it.

There was no sign of the jungle fairies, and she was just worrying that they might have lost interest and fluttered off somewhere when a movement drew her eye. She saw the four fairies had set up some kind of makeshift mini-golf course on top of the ice dragon—using little sticks of ice to knock a tiny round shell around the dragon's claws and over her tail.

"Hey!" Stella called to get their attention.

Hermina dropped her golf club, startled, and then exclaimed in delight at the sight of Stella. The next second, all four jungle fairies came tumbling down from the dragon in a tangle of big hairy feet and excited grins. They fluttered straight over to the explorers, dancing and cartwheeling in excitement. Stella grinned and waved at them before hurrying over to the wall.

"Felix!" she cried, banging on the ice with her fist. "Are you still in there?"

There was a muffled exclamation from the other side, and then Felix's voice called back. "Stella? My darling girl, is that really you, or have we finally lost our marbles in here?"

"It's me!" Stella replied, grinning.

"Beanie?" Joss's voice called out at the same time that Beanie called for her.

"Quick, Stella!" Beanie exclaimed. "Get them out."

Stella was already reaching for the star charm at her wrist and reciting the spell from the Book of Frost:

"This shard of ice shall be no more,

"Revert to how it was before."

Of course, it wasn't actually a *shard* of ice this time, but a great thick wall, and so it took Stella several attempts before the ice was finally thin enough for them to break through with their boots.

Stella was feeling decidedly wobbly by then, but the next moment Felix's arms were around her, and she sank against him in relief.

"You extraordinary girl!" he exclaimed, before holding her out at arm's length. "Are you all right?"

Stella reassured him she was fine. "Are *you* okay?" she asked. She saw that he had rather a scruffy layer of stubble, but the eyes twinkling at her over the top of it were exactly the same.

"I hope I never see a piranha cupcake again," he told her. "But other than that we are both well. The jungle fairies were magnificent."

Stella looked over to where Joss knelt before Beanie, gripping his shoulder and having a similar conversation. Then Beanie glanced behind him and said, "Mum, there's someone else here who wants to see you."

Joss followed the direction of his gaze, and a gasp caught in her throat. A few yards behind Beanie stood a tall, broad-shouldered man dressed in Polar Bear Explorers' Club robes.

"It . . . it can't be!" Joss exclaimed in a whisper.

Adrian Albert Smith walked slowly forward. He looked tired and still a little dazed, but a smile spread over his face, making crow's feet appear at the corners of his eyes. "Joss," he said, his voice shaking and hopeful and uncertain all at the same time. He reached out a hand tentatively toward her. "It really is me."

Joss shook her head and blinked hard, as if expecting this to be a mirage, but when he didn't vanish into the air, she leapt to her feet with a cry—a sound of raw, unspeakable happiness. And the next second she was running straight to him, throwing her arms around his neck and clinging to him tightly with one arm as she gestured frantically for Beanie to join them with the other. Stella knew her friend didn't normally like to be touched, but he made an exception this time, standing between his parents and gripping them both by the hand. He was trembling from head to foot, and Joss was openly sobbing as she covered her husband's face in kisses.

"You broke my heart!" she told him. "I love you too much and you completely broke my heart!"

"I know." Adrian sighed into her ear. He closed his eyes and said, "But I'm going to put it back together again. I'll make it up to you both."

"Good gracious, Stella," Felix said as she leaned against his arm. "What in the world have the four of you been up to?" He looked down. "And who is this fine fellow?"

Stella saw Melville standing at their feet, doffing his bowler hat. "Melville Montgomery—of the Bayside Montgomerys—at your service," he said.

"He's from the Islet of Gentleman Flamingos," Stella said.

"But . . . there's no such thing," Felix said. He looked back at Melville and said, "I beg your pardon. Of course I'm delighted to meet you, but the Islet of Gentleman Flamingos was disproved and removed from the map years ago."

"Ah," Stella said. "About that. There are a few things we need to tell you."

EPILOGUE

Three Months Later

IT WAS A BRIGHT, crisp sunny day, and Stella was in the garden doing cartwheels with her polar bear when Felix called to her from the veranda. She got up, brushed snow from her dress, gave Gruff a great big kiss on the side of his head, and then made her way over to where Felix stood waiting for her with a newspaper in his hand.

"I thought you might like to see this," he said, holding it out to her with a smile.

Stella looked at the paper warily. Since they'd returned from their expedition with news of the Collector and the Phantom Atlas Society, there had been an uproar, to say the least. The revelation of what was really on the other side of the Black Ice Bridge had spread like wildfire. An emergency meeting was called at the Polar Bear Explorers' Club, attended by representatives from the other clubs, as well as the members of Stella's own expedition.

There had, at first, been a great deal of skepticism regarding their story. The president of the Jungle Cat Explorers' Club even suggested that Beanie's dad had lost his marbles during his time on the bridge and, what's more, that the entire thing was an elaborate lie in order to avoid Felix's and Stella's arrest.

"My dear sir," Felix protested, "you can see a great flock of phoenixes out there with your own eyes!"

Since they'd arrived back in civilization, the phoenixes had stayed glued to Stella's side, which had made it rather difficult for anyone thinking of arresting her. A phoenix had a strong, savage beak, and their bite could take a hand off if you weren't careful.

"No one denies that the young people managed to discover a flock of phoenixes, but that doesn't make the rest of their story true," President Fogg said.

"And what about Melville?" Stella gestured at the gentleman flamingo, who had also come to support them.

"Probably just a strange anomaly you picked up somewhere." President Smythe sniffed.

"Well, I never!" Melville exclaimed indignantly.

"You can't seriously expect us to believe that this snow globe contains the Land of the Giants," President Fogg said, picking up one of the snow globes that had been spread out on the table and squinting at it. "Or the Island of Lady Swans," he said, moving on to the next one. "Or the Sky Phoenix Explorers' Club, for heaven's sake!"

"We certainly believe that to be the case," Felix replied calmly.

"Well, if that's so, why don't we just open one right now and find out?" President Smythe said, already reaching for the snow globe containing the giants.

"No, no." Felix shook his head. "You can't simply open it here."

"And why not?" President Smythe asked suspiciously.

"Use your common sense, man," Felix said. "It's the Land of the Giants. If it springs back into life here, it will flatten us all. There isn't room for it."

"How terribly convenient for you," President Smythe said, replacing the snow globe with a sneer.

"On the contrary, it is most inconvenient," Felix said sharply. "Nevertheless, we must endeavor to be sensible if we can." He picked up the Phantom Atlas, which had also been laid on the table. "This book shows where these places were collected from. The globes must be returned there and put back. Look, the Land of the Giants is meant to go here." He pointed to a page on the map. "Someone traveling by dirigible could make it in under a week. And the Sky Phoenix Explorers' Club is only a few more days away from there."

Finally, after much discussion, it was agreed that the two snow globes Felix had mentioned would be taken to their correct locations and opened. Much as Stella pleaded, they refused point-blank to allow her or Felix to go since they were both technically expelled from the club.

"I will take them," Ethan's father, Zachary Vincent Rook, offered. "Look at the geography." He gestured at the atlas. "It'll be faster by submarine."

Since everyone was able to agree with this choice, Zachary assembled an Ocean Squid Explorers' Club expedition without delay, and Ethan accompanied him. Stella and Felix were allowed to return home with the phoenixes. Beanie and his family also went home since they still had a lot of catching up to do. And Shay's mother arrived to collect Shay, who also very much needed to spend some time with his family.

"They did it," Felix said now, looking down at Stella as she took the newspaper from him. "Ethan and Zachary did it."

Stella looked at the newspaper headline, which read:

ICE PRINCESS SAVES FORGOTTEN EXPLORERS' CLUB

The article went on to detail how Zachary Vincent Rook's expedition had released the Sky Phoenix Explorers' Club from the snow globe. There had been a dozen explorers trapped within the clubhouse when it was collected, and the newspaper had printed quotes from some of them.

"We can't thank the ice princess enough."

"If it wasn't for her, we'd still be imprisoned."

"We may have lost most of our members, but the Sky Phoenix Explorers' Club will rise from the ashes."

"New applicants welcome."

"Stella Starflake Pearl may join our ranks anytime she likes...."

"The papers are all full of it this morning," Felix said. "The Land of the Giants has been set free as well. I'm sure you have Ethan to thank for making sure they knew who was responsible."

"It wasn't just me," Stella said. "It was all of us."

"Well, you were the only one who was facing arrest," Felix replied. "And now the papers are calling you a hero."

"Tomorrow they'll probably be calling me a villain again," Stella said.

Even so, she couldn't prevent a rising sense of excitement as she gripped the newspaper.

"That, I think, is a problem for another day," Felix said. "For now, public opinion is with us. There are snow globes that need to be returned to their places on the map, a Collector to catch, and a Phantom Atlas Society to thwart. In the meantime, I have received a telegram from President Fogg offering us both full membership of the Polar Bear Explorers' Club once again, if we want it. There's also a telegram from the president of the Sky Phoenix Explorers' Club—a nice chap by the name of Alistair Fox Jacob—inviting us to take tea at their club. The king of the giants also sent a letter, which the servants are currently rolling out on the front lawn—it's rather large—but I imagine that will be an invitation too."

He looked down at her. "So, what do you want to do?"

Stella folded the paper and tucked it under her arm. Then she looked up at Felix as a grin spread over her face. "I want to do all of it," she replied. "Be an explorer again. Visit the giants and the Sky Phoenix Club. Return the snow globes. And stop Scarlett Sauvage before she can do any more damage."

"Right," Felix replied, rubbing his hands together. "Then we have a lot to do. I suggest we share a pot of tea and cookies in the library. And then, my dear, I think we'd better get started."

Acknowledgments

Many thanks to the following wonderful people:

My agent, Thérèse Coen, and the Hardman and Swainson Literary Agency.

The lovely team at Simon & Schuster Books for Young Readers—especially to my editor, Amanda Ramirez—Justin Chanda, Tom Daly, Katrina Groover, Martha Hanson, Jenica Nasworthy, and everyone else behind the scenes.

My two Siameses, Suki and Misu, and my husband, Neil Dayus.

All of the children's booksellers and teachers who take the time to champion books and nurture a love of reading in young people.

And, finally, to all of the children who have read and enjoyed Polar Bears. When you dress up as the characters, or write letters to me, or create things in the classroom, or share your amazing ideas at events, you remind me of what a special thing it is to be a children's writer. I hope you enjoy this book too.